Praise for

'Jaime Clarke pulls off a sympathetic act of sustained male imagination: entering the minds of innocent teenage girls dreaming of fame. A glibly surreal world where the only thing wanted is notoriety and all you really desire leads to celebrity and where stardom is the only point of reference. What's new about this novel is how unconsciously casual the characters' drives are. This lust is as natural to them as being American—it's almost a birthright. Imagine Britney Spears narrating *The Day of the Locust* as a gentle fable and you'll get the idea'
Bret Easton Ellis

'*We're So Famous* smartly anticipates a culture re-configured by the quest for fame. The starry-eyed girls at the center of this rock-and-roll fairy tale are the predecessors of today's selfie-snappers. With biting wit and wry humor, Clarke brilliantly reminds us that we've always lived for likes'
Mona Awad

'Daisy, Paque, and Stella want. They want to be actresses. They want to be in a band. They want to be models. They want to be famous, damn it. And so … they each tell their story of forming a girl group, moving to LA, and flirting with fame. Clarke doesn't hate his anti-heroines—he just views them as by-products of the culture: glitter-eyed, vacant, and cruel. The satire works, sliding down as silvery and toxic as liquid mercury'
Entertainment Weekly

'Jaime Clarke is a masterful illusionist; in his deft hands, emptiness seems full, teenage pathos appears sassy and charming. *We're So Famous* is a blithe, highly entertaining indictment of the permanent state of adolescence that trademarks our culture, a made-for-TV world where innocence is hardly a virtue, ambition barely a value system'
Bob Shacochis

'Clarke seems to have created a crafty book of bubble letters to express his anger, sending off a disguised Barbie mail bomb that shows how insipid and money-drenched youth culture can be'
Village Voice

'Jaime Clarke's novel *We're so Famous* follows Stella, Paque, and Daisy—three utterly talentless girls from Phoenix who share a near-horrifying affinity for Bananarama. But it's only after Daisy and Paque's unwitting connection to a double murder helps skyrocket their band, Masterful Johnson, to nationwide stardom that the story really gets going. Through a string of pop-culture references (Neve Campbell, Dennis Hopper, Jennifer Grey's nose job) and mishaps (an unfortunate lip-synching tragedy a la Milli Vanilli, movie deals, smack), Clarke keeps the satire sharp and his heroines clueless'
Spin Magazine

'Darkly and pinkly comic, this is the story of a trio of teenage American girls and their pursuit of the three big Ms of American life: Music, Movies and Murder. An impressive debut by a talented young novelist'
Jonathan Ames

'This first novel is plastic fantastic. Daisy, Paque and Stella are talentless teens, obsessed by Bananarama and longing for stardom. They love celebrity and crave the flashbulbs and headlines for themselves. The girls become fantasy wrestlers, make a record, get parts in a going-nowhere film, then try to put on big brave smiles in the empty-hearted world of fame. Sad, sassy and salient'

Elle Magazine

WE'RE SO FAMOUS

JAIME CLARKE

For Philip Pavir —
Hope you like this
(esp the part that takes
place at the
Chateau!)

ℬℛ

BLOOMSBURY READER

LONDON · OXFORD · NEW YORK · NEW DELHI · SYDNEY

First published in Great Britain in 2001 by Bloomsbury Publishing Plc

This edition published in 2016 by Bloomsbury Reader

Bloomsbury Reader is an imprint of Bloomsbury Publishing Plc

50 Bedford Square, London WC1B 3DP

www.bloomsburyreader.com

Bloomsbury is a trademark of Bloomsbury Publishing Plc

Bloomsbury Publishing, London, Oxford, New Delhi, New York and Sydney

ISBN: 9781448216505
eISBN: 9781448214358

Visit www.bloomsburyreader.com to find out more about our authors and their books.
You will find extracts, author interviews, author events and you can sign up for
newsletters to be the first to hear about our latest releases and special offers.

You can also find us on Twitter @bloomsreader.

For David Ryan

Contents

Introduction

We met in graduate school, while attending a master of fine arts program for creative writing. If I'm being entirely accurate, it was a low-residency program—you went for a couple of weeks every six months but handled most of the writing work through monthly correspondence with that semester's professor. Both Jaime and I had applied in no small part because this particular college had a famous name. Actually, that is to say the undergraduate program was *infamous*, a small and isolated den in Vermont where artistic black magic was practiced, and from which emerged writers with gaudy and nefarious reputations: One of its freshman students had written a bestselling novel that had become an R-rated Brat Pack movie with an amazing sound track. This particular young author had become hugely famous, his name appearing in book reviews and gossip columns alike. But he wasn't alone. At least two of his friends from undergrad writing workshops also published novels. Bret Easton Ellis, Donna Tartt, and Jonathan Lethem, all of them had come through Bennington's writing workshops. So, separately, Jaime and I had decided to enroll in the next-best thing, Bennington's mail-order correspondence graduate school deal. We were going to be writers too. We were in our twenties. This is how things went.

Fast-forward a bit. Summer of 1996. The back pages of an issue of the now-defunct fashion and culture magazine *Details*. A photo spread featuring two attractive young women. The pair called themselves Shampoo, but Jaime couldn't quite figure out if they were models, singers, a band, or what. It seemed to him that these two, their fake names and personas and very pulses and souls, had been entirely devised explicitly for the purpose of becoming famous. However fame happened, Shampoo couldn't have cared less. This idea seemed novel to Jaime. Their bold absurdity, their willfully oblivious and naked ambition.

Fast-forward a bit more, to 1997. Way down in Hattiesburg, Mississippi, the very excellent writer Mary Robison fished out, from among the entrants to a short story competition, a tale of three talentless girls who wanted to be famous. The piece was soon named a finalist for *Mississippi Review's* annual prize and was published in that excellent literary magazine, then edited by Frederick Barthelme, marking it as the first fiction among our peers in grad school to see the light of day in any kind of respected literary magazine. Back in Arizona, Jaime set to expanding the story, in the hopes of making a book of it. 'I remember the dilemma at the outset,' wrote Jaime in an e-mail, 'was how to write a book that was borne of my loathing of celebrity culture without it turning into a scathing screed that only like-minded individuals would get and nod their head to. So I tried to create a more charming narrative that still seethed with disdain for celebrity worship at the expense of everything real. And then who would be the messenger?'

The messengers ended up being Paque, Stella, and Daisy, three high school friends from Phoenix. On the pages that follow, you will meet them—they start out living together in a model home in an unfinished housing community at the base of a mountain. The girls have dropped out of school because why not? Sometimes they ride around town in limousines because a friend's dad has a limo service, and business is usually slow. Back in the eighties, being willfully ironic on television was new and daring and a way of saying, *I am not a part of this bullshit.* Like so many of us who grew up at that time, the girls look to David Letterman, without any irony, as their icon of ironic humor. Quotes from *When Harry Met Sally . . .* are a way of punctuating conversation. Not ten pages into the book, one of our trio, Paque, voices what seems to be as much of a treatise or agenda as these girls possesses:

> Everyone is sick of today's hyper-ironic music. People crave fun, we think. And the music of the '80s *was* fun. 'The Perfect Way' by Scritti Politti was a song you could dance your ass off to, and 'Safety Dance' by Men Without Hats was another one. Me and Daisy do like some '90s stuff, but most of it isn't fun . . . Putting the fun back into music is the answer. Fun: 'Love Shack' by the B-52's. Not fun: anything by Metallica. Fun: 'I Want Candy' by Bow Wow Wow. Not fun: Smashing Pumpkins. The all-time most fun song ever: 'Come On Eileen' by Dexys Midnight Runners. Whenever me and Daisy hear that song we dance our asses off. If the music makes you want to jump out of your skin and dance (for instance, anything by Madonna from the '80s and early '90s), then it's good.

Harmless, right? An equation as simple as girls just wanting to have fun. Early name-dropping of Tower Records also feels right for this time period, because Tower Records was where teens went to check out all the record covers that had nearly naked women on them. My nostalgic delight-o-meter was set atingling that much more in the early pages with another reference: Millers Outpost, a basically forgotten chain of stores that appeared through the southwest in the eighties—if you were in junior high school back then, you bugged your parents to take you there for your Levi's jeans, your shirts from Ocean Pacific.

So then, from the opening pages this book is filled with signifiers, specific markers from what seems a quite specific and innocent time. But don't be fooled. There's more at play. Two of the girls form a band named Masterful Johnson, and though they have no discernable musical abilities, the group somehow manages a shot at stardom. This ends with a lip-synching fiasco at a summer concert, an event very much inspired by the pop duo Milli Vanilli, who were caught and excoriated for lip-synching during the early nineties, when grunge kicked in and authenticity—or at least a pose of authenticity—was key to success. Soon after, there's a shooting, maybe a murder. The girls get out of town briefly, to Manhattan. Stella lands in Hollywood, where she takes a crazy, mixed-up whirl at acting. Understand, during recording sessions, we never get one word about musical integrity; during talks about auditions and acting, nothing about craft or art is put into play. Rather, Stella turns out to be big on dead pools and participates in message board discussions about which celebrities will kick the bucket next. Stories of famous and rare celebrity deaths—Bob Crane from *Hogan's Heroes* and his autoasphyxiation tragedy; Jayne Mansfield's beheading—start creeping into her conversations. In her search to track down a burned-out rocker for her dead pool, Stella sets to writing letters to celebrities—Axl Rose, Jennie Garth—who've come in to get photos developed at the booth where she works her day gig. Of course Stella ends up meeting the crashing rocker. Of course they shack up, just off of Sunset Boulevard, fading in and out of a high in one of the cabanas at the Chateau Marmont. Naturally, these scenes are captured as the pages of a screenplay.

Taking on the subject of fame is a way of addressing the culture while also delving into that universal desire to have our own name known. Fame connects to the need for attention, to be *seen*, that is part of us from infancy onward; for the teacher to bestow attention on *me*; the fantasy worlds of being the best, celebrated, being beloved. This is worth thinking about and wrestling with. Usually, as we mature through teendom and into adulthood, our need for attention gets redirected, at least a bit, in some way: We still want all the fame, and want to be known, we want love. But we also run, in a critical and pragmatic manner, into just how the world works. Maybe we want to do something significant, something that *earns* attention. We get older and the price has to get paid, and while it's not like anybody's necessarily turning down the chance to become famous, sustenance—both emotional and physical—becomes a priority. Sooner or later, the idea of fame, or rather, the importance of it, has to take a backseat to the dreaded details and demands of the specific life we are living. When this backseat-taking doesn't happen, what does that mean about Johnny or Jenny X? What does that say about him or her, when he or she clings to childlike illusions?

When he wrote *We're So Famous*, Jaime wrestled with those questions through the form and medium of fiction, while at the same time engaging with the parameters of the form of the novel itself. And so this novel has three narrators—Paque, Stella, and Daisy— each of whom gets her own section, speaking in a voice that has empty similarities to her friends', but is still uniquely clueless in its own right, and that tells its own particular part of this larger, comic, mildly tragic tale. We get the time-capsule-preserved cultural references, the expertly dropped names of yore, the hints and influences of those writers Jaime loves and by whom he was influenced (Ellis, F. Scott Fitzgerald). Also a litter of epistolary sections, chat room discussions, those screenplay pages.

My own favorite character is shy, gentle Daisy, whose name carries a distant echo from *The Great Gatsby*. Daisy is the girl who laughs at every reference, who turns her back at the doorway where a grisly celebrity murder happened. She is the sensitive, squeamish one, the most decent one, the one who isn't ambitious or lovestruck, but is just kinda, well, overwhelmed. While everything is circling the drain for our friends, she writes for advice to the pop band Bananarama, care of their fan club. Once you understand just how sweet and toothless Daisy's gesture is, you see the perfect angles of this construct. A joke that, even with time, remains too perfect to be funny.

I've known Jaime for twenty years now. The man has worked and evolved and willed himself into something of a literary entrepreneur, putting together numerous anthologies and cofounding the literary magazine *Post Road*, which is now run out of Boston College. He also rescued a bookstore in Boston, Newtonville Books, with his wife, the hilariously sharp Mary Cotton. Jaime wrote three more novels, the Charlie Martens trilogy that features *Vernon Downs, World Gone Water,* and *Garden Lakes*. But his love for writers is real. Writers come in and out of the bookstore, in and out of his anthologies, in and out of the book trailers he makes for his books. He's shown a true talent for sensing potential and finding a pulse, for cultivating talent, running with ideas. It's no exaggeration to say he's woven himself into our national literary fabric.

It is the spring of 2016, and there have been other evolutions as well. Paque, Stella, and Daisy have long given way to *1 Night in Paris*, the misadventures of Khloé and Lamar, the Kardashian game app, and the Adidas Yeezy Boost. In the same way that our technology has accelerated, and our news and entertainment and consumptive cycles have accelerated, it also seems that the appetite for fame has accelerated, as has its residual price. This doesn't mean there aren't any more sweet, innocent songs that make us want to get up and dance; certainly there are. It doesn't mean that things are only headed in one horrid direction. But the scales in this equation have indeed tilted. The darkness and willful vacancy also seem to have coalesced and metastasized. My sense is that the sweetly curious narrators you will find in these pages provide more insight as to how we got to this cultural moment than many more-heavy-handed books. This alone makes *We're So Famous* worthwhile. And what follows will surely make you want to jump out of your skin and dance.

—Charles Bock

Paque

If you haven't heard of us, your friends probably have. You might have a copy of our album, *We're Masterful Johnson*. But there are a lot of bad rumors and gossip about us and how we became famous and what happened, so this is for the record.

The most untrue thing said about us is that we're rich kids, which makes me and Daisy so mad we can't talk. The snobbery in that suggestion is maddening. Plus it implies lazy afternoons by the pool waiting for our favorite video to come on MTV. We resent that. Anyone who's ever done anything knows it takes a lot of hard work and always a little luck and when someone is an overnight sensation they've really been at it for years.

Just because we rode around Phoenix in limousines people assumed we were rich. But no one ever knew where the limousines dropped us off at the end of the night, at my house at Estrella, where I lived with Ma Bell and Birdy, two tip-top guys me and Daisy met after dropping out of high school.

Me, Ma Bell and Birdy lived in the only finished house in the development, which had been deserted since the guy who owned it went to prison. Estrella was supposed to be a dream community for affluent families who wanted to live west of Phoenix, away from the center of the city which, since the earthquakes in California and the floods in the Midwest, was spreading like a stain. Estrella was hidden by the Estrella Mountains and far enough out that we never saw anyone except ourselves. Once in awhile a car would park on one of the deserted streets on a Friday night and we could hear the radio blasting from the car while who-knows-who made out. All the paved streets had names like Buena Vista and Morning Glen, or Wonderview and Cactus Wren.

Like I said I lived there with Ma Bell, who was twenty-three and worked for Motorola, a huge technology company. I'm not sure what exactly they make or do, but Ma Bell was the first to move into the house. He had the master bedroom upstairs, which someone had

10

tastelessly decorated in blue pinstriped wallpaper (to match the blue carpet). It could've been black for all you knew, though. Ma Bell never turned on the lights because his bank of computers gave off enough light for him to see by. He worked from generators (we didn't have any electricity) and cell phones (or phone service). Anytime I asked him what he was working on all he said was, It's something for work.

Birdy, on the other hand, didn't have a job. He was seventeen and he sometimes lived with his family, who I guess didn't care much for him. He had dropped out like me and Daisy and he mostly listened to his music or slept during the day because he was out all night tagging under passes with his name, which he could do very elaborately in multicolored spray paints.

It was Birdy who got the limos for us. His old man ran a limo company, King Limos, and all we had to do was call up and a limo would come for us. Practically every Saturday night me, Daisy and Birdy got picked up by the limousine—sometimes white but usually black and stretch—and we cruised the malls until they closed, hanging out the window, yelling at people we knew, or cuties, and then on to Mill Avenue where we usually attracted everyone including the cops, who told us time and again that we couldn't hang out the windows.

Me and Daisy felt famous in the limo and it was part of how we fantasized it was to be famous, which was having nice cars, wearing really nice clothes, living in a nice neighborhood and basically just having the things you wanted. And people would give you things. In magazines and on TV it never looked like any celebrity was hurting for anything. We couldn't imagine Madonna eating a hot dog at an A&W, or waiting in line for tickets to a movie. Not that she *couldn't* do those things if she wanted to, but Madonna wanting a hot dog wasn't the same thing as me and Daisy wanting a hot dog.

Daisy lived at home with her mother, who was a stewardess and was never home. I spent a lot of time at Daisy's house, which I liked for a number of reasons including the fact that I could take a hot

11

shower. I'd come over and the limo would wait while we got dressed to go out, Daisy always wearing her mirrored sunglasses that I kidded her by calling her serial killers. Eventually I just moved all my stuff into Daisy's bedroom.

We liked to dress outlandish like rock stars, which is what we wanted to be. We wanted to be a real band, for sure, but we weren't really *musical*, that was the problem. That was the problem from the beginning, when it was the three of us. Me and Daisy and Stella wanted to be just like our favorite band— probably the best band in the entire world, Bananarama. See it was perfect. Me and Daisy are sort of opposites like how Sara Dallin was the blonde one and Keren Woodward the one with the dark hair and exotic features. And Stella looked just like Siobhan Fahey (it's spooky how much she resembled Siobhan: she had the same small mouth and wide eyes, except her eyes were blue. That's what guys liked most about Stella, her eyes. Guys said she looked like a doll, and Stella liked that). Most people don't know Bananarama's real names, but there you are. So our idea was to start an all-girl band in America (little-known fact: Bananarama is in the *Guinness Book of World Records* as Britain's most successful all-girl group) and become famous, maybe do a tour with them. We wished we were aware of Bananarama when they were in their heyday, but me and Daisy were just born when their first album, *Deep Sea Skiving*, came out in 1983. We're pretty sure that like everything else from the '80s, Bananarama will have a renaissance. It just feels like the right time. Everyone is sick of today's hyper-ironic music. People crave fun, we think. And the music of the '80s *was* fun: 'The Perfect Way' by Scritti Politti was a song you could dance your ass off to, and 'Safety Dance' by Men Without Hats was another one. Me and Daisy do like some '90s stuff, but most of it isn't fun. And the Spice Girls are shite. (We don't acknowledge the Spice Girls, who are basically ruining the advancements Bananarama made for all-female groups.) Putting the fun back into music is the answer. Fun: 'Love Shack' by the B-52's. Not fun: anything by Metallica. Fun: 'I Want Candy' by Bow Wow Wow. Not fun: Smashing Pumpkins. The all-time most fun song ever: 'Come On Eileen' by Dexy's Midnight Runners. Whenever me and Daisy hear that song we dance our asses off. If the music makes you want to jump out of your skin and dance (for instance, anything by Madonna from the '80s and early '90s), then it's good. 'Too Shy' by Kajagoogoo comes to mind, too. That's my and Daisy's opinion.

A little known fact about Masterful Johnson is that we made a single when it was the three of us, long before *We're Masterful Johnson*. Stella's father loaned us the money to do it and we spent months on the lyrics. I can take credit for the first line, 'You are my end,' which wound up being our title for the song, but we were stuck after that and Daisy and Stella helped out by looking up some poetry. We studied Yeats and Keats and Wordsworth; those guys knew how to melt hearts. I don't know how much it helped us in the end, though. We paid some studio guys to come up with the song, which was called 'What the—, Who the—, Hey!' I think between me, Daisy, Stella and Stella's father we still have the 500 copies we paid for. But we weren't down about our singing career. It doesn't happen overnight.

In the meantime Daisy got the idea that we should become models and found a modeling agency to represent us: StarryEyed Productions. Brad Johnson, who looked like the stereo salesman from *Fast Times at Ridgemont High*, told us he thought we could be supermodels. We were pretty excited about that. The wood-paneled walls of StarryEyed Productions were covered with pictures of beautiful women and handsome men, but we never saw anyone else in Brad's office except Jimmy Rider, a seven-year-old cute-as-pie punk that me and Daisy and Stella grew to hate. Jimmy's real name was Hayworth Rhoades, but his parents thought Jimmy Rider sounded more like a movie star's name than Hayworth Rhoades, which is what his parents wanted him to be.

Brad booked the four of us in a fashion show at Thomas Mall on 32nd St. Brad got a couple of the merchants in the mall to sponsor the show, so the Gap and Miller's Outpost loaned us the clothes to model on the makeshift stage put up by mall maintenance. You could see people in the mall wondering what was going on. Our dressing room was the shipping and receiving area at Miller's Outpost, a small cement room stacked with cardboard boxes. The floor was littered with that styrofoam popcorn stuff. Brad warned us we should wear deodorant so we didn't sweat up the clothes so Daisy ran to the Osco Drug in the mall to buy a stick. Antiperspirant, Brad called out after her.

We each had two outfits for the show. But we didn't really have any idea about runway work. Our only reference was what we saw on *House of Style* on MTV and that looked pretty easy. You just sort of went out there and had a rhythm. But because the stage was so small, me and Daisy and Stella had problems keeping the right amount of space between us. And that pip-squeak Jimmy Rider was doing some sort of gymnastics routine between us. The fact that the speakers pumping out the music above us were weak didn't help either. People stopped to look but between Jimmy Rider thumping the stage with his somersaults and the three of us dancing into one another, no one was particularly interested. Brad thought it went off great and beamed at us that the show was the start of our careers, but we knew better. Brad wasn't so happy though when he collected our outfits. Which of you is wearing perfume, he demanded. We sniffed ourselves and just then noticed we smelled like lilacs. Daisy pointed at the stick of antiperspirant: floral scent.

We laughed about that story for a long time and any time we laughed it made me and Daisy miss the old days, the three of us. We agreed we'd visit Stella (who moved to Hollywood to become an actress) after we'd restarted Masterful Johnson as a duo, like Bananarama had to do when Siobhan left the group to form

14

Shakespear's Sister. We weren't really in touch with Stella then because we resented Stella selling out Masterful Johnson and moving to California. Plus Stella's obsession with celebrity deaths creeped us out. Stella keeps three separate notebooks, a Murder Book, a Suicide Book and an Accidental Death Book. At first she just had the Murder Book but when we met her, when she was nineteen, she had just added the other two. She used to let us bring the Murder Book to school. The first half was dedicated to details concerning John Lennon's death outside the Dakota in New York, with subsections on Mark David Chapman and *The Catcher in the Rye*. (Chapman was reading *Alice and Wonderland* before *Catcher* and just happened to finish it the day before he shot Lennon. Stella found that out.) The second half is all about celebrity murders. Political murders don't interest Stella. JFK. King. Bobby Kennedy. Gandhi. People killing other people over ideas was an historical fact, Stella said. None of it interested her, except Hitler. Stella was fascinated by a story about how Hitler almost committed suicide before he really rose to power. The *Munich Post*, an anti-Hitler paper, printed a story about how Hitler's beautiful half-niece was found dead, a bullet through her chest. The bullet was fired from Hitler's gun, which lay at her side. The death was called a suicide but people had heard Hitler and his half-niece arguing at his apartment the day before she died. There were rumors that Hitler and his half-niece were sexually involved, a rumor some people believed when it became known that the half-niece's nose was broken when they found her.

What if Hitler *had* committed suicide, Stella liked to ask. Can you imagine?

It was too big of an idea for us to imagine.

Right after Lennon in the Murder Book was Bob Crane, Colonel Hogan from *Hogan's Heroes*.

Stella used to visit the site in Scottsdale where the colonel was murdered. It's right by the all-time best mall in Arizona, Scottsdale

Fashion Square. Once she dragged me and Daisy out there and we stood next to the irrigation ditch and tried to look in over the trees. The place has been remodeled since, Stella told us, but it's basically the same layout. She pointed to the bungalow where Hogan was staying. She told us how he was in town that summer in 1978 to do a play called *Beginner's Luck* at the Windmill Theatre on Scottsdale Road (the theater isn't there anymore). The Windmill put the star of their plays up in the bungalow and when Crane was in town he rigged the bungalow with then state-of-the-art video equipment so he could videotape himself having sex with various women. (Stella was on to a bootleg of one of the tapes, but me and Daisy don't know if she ever got one.) Stella didn't believe the theory the cops came up with, that it was John Carpenter, a friend of Crane's from L.A. who ran a video equipment business, who killed him. The police said Carpenter was a hanger-on who Crane included in his partying. But Carpenter was also bisexual and, according to the police, Crane sensed some weirdness—or maybe there was a bad party scene— and he started to distance himself from Carpenter. So Carpenter, feeling pushed out, bashed Hogan's head with a tripod. The police never found a murder weapon, but they knew enough to know it was a tripod (a corner of the flower print sheets on the bed where Hogan lay in his own blood, his temple crushed, a cable wrapped around his neck, tied in a bow and cut cleanly with a knife showed where the killer had wiped the murder weapon clean. The police originally suspected a tire iron or pipe). And there supposedly were swatches of blood taken from the trunk of Carpenter's rental car, brain pieces maybe, but true to the law in the wild west, the police couldn't get it together enough to prosecute Carpenter (though they did finally try in 1994, but Carpenter was found not guilty).

Stella said, Let's walk by the room. The three of us snaked single-file down the narrow sidewalk, stopping in front of what would've been #132A, Colonel Hogan's apartment. Me and Daisy were standing in front of the door thinking about Stalag 13, about Schultz, Colonel Klink and his monocle, Newkirk and Sergeant Carter and Kinchloe. We could hear Major Hochstetter; we could see the impatient look on General Burkhalter's face. We remembered noticing when Klink's original secretary, Helga, was replaced by another actress, her character name switched to Hilda. That was his wife, Stella said, and when Crane was killed they were getting a divorce. Stella thinks Hilda had something to do with Hogan's murder. She also thinks the colonel knew it might end badly in Phoenix. Stella said Crane had messed around with a married woman in Phoenix in the early seventies and the woman's husband was someone rich and powerful. Whoever it was that killed him, Stella said, Crane *knew* them. She paused and let us think about that. Crane was obsessive about locking his door, Stella went on, but when they found him his door was unlocked with no signs of forced entry. She walked us through the facts. Crane was killed in his sleep and then strangled after he was dead. That morning's paper was *inside* the apartment. Crane was killed around 3 A.M. A mystery bag that everyone knew held a photo album filled with Polaroids of women, the face-out photo a clothed shot with a nude shot tucked behind it, was on the bed, empty of its contents. Most of the pornographic tapes and photos were gone too but a tape of *Saturday Night Fever* Crane had edited for his son remained (Crane edited out all the cursing and questionable scenes). Undeveloped photos were left behind in the makeshift photo lab Crane had set up in his bathroom. Crane didn't use drugs and drank infrequently, yet there was a six-pack of Coors in the refrigerator and on the kitchen counter a bottle of gin and an opened bottle of Scotch. Sixty cents had fallen out of a pair of white trousers draped over the back of the couch. The Colonel's wallet was still in the pants. Crane himself was found in the master bedroom in a half-fetal position, his right hand under a pillow. Dried blood was crusted around his head. Fresh blood ran from his nose. On his left thigh were blobs of semen. Daisy turned her back on the door of #132A but I stared at it, imaging the long hall behind it, past the kitchen on the right, the guest bedroom on the left, past the living room, towards the television and video camera against the far wall, towards the master bedroom—like I'd seen it diagrammed in Stella's notebook. I wondered what the walls knew. Daisy pretended to be interested in the sky and the three of us moved down the sidewalk, away from the secrets kept behind the gold-curtained windows.

So the next thing that happened was we met Rick, who saw us dancing at Planet Earth, and we thought he was just another perv but he turned out to be this really sweet, sad kind of guy who just wanted to help make us famous. 'If that's what you want,' he said when we told him. 'I can tell you have your heart set on it.' Boy, did we. Daisy told him sometimes she fell asleep with her fingers crossed.

We flat-out asked Rick if he had connections and we appreciated his honesty when he said he didn't. Rick said he lived in Chicago and only came to Phoenix in the winters to golf and that he'd only been to California once in his entire life. Imagine only ever going to California once in your life. We didn't see the logic in Rick's travel pattern. Me and Daisy wanted to be buried in California.

'Some guys I golf with have a recording studio in their house though,' Rick said and we got pretty excited.

Rick's friends, Elliot and Hunter, lived in one of those two-story tract-type houses on a street where all the houses looked the same and most of the yards were still dirt.

Elliot and Hunter said they were pleased to meet us. Hunter couldn't take his eyes off Daisy, who twisted shyly on the carpet in the furnitureless room.

'Did you bring some songs with you,' Elliot asked.

Rick explained the situation, practicing his golf swing with a club from a bag leaning in the corner. He hit imaginary golf balls and watched each one's flight until it was time to tee up another. 'These girls need some material,' he said.

'Let's get high and we'll write some songs,' Elliot said.

Me and Daisy thought that was a pretty good idea and Rick went out for Doritos and Mountain Dew while the four of us hunkered down to do some songwriting.

Maybe because of the equipment or maybe because Elliot and Hunter knew how to produce, our singing didn't sound all that bad and even though we were fried out of our gourds we managed to each come up with a song. Daisy wrote 'I'd Kill You if I Thought I Could Get Away with It' and I wrote one with Elliot called 'Do Fuck Off,' a love song.

Elliot and Hunter kissed us goodbye and promised to make copies that we could send around to record companies. 'They're good guys,' Rick said as we pulled away. Rick had to catch a plane back to Chicago but before he left he told us we should probably think about finding an agent to represent us. We liked the idea of having an agent, someone who could get us parts in movies and who could arrange to pick us up in limousines and take us anywhere we wanted to go. 'An agent looks out for your interests,' Rick said. We said we wanted Rick to be our agent because he seemed to be looking out for us but he told us no, he wasn't an agent, but he'd try to find someone to represent us. Maybe we'd see him in a month or so, he said. Goodbye, girls, he said. He looked sad.

Daisy's mom could get us tickets to fly for free, and when Daisy's brother Chuck called from New York and said he wanted us to be in a film he was making, her mom came through with two roundtrip tickets. Chuck is Daisy's identical twin. He's a film student at NYU and Daisy loves him like a brother.

Neither of us had ever been to New York City before, even

19

though we'd seen it on TV (we love *Letterman*). Our plane tipped its wing and the black night outside the window was suddenly lit with a million lights so bright we thought we were landing on the moon. Daisy said, Look, there's the Empire State Building and I followed her finger towards the skyscraper lit yellow.

Chuck met us at LaGuardia and we got a cab into Manhattan. Chuck lives in the West Village and the cab driver let us off right where Sally let Harry off in *When Harry Met Sally*, at the Washington Square arch. 'You were the only person I knew in New York,' I said as the cab drove away and Daisy laughed.

Chuck's roommate, Bertrand, was a film major, too. Bertrand was a lot older than Chuck. He said he had four degrees already: a bachelor's in creative writing and another bachelor's in philosophy; he also had an MFA from Vermont College in poetry as well as a Ph.D. in American history from a college he kept calling Ball State. He had another year to go at NYU. Daisy asked him why he had so many degrees and he said, I have to stay in school until I get my big break so I can pay off all my student loans. Plus, he said, you get all the great connections in school.

Where Chuck wanted to be a director, Bertrand wanted to be a screenwriter. Together they were working on Chuck's student film, *Plastic Fantastic*, which is also the name of Chuck's all-time favorite Flesh for Lulu album. Chuck and Bertrand's friends were helping on the film. A girl named Chloe, a sociology junior from Hatties-burg, Mississippi, was playing the lead, a girl whose name was also Chloe and who was also from Mississippi and was also a sociology major at NYU. Chloe's friend in the movie was a character named Melinda, whose name was really Melba. She was a film major too and me and Daisy suspected she was Chuck's or Bertrand's girl-friend, we couldn't tell which. The film took place inside this New York night club called XOXO in the movie but was really called The Cellar. It was in the meatpacking part of Manhattan. Bertrand knew the owner who let us film while the bar was open. Me and Daisy played friends of Chloe and Melinda's at the club and the movie was about how men see women in bars and, as Bertrand explained, 'how that translates to life.' We liked Chloe and Melinda a lot so it was easy to act like we were their friends. Chuck said it was okay if our characters were named Paque and Daisy, so we went with that.

Because the owner was letting us film in his bar, Chuck had to give the owner's son Jeff a part so Chuck made Jeff one of a series of assholes who were to appear throughout the film. In the scene at The Cellar me and Daisy are dancing together and Jeff comes up and starts dancing with us and we innocently dance him into our circle. But when the song is over and me and Daisy have said thanks, Jeff won't let us alone and he harasses us out of the club, onto the street and into a cab. Chuck and Bertrand wanted Jeff to follow us in a cab, but Chuck decided that was too difficult and expensive an idea to shoot.

We had to admit that we were bored much of the time. Chuck would spend a half an hour fiddlefucking around with the lights and microphones while me and Daisy just stood there. Finally we asked the DJ to play some music so we could dance, just to keep warmed up. Chuck said, OK, let's shoot and we went in front of the camera but had to stop right away. You're dancing out of the frame, Chuck said to Daisy. But that's how I dance, Daisy said. Chuck explained to us that with the one camera if we danced too far apart he wouldn't be able to get us both in the scene. So the DJ started the music again but this time we were so nervous about staying close to each other that we didn't look natural and Chuck made us stop. He told Bertrand to tape a square this long by that wide on the floor. Just stay in the box, he said. That helped us out and we got a glimpse of how good a director Chuck is going to be one day. He already knew what me and Daisy learned, that it isn't so easy to be a movie star. You have to worry about a lot of things that people who see your movies sort of take for granted. We didn't talk about it, but after spending hours just to get two or three minutes worth of film, we felt a deeper appreciation for what Bananarama had to go through to make all those wonderful videos.

Chuck told us we were really great and me and Daisy decided to go out and celebrate. We hopped in a cab and told the cab driver to take us to Times Square. We felt like Alice in Wonderland when the cab let us off right by the giant, flashing Cup-O-Noodle and the big screen TV showing the news. Even though it was after midnight the sidewalks were jammed with people. We passed a guy selling nuts but didn't get any because some of the nuts had burned and it smelled like shite. We had to put our hands to our mouths in order to get by him.

Daisy grabbed my arm and said, Look. She pointed at the numbers 1515 on the building in front of us and it gave us the goosebumps. We were standing in front of MTV, the all-time best channel on TV. We tried the doors but of course they were locked. We put our hands to the glass and peered inside but couldn't see anything. Neither of us said anything as we silently thought about all the famous people who had passed through those doors. Daisy touched the handle again and just held on to it. I started singing, 'Video killed the radio star' which made Daisy laugh.

Our next cab driver was a little bitter when we asked him to take us to the Ed Sullivan Theater but we didn't know it was within walking distance. We were amazed at how it looked exactly like it does on TV. Standing under the glowing yellow and blue neon sign we had a past-life feeling, a feeling that we'd stood where we were standing a hundred times before. We *have* to get tickets, Daisy said. The sign taped on the door told us to try waiting in line early in the morning, that we had to write in six months in advance if we wanted guaranteed seats.

We agreed we would come back and stand in line around 2 A.M. but until then we should go out and see more of New York. We went to Rockefeller Center and pressed our noses against the *Today Show* studio glass window. It looks like a small apartment, someone walking by said. The flags around the ice skating rink flapped loudly like applause.

We walked up Fifth Avenue. Daisy pointed out Tiffany's and we stood in front of the sign and said 'oh dahhling' over and over. Daisy's neck is long and smooth like Audrey Hepburn's, which we noticed on our ten millionth viewing of that movie (Daisy's mom owns it).

Me and Daisy skipped the block between Tiffany's and Central Park when Daisy stopped cold. Look, she said. She pointed at a hotel that looked like a castle. What is it, I asked. It's where Gatsby confronted Tom, remember, she said. Then I figured it out. The Plaza Hotel. *The Great Gatsby* is Daisy's all-time favorite book; she's read it more times than some people have read the Bible. She was in the middle of reading it the first time when we dropped out of school. Sometimes guys accuse us of being dumb and if they do, Daisy starts right in talking about how many times she's read *The Great Gatsby*.

Me and Daisy gawked at the chandeliers in the lobby, which was like looking up at stars. Because it was so late there was no one around. Daisy asked the waiter if we could please please please sit at a table and he smiled and said sure. The waiter's eyes were sunk in so far his head looked like one of those Halloween skull masks. We ordered Cokes and sipped them, imagining all the shiny people who must have passed through the lobby of the Plaza and wishing we were them.

Our waiter, Mel, made sure our Cokes were bottomless. We got the feeling he liked having us around. He kept walking by our table and making funny comments about people who were walking by. Better give them the penthouse he said about an enormously fat couple. Things like that. We found Mel more amusing than hand-some and it was fun just to sit and watch and laugh. Finally Mel came to our table and didn't say something funny. You guys have to go, he said. I'm getting off now if you want to go get a beer or something, he offered. We said sure, we could do that, and Mel took us back to the West Village, to a dark wood bar called Minetta's. Mel knew the manager, Taka, a squarely built man with a friendly smile. While Mel and Taka shook hands me and Daisy looked around at all the great pictures on the walls. They had old-time cartoons up with real pictures of people we didn't recognize. Daisy pointed out a small picture on the wall. It was a picture of the actor Alec Baldwin and his actress wife, Kim Basinger. What was funny about the picture was that it was hung right where it was taken so you could see Alec and Kim sitting next to each other in the spot you were standing in front of. Daisy sat where Kim was sitting in the picture and said, Oh Alec, in a southern accent that was so funny Mel and Taka started laughing.

What happened next was the subject of an argument the next day about what exactly Mel said. It started with us noticing how Mel seemed to be a sort of big shot in Minetta's. The bartender, Donna Marie (who is herself an actress—she played De Niro's girlfriend in that movie about the mob guy who goes to the shrink; we asked her if Bobby D. liked that Bananarama song about him but she said she didn't know), sent drinks over without Mel having ordered them. Mel looked different out of his all-white Plaza outfit too. Less of an angel. At some point Daisy asked what time it was; it was after one. Remember we have to go line up for *Letterman*, she said. I said, Yeah, that's right. I noticed Mel didn't say anything and I thought he would at least ask us about it. He pretended like he didn't hear us. We'd seen that look before, the look some men get when you say you have to get home at a certain time, or that you have to get up early the next day. Suddenly there was a buzz in the bar and people craned their necks to look out the window. We looked too and saw the big white limo idling at the front door. It must be Alec and Kim, Mel said. But the doors didn't open and we saw Taka go out and talk to the driver and come back in.

I'm going to A.C., Taka said. Who wants to go?

Mel laughed. How about it girls, he asked. Want to do some gambling?

Me and Daisy communicated with our eyes how much we wanted to ride in the limo. But we didn't necessarily want to go to Atlantic City. Once we went to Las Vegas to party with these friends of Rick's who were in commercial development. We thought he meant making commercials but it turned out they had something to do with construction and building offices. These guys had another girl—Veronica something—with them at the hotel. After a night of watching these guys gamble we all went up to the suite and partied. The office guys had some coke and we did it. They had a bar and we drank. We partied pretty late with them and at some point Veronica something said she had to go. Me and Daisy were surprised because we thought she was the black guy's girlfriend—she spent the whole night hanging off him and she partied with him back at the suite—but it turned out she was a hooker. The black guy, I think his name was Hank, said he'd drive her home but the hooker smelled something fishy and wanted to be paid. Hank said, Relax, bitch, I'll pay you and he smacked her across her face. Me and Daisy closed our eyes but we heard that sound in our ears. The other guys just laughed and Hank pushed the hooker into the bathroom and slammed the door but we could still hear him punching and kicking the hooker, whose crying became less and less until it just stopped. Me and Daisy ran out of the hotel when the others weren't looking. We had to call Daisy's mom to get home and what we told her was that we got really sick on some food and thought we might have to go to the hospital. It was the best story we could come up with.

So we didn't want to go to Atlantic City because we didn't even know Mel or Taka but we really wanted to ride in the limo. What about *Letterman*, Daisy asked.

I know someone who works there, Mel said. Of course we weren't surprised later—after we'd gotten separated from Taka and Mel, who disappeared from the blackjack tables—that Mel was lying. (We even went straight from the Port Authority to the Plaza the next morning looking for him but the manager said no one named Mel worked there.) But Mel convinced us to go and we followed him out to the limo as Taka grabbed two bottles from behind the bar.

Mel and Taka sat by the doors of the limo and me and Daisy sprawled out on the leather bench in front of the bar, which had a long electric blue neon strip running across the top. A little TV built into the bar stared at us like an eye that never blinked. Daisy unsecured one of the glass tumblers. Don't drink their booze, Taka said, it's too expensive. He produced the bottles of wine he'd taken from Minetta's and we toasted our impending success in Atlantic City.

Veterans that we are, me and Daisy drank almost a whole bottle between us. Men will let you drink all the liquor you want; we learned that a long time ago. Without saying anything we stood up and stuck our heads out the moon roof. The limo accelerated to pass a slow car and our hair blew into our eyes. We're flying, Daisy said. She stuck out her arms like Superman and laughed. I laughed too and then suddenly Daisy's laugh turned to choking and then she vomited over the side of the limo. The wind caught the chunks and blew them against the limo, scattering the vomit in a yellowish-orange spray across the trunk. Daisy coughed twice and then smiled, mouthing, Sorry. We ducked back into the limo and she passed out. Mel turned on the TV and we sat and just stared, transfixed by the flickering images no bigger than the size of a hand.

The casino looked like a cafeteria in a shopping mall; the green and beige diamond shapes in the carpet gave us vertigo. The bright light burned our eyes too and made everyone white like ghosts. We arrived sometime after 3 A.M. and pretty much the only people gambling after 3 A.M. were people serious about dice and cards.

Mel and Taka sat at the baccarat table and me and Daisy were like Bond girls, standing behind their chairs, inhaling cigar smoke. We tried to follow the game—we wanted to know how hard a game whose minimum bet was $100 was—but it was near impossible to figure out that shite game. Taka won right away and the others at the table, men with bags under their eyes that looked like coffee cups filled to the brim, shot him a dirty look. Daisy said why don't we try our luck at blackjack and so we did but we found out we didn't have any luck and the most fun we had that night was telling this old fart that we were showgirls. When he asked us at which hotel Daisy said, Hotel California. The old fart nodded like he knew exactly where it was.

At a certain point Mel and Taka drifted away from us and Daisy was the one who said, Let's head back. I agreed with her. On the bus ride back to New York it started to sink in that we probably weren't going to see *Letterman* after all but we decided we would try calling the Ed Sullivan Theater from the Plaza pay phone to see if there were any extra tickets, but no one picked up.

After an afternoon nap, we completed a second night of shooting, which was basically us reshooting the scenes from the night before. Then Chuck took us to see the actor Paul Newman at the New School. Paul Newman had started a program there for people who wanted to be in the movies. Me and Daisy have only seen one Paul Newman movie: *The Hustler*. It was Paul Newman from *The Hustler* we had in mind when we went to the New School with Chuck. We were surprised that Paul Newman *in person* looked like he was a million and a half years old. He reminded Daisy of her grandfather the way he just sort of sat up there and stared like he was trying to contact other worlds.

The event had a moderator, an old bald guy who probably wished he was a famous actor but settled for being the friend of a famous actor. We sat in the back of the classroom because all the ass kissers crowding the front of the room around old Paul made us sick. That's the thing about all these shiteheads in college; they pay a gazillion dollars to go to film school on the off chance that they'll rub shoulders with someone, whose ass they'll kiss, hoping that person will make their career for them. Me and Daisy said fuck that. If you want to do something, you do it. For instance, before they were Bananarama, Keren worked for the BBC and Sara and Siobhan studied journalism at the London College of Fashion. But they realized how much working sucks it out of you and how you can get only so close to your dream that way. So they started spending their nights singing to backup tapes in London clubs, knowing that sooner or later either word-of-mouth would spread or someone would see them and make them famous. Which, of course, is what happened.

Inevitably one of the ass kissers asked Paul how he got started in the movies. How many times has Paul Newman had to answer that one? But Paul was gracious and said what he'd probably said a hundred times or more. Another ass kisser, one positioned virtually at Paul's feet, asked what advice he had for aspiring actors. The room shushed and everyone stared straight to the front of the room. You have to want it more than anything, Paul said. You have to never give up, never let anyone tell you that you're no good, Paul said. The crowd of ass kissers clapped like old Paul just told them they were going to live forever.

Chuck asked Paul what he thought the difference was between working in front of the camera and working behind it. Paul made the usual joke about actors really wanting to direct and said something general about how much harder it is behind the camera than in front of it. I looked over at Daisy and she wasn't paying attention either. We were both thinking about getting home in time to watch *Letterman* when we heard our names. Chuck was telling Paul about our movie, pointing at me and Daisy as the stars. Paul craned his neck to get a look at us and Daisy just sort of waved, embarrassed. The guy filming the whole thing for the school turned the video camera on us. We could've killed Chuck. When the deal was over Chuck rushed to the front of the room to join the crowd of ass kissers and me and Daisy went downstairs to the cafeteria to find a TV but there wasn't one. I pulled an Almond Joy from the vending machine and we sat at a table in the cafeteria listening to the lights overhead hum, Daisy drawing her name in spilt salt with her fingers.

Back in Phoenix, we were anxious to get our tape. We dialed Elliot and Hunter's number, but their number was disconnected. We hadn't heard from Rick in forever so we called him to find out what was going on but his phone number was disconnected, too. Daisy turned on the television while I checked the number with information and Daisy said, Look, it's them. And sure enough over the shoulder of the anchorwoman was a picture of Elliot and Hunter with the caption SENATOR'S SON SLAIN.

Turn it up, I said.

Daisy hit the remote and the anchorwoman's voice rose in the living room. The details of the murder were scarce. As far as the police were able to determine, Hunter and Elliot were shot to death in their home somewhere around midnight. Daisy noted that it was the day after we recorded with them. Holy shit, Daisy said, look at that. A picture of Elliot at the White House with his father, Senator Hawkins, flashed in a succession of pictures, mostly of the senator and his wife at various parties. The anchorwoman came back on and over her shoulder appeared crude sketches of people the police wanted to talk to. A neighbor woman told the police they were the last people she saw at the house. We couldn't see it at first—Daisy was the one who really saw it—but sure enough the sketches were of me and Daisy and Rick.

Daisy said, Try Rick's number again. Her hand shook as she beamed the remote control at the TV, switching it off. I dialed Rick's number and the disconnection recording played in my ear but Daisy started to freak out, pacing the room, looking out the window like she was in the government witness relocation program.

I hung up the phone. Look, I said, we didn't do anything, we don't know anything. Daisy looked out the window again. We should call the police, I said.

But they're gonna ask about Rick and now Rick's disappeared and they're gonna want to know why, Daisy reasoned.

I said we didn't know why and that if we didn't go to the police it would make us look guilty of something. We agreed to wait until the morning to call the police because we secretly hoped the police would figure it all out overnight or we'd hear from Rick. Once that shite was straightened out, we hoped to get our tape back. (We *did* feel sympathy for Elliot and Hunter, who were, as far as we knew, nice guys, and they certainly didn't deserve to be murdered—if we could, there'd be a ton of things me and Daisy would like to undo.)

We called Stella and asked her advice. When we told her, the first thing Stella said was that now she could add us to her Murder Book. She laughed and you could almost hear the ocean in the background. We wished we were there instead of in Phoenix. We wished we were kicking through the waves and laying out in the sun.

Before we could ask Stella for her advice she launched into the latest target of her celebrity death obsession: Jon-Erik Hexum, the actor who starred in the early '80s TV shows *Voyagers* and *Cover Up*. Me and Daisy remembered watching the shows when we were kids but we didn't know right away who she was talking about. The really good-looking guy, Stella said, the one that looked like a model. We said we remembered even though we weren't sure and Stella told us how in 1984 on Stage 17 at the 20th Century Fox lot, the set of *Cover Up*, there was a half hour break between takes of a scene involving Jon-Erik Hexum's character, a weapons expert, and another actor. (Stella had a copy of the script.) Hexum was supposed to be trying to infiltrate an enemy group as a spy and in order to win over the enemy's confidence he was to load his .44 Magnum with blanks and shoot one of his partners, who was posing as a jewelry smuggler in a Miami hotel room. So between takes Hexum was fooling around with the gun on the set when it accidentally went off. The noise startled everyone and, being a practical joker, Hexum sat on the bed in the makeshift hotel room, spun the barrel of the gun and put it to his head and said, 'Let's see if I've got one for me.' Hexum pulled the trigger and fell back on the bed, blood gushing from his temple where a quarter-inch piece of cardboard lodged itself in his brain. Someone got a towel and a guest star put his fingers in Hexum's mouth to keep him from choking on his tongue. There wasn't time for an ambulance so Hexum was thrown in the back of a station wagon and rushed to Beverly Hills Medical Center, where six days later he was pronounced brain dead. He donated his heart, kidneys and corneas, Stella said. Apparently the heart had been donated to the owner of a Vegas escort service. There was supposed to be something funny about that but we didn't see it. If you didn't stop her, Stella would go on and on like that.

It was good to talk to you, Stella, we said.

She said, Come visit soon.

We were so tired we couldn't sleep.

We had finally dozed off when there was a knock on Daisy's front door. Me and Daisy jumped up, frightened, and crept towards the door. The

31

sun was coming up like headlights way off in the distance and we could barely see the man on the porch, a tall, thin man with his red hair in a ponytail. His skin was so white it glowed and his nostrils flared.

The man raised his fist and knocked again. Daisy looked at me and I shrugged. She reached for the portable phone and with it securely in her hand she swung open the door, startling the man, who introduced himself as Fred Meyers, a reporter for the *Arizona Republic*. A second man stepped out of the shadows and introduced himself as Buttrey. I'm the photographer, he said.

Daisy checked to see if her mom was home, but she wasn't. Then we all sat at the kitchen table and told Fred Meyers our story. He didn't get too interested until we got to the part about Rick and Elliot and Hunter. Fred asked us if we ever saw any guns in the house. We said no. He asked us if we ever saw any drugs, or if anyone delivered a package while we were there. We said no. He wanted to know if we overheard Elliot or Hunter on the phone. Again we said no.

Buttrey said, I have to get to another shoot, so do you mind if I take your pictures now?

Me and Daisy said we didn't mind but we did want to fix ourselves up a little. Buttrey said, Okay, but hurry. We changed clothes and made ourselves presentable and Buttrey took a picture of us sitting next to each other on the couch.

Fred gave Buttrey some instructions about what to do with the film and Buttrey took off. Fred said, I want to ask you girls some more questions. He ran through a list of names but there was no one we had heard of.

We volunteered that we didn't know where Rick was either, that we tried to call him but his phone was disconnected. Daisy said, We can give you his phone number so you can track him down and he'll tell you exactly what we told you.

Fred scrunched up his face and then looked down at the table.

When he looked at us again he said, They found Rick this morning in a hotel room in Chicago, shot in the back of the head.

It was like being run over by a semi. Me and Daisy didn't look at each other and I felt tears coming out of the corner of my eyes. Daisy put her head in her hands and started sobbing. It felt like we were in a really horrible movie. Fred said he was sorry and set down his notepad. We sat like that for some time and then we told Fred we didn't want to talk anymore. I understand, he said, but we have to call the police now.

Why, Daisy asked, standing abruptly.

You girls are wanted by the police for questioning and I think it's best if you just tell them your story, he said, to clear your names.

Fred got us to agree to let him call the police. He told them he would bring us down himself but wanted to 'come in through the back.' That phrase frightened us because we saw no reason we couldn't just walk right in, tell our story, and walk right out. Suddenly we were very nervous about the idea of handcuffs.

Fred's precautions turned out to be necessary though. Someone at the police station leaked to the media that 'the two women sought in connection with the murder of the senator's son' were turning themselves in and man, you should've seen the mess. We did try to go in through the back, but there were an equal number of reporters around back as there were in front. Of course all those in front chased around to the back once they saw the ones in back crowding around our car.

Get back you wolves, Fred said as he slowed the car.

For a moment we just sat there and nobody moved or said anything. A million faces pressed against the window of Fred's car, but luckily the windows were tinted. A reporter crawled on the hood of the car and took a picture through the windshield but Fred stuck his face in front of the lens as me and Daisy ducked down.

Fred's cell phone rang and when he hung up, he put the car in drive and rolled us out of the crowd. There's a change in plans, Fred told us.

The change in plans was that we'd meet with the police at a prearranged meeting place, which turned out to be the Royal Palms Inn off Camelback. The police were already waiting for us in a cabana off the pool and Daisy said something about wishing she could go for a swim instead of talking to the police, who wouldn't let Fred stay in the room with us. We protested and they said, Fine, you can call your lawyer, which should give the rest of the press enough time to find you here. We agreed that wasn't such a hot idea, so we told them what happened. They nodded and took notes, stopping us to ask us to repeat ourselves, over and over. They kept asking us about the lyrics in the song 'I'd Kill You if I Thought I Could Get Away with It.' They wanted to know which one of us wrote it and we said we all sort of did. They kept repeating the lyrics: *They'd find you and they'd know it was me / Our love is obvious / It's so plain to see / It all points to me / It's you I'd like to hit / I'd kill you if I thought I could get away with it.* It sounded funny when they read it instead of singing it but they didn't see that it was very funny.

Before we left we asked the police if they could give us our tape. It's our property, Daisy said. The police looked at us squarely and said they'd see what they could do.

That night we saw ourselves on the news. After a picture of Rick they had footage of Fred's car out back of the police station. You could see Fred in the driver's seat, but that was all. The anchorwoman, Judy Kern, told the viewing audience that 'two singers have come forward as the mystery women in the senator's son's home the day before Elliot Hawkins met his fatal end.' Me and Daisy just looked at each other.

The next morning we had to walk to Smitty's to see our picture on the front page of the paper. (Because she was gone so much, Daisy's

34

mom didn't get the newspaper. I forgot to mention that Daisy's mother was a freelance stewardess too, and sometimes in between flights for America West she hired out for private trips to Europe or wherever.) You know how sometimes pictures in newspapers look terrible, like mug shots? That's what we expected. We were surprised at how, well, *glamorous* the photo was. In our minds we imagined the two of us sitting on the couch, straight as arrows, staring into the lens like deer caught in headlights. That was how we felt. But maybe because of the equipment, or maybe because Buttrey knew how to work a camera we looked totally relaxed and confident. We were leaning in towards each other, our faces slightly tilted up. We weren't smiling, but we weren't frowning, either. The headline read: MYSTERY WOMEN FOUND.

What do you think happened to Rick, I asked. Daisy shrugged. Could it be a coincidence, she asked. I said I didn't think it could.

Sometimes when we're down in the dumps, we get hot apple pies from McDonald's to cheer us up. We're cheered if the pie is really hot, the flaky crust melting away so the warm apple filling oozes into our mouths. We're less cheered, however, if the pie has been roasting under a heat lamp and falls out of the box like the last greasy burrito at an all-you-can-eat buffet.

So we decided to get pies and while we were waiting to give our order, a little Mexican girl tugged on Daisy's shirt. Can I have your autograph, she asked. Except she said, ah-oh-graph. Daisy looked at me and I said, Maybe she thinks you're one of the Spice Girls. Daisy laughed and asked the little girl her name. Marguerite, the little girl said. Daisy took the pen and signed the McDonald's napkin Marguerite held out for her. I spied Marguerite's parents at a table piled high with burger wrappers and Cokes. They waved when I pointed them out to Daisy.

Marguerite asked me for my ah-oh-graph too and I signed below Daisy's name. Thank you, Marguerite said and bounced the way happy children do. She ran back to her table, her little pink jellies clip-clopping against the tile floor.

We were so freaked out we took our pies to go.

Just when we were wondering, What next? we turned on the radio and heard one of our songs, 'Do Fuck Off,' coming through the speakers. It sounded great. Me and Daisy stared at each other, amazed. We remembered all the times we dreamed of having a song played on the radio. When the song had finished, House Hausler, the DJ, said, That's a track from Masterful Johnson's demo tape, recorded at the late Elliot Hawkins's studio, an exclusive here at KUKQ. He said, I can't say the real title on the radio, but we're calling the song 'D.F.O.' The only thing that could've topped our being on the radio was if House played 'Cruel Summer' by Bananarama after us. But he didn't.

How did he get our tape, Daisy asked. She looked a little hurt. I said probably someone from the police gave it to them. We agreed we wished we had an agent to handle things. The radio station was playing our song but you couldn't buy our record anywhere and we weren't making any money. We started to feel a little ripped off.

After a Taco Bell commercial, House said, Go ahead, caller. Is the song called 'Day Fades Out', the caller guessed. House laughed. (When we recorded the song, Elliot thought it was cool to call the song 'Do Fuck Off' without actually putting that lyric in the song— which shows you Elliot's sense of humor.) Another caller guessed the title was 'Don't Forget the Ointment'. House was having such a good time he invited everyone to call in and make a guess.

Go ahead, caller: 'Dog Fights Orange.'

Go ahead, caller: 'Delia Fakes Orgasm.'

Go ahead, caller: 'Dancing for Oreos.'

Caller: 'Dental Freak Out.'

Me and Daisy were in near stitches we were laughing so hard.

Daisy decided to call in and solve the puzzle but the line was busy. House played an old New Order song. (Ian Curtis, the lead singer of New Order when New Order was called Joy Division, hung himself right before the start of Joy Division's 1980 world tour. He's in Stella's Suicide Book along with a fiber of rope that's supposed to be *the* rope Curtis used.) Daisy kept trying until she finally got through.

Go ahead, caller, House said.

It's called 'Do Fuck Off', Daisy said. She said it so fast that even with the five second delay House couldn't bleep her out.

How did you ever guess that, House asked.

I'm the one singing it with Paque, Daisy said.

House's radio voice crescendoed. Holy smokes kids, he said, it's Masterful Johnson on the line. Which one are you, he asked. Daisy said she was Daisy and I turned down the radio and picked up the black and white Swatch phone next to Daisy's bed. Hello it's Paque, I said. We told House we were huge fans of the station, not just because we were but because that's what a band's supposed to say whenever a DJ interviews them in their hometown. House asked us about our musical background and we told him about how we started Masterful Johnson in high school and that Elliot and Hunter gave us our first real break. House asked if we could tell them anything more about the murders but Daisy told him our lawyer told us not to say anything, even though we didn't have a lawyer. Do you have plans to release an album, House asked. We said we'd like to but that we didn't have a label. We didn't tell him that we didn't have any other songs besides the two on the demo. We told him that Rick was our manager and was really the one behind us the whole way and we were a little lost without him. It choked us up a little to talk about Rick so House didn't ask us anymore questions.

Here's a second cut from the pride and joy of Arcadia High School, Masterful Johnson, House said in his radio voice.

I'd like to have you down to the station when you do release an album, House said off air. His radio voice was gone and his regular voice made you think of bees swarming. We said we'd love it and we'd call if that happened. Hey House, Daisy said, will you play some Bananarama? House said he would and we felt as powerful as the president of the United States when the next song came on and it was 'Robert De Niro's Waiting' from Bananarama's 1984 self-titled album. It's the first-best album, followed by 1991's *Pop Life*. Really they never put out a shite record, but me and Daisy love 'Venus' from the 1987 album, *Wow!* Daisy said we should've asked House about the U.S. 'Wild Life' mystery and thought about calling him back but didn't want to wear out our welcome. Besides, Stella investigated it and came up with what is probably the best explanation. She said that when *Bananarama* was released from London/Polygram in 1984 the album and cassette featured the full-length version of 'Hotline to Heaven.' When the record was re-pressed shortly after, the full-length version of 'Hotline to Heaven' became a 12" single and the album featured an edited version (3:45), about half the play length, along with 'The Wild Life' (3:50). But when the U.S. edition was pressed, the first release was used and so 'The Wild Life' doesn't appear on any U.S. release. There is, however, a U.S. 7" single (3:17) with 'The State I'm In' as the B-side. Stella said she tracked down a 12" U.S. promo with the 3:17 version on both sides. She said there's rumored to be a Canadian 12" with the dub mix and she thinks maybe there's a Canadian 7", but she wasn't positive. Me and Daisy are always on the lookout for it though. We even stop at garage sales on the off-chance someone is throwing away gold.

No sooner had we hung up with House than the phone rang again. It was someone named Ian Black from Cactus Records, a local label we recognized because they put out records by some of our fave local bands like Dead Hot Workshop and Wise Monkey Orchestra. House gave Ian our number (we wondered how House knew it but Ian told us the radio station had caller ID) and Ian suggested we meet. So me and Daisy went to Cactus Records in Tempe, the college town built up around Arizona State University, a shite college we couldn't get into when we were thinking about studying music.

Ian was surprisingly young. He was small but had an intense face, small dark eyes and a forehead like a movie screen. He said he was very glad to meet us and thought it would be great to work together. We toured the studio, which was a small two-room adobe with wood paneling on the inside.

Let me introduce you to Jammin' Jay Jasper, he said. Jammin' Jay was blond and tan and looked like he belonged on the beach in California instead of behind the mixing board. Jammin' Jay looked familiar too and sure enough he said he was the bass player for Phantasm, a one-hit-wonder band back in the early '80s.

Ian wanted to put out a record as soon as possible, to capitalize on the recent press. People's minds are like sieves, Ian said, so we have to act fast. He asked us if we thought we could come up with some more songs. We said we thought we could but we'd need help and it might take a little while. Jammin' Jay suggested we release a single with the two songs we already had and Ian agreed this was a good idea. 'D.F.O.' was the most requested song on House's show that week, so that would be the A-side and 'I'd Kill You if I Thought I Could Get Away with It' would be the B-side. We all agreed that, due to recent events, the title should be changed. After some serious brainstorming we came up with the substitute title 'You're No Fun.'

We let House dub the demo tape and he returned it to us. It still had a PROPERTY OF PHOENIX POLICE sticker on it. We talked about hiring studio musicians to re-record the songs, but Ian wanted to get the single out *literally the next day*, so Jammin' Jay cut our single from the demo tape. He let me and Daisy hang around while he worked. We asked him about Phantasm and he told us some pretty cool tour stories. We didn't know it, but Phantasm was still huge in Europe and Jammin' Jay said they played just about every city in every country over there. He told us he played in East Germany before the wall came down. We asked him what it was like to be famous and he just smiled. It's everything you think it is, he said, but it's also things you don't think it is. We asked him what he meant and he said there was a really awful side to being famous. Like being mobbed in a restaurant and stuff like that, we said, nodding our heads that we understood. But that's not what Jammin' Jay meant. People do things they wouldn't normally do, he said. He told us a story about playing in Louisiana—he couldn't remember where exactly—and how after the show they discovered a group of thirteen-year-old girls waiting backstage to meet them. The group recognized that these weren't your average poster-plastered bedroom wall fans. The thirteen-year-old girls were painted up with heavy make up and wrapped in revealing dresses and low-cut costumes. Here's the really horrible part, Jammin' Jay said, the girls were wrapped up like Christmas presents by the women standing behind them, who were trying to drop them off with promises to pick them up later. Their mothers.

Jammin' Jay just sat there shaking his head. The story reminded us of the end of the *License to Ill* tape of Beastie Boys videos where the Beasties are backstage with these chicks who obviously are in love with them. The Beasties chase the girls around the room and after being caught one of the girls asks Mike D or Ad Rock or MCA—we can never keep those guys straight—to sign her stomach. So whichever one it was takes a marker and starts to sign but pulls back the girl's stretch pants and 'accidentally' drops the marker inside. Then he goes in after it. It was probably one of those moments that shouldn't have been taped, like that night in Rob Lowe's Atlanta hotel room. Stella has a pirated copy of that tape and she showed it to me and Daisy. We *love* Rob Lowe. We think it's a shame what that tape did to his career, though maybe it's been long enough now everyone has forgotten. We hope Pee-Wee comes back, too. Last thing we heard, Stella was going to keep another notebook, Career-Ending Scandals, and she was going to put Rob and Pee-Wee in it, along with Roscoe 'Fatty' Arbuckle. Me and Daisy had never heard of Fatty Arbuckle until we got a letter from Stella, postmarked from San Francisco. Apparently Arbuckle was the biggest star of his day. There's no one to compare him to now, Stella said. She was in San Francisco doing research on that day in September 1921. Stella said Arbuckle had three adjoining suites on the twelfth floor of the St. Francis Hotel. His roommate, Fred Fishback, arranged for the party—not Arbuckle like everyone thought. Fishback had invited an actress named Virginia Rappe who Stella said was also a prostitute. Rappe's madame came too, Bambina Maude Delmont (who the state of California had charged with fifty counts of extortion, bigamy, fraud and racketeering). Arbuckle later said he expressed concern about Rappe's presence at the party. It was known that Rappe had had five abortions before she was sixteen years old and she and her lover had been thrown off the lot of *Keystone* because of venereal disease problems. Apparently the producer had the lot fumigated. Anyway, the party took place in suite 1220—the sitting room. 1219 and 1221 were adjoining bedrooms which people traveled in and out of as that's where the bathrooms were. Even though it was the early years of Prohibition, Fishback had secured liquor, a couple of bottles of Scotch and a bottle of gin. Orange juice and seltzer were sent up from downstairs and everyone was drinking. Virginia Rappe was drinking orange juice and gin.

Arbuckle had a driving engagement and went into his bedroom, 1219, to change clothes. He locked the door because he didn't want anyone coming in while he was changing. He found Virginia Rappe passed out on his bathroom floor. He helped her to the bed and,

41

thinking that she was drunk, elevated her feet to help the blood to her head. Arbuckle went back into 1220 to find Maude Delmont, but didn't see her. He told another guest 'I think Virginia is sick' and when Arbuckle and the guest reentered 1219, Virginia Rappe was sitting up on the bed, screaming and tearing at her clothes. Mrs. Delmont finally appeared, drunk, and Arbuckle asked her to make Rappe stop tearing her clothes. Rappe's shrieks grew in intensity and Arbuckle tried to quiet her. One of her sleeves was hanging by a thread and Arbuckle said, 'All right, if you want it off, I'll help you' and tore off the sleeve. Stella said they used that statement against him in the trial. They also said Arbuckle threatened to kill Maude Delmont. When Fatty returned to the room he found Rappe nude on the bed with Maude Delmont rubbing an ice cube over her body. Arbuckle said he thought Rappe needed real medical attention and Delmont yelled at him to shut up and mind his own business. Fatty didn't like her tone and told Delmont to shut up or he'd throw her out the window. They tried to turn that into something against him at the trial, too. Finally Virginia Rappe was carried into a room down the hall, 1227, with the help of hotel management. Maude Delmont passed out on the bed next to her. Four days later Virginia Rappe died of peritonitis. Her fallopian tubes had ruptured because of pus accumulation from gonorrhea. But Maude Delmont told the police that Fatty raped her and because he was so huge, he flattened her. Me and Daisy sort of remembered the story after Stella told us but we remembered something about a Coke bottle or a champagne bottle being stuffed between the prostitute's legs and that Arbuckle had kicked the bottle to wedge it up in there. Stella said a lot of people thought that but that it wasn't even close to being true. The saddest thing of all, Stella said, was that after a couple trials where Arbuckle was found not guilty, he was going to make a comeback. But he was already an alcoholic and he had a heart attack in New York City.

You can really learn a lesson from what happened to Fatty, Stella ended her letter. Me and Daisy thought, Yeah, you really could.

Ian's girlfriend Marika designed the cover for our single. She was also a singer (Ian was producing her first album). She used the photo from the *Arizona Republic* but enhanced the colors on her computer so that everything including Daisy's pink shirt was bright. We told her it looked really great and she was glad we liked it. We met Ian on Sunday and by Tuesday morning 'D.F.O' was in every Tower Records in Phoenix. By Wednesday it was in every major record store in the state. Suddenly it wasn't just House playing our record; flipping through the stations, FM *and* AM, we could pretty much find it any time of the day. We went to the Tower Records on Mill Avenue—the one by the college—and watched people come in and buy our record. Tower Records had it right up at the register. Mostly it was teenagers and college kids, but some older people bought some too and that made us happy. We wanted everyone to listen to it and thought anyone who liked good music would enjoy it. We gave a bunch to Daisy's mom, who called it danceable, which, coming from someone older tells you something. But she was still concerned about Elliot and Hunter and called a lawyer she sometimes freelanced for and the lawyer called down to the police station but the police told him me and Daisy weren't suspects. We were all relieved.

Meanwhile, we were hard at work in the studio recording our full-length album. We were having trouble coming up with songs. Jammin' Jay co-wrote one with us called 'We Love Goo,' a sort of rock anthem. We had a lot of fun singing that one. Too much fun, in fact. It took us many, many tries to get that one 'waxed' (that's recording talk for 'recorded'). We would get so excited we'd start yelling the lyrics and laughing and Jammin' Jay constantly reminded us about the schedule.

Ian was busy promoting us around town. He visited all the radio stations and the record stores to meet the people who were handling our record. He said he even knew the guys in the warehouse and that's what made him a good promoter. We asked Ian if he'd be our agent and he said he was already like our manager and that reminded him to have us sign a contract with Cactus Records. Daisy made a flower out of the dot above her *i*. That's my new signature, she said.

Ian booked us in a Tempe music festival called SaltBed, which was held every year in the dried river bed of the Salt River that runs along the border between Phoenix and Tempe.

Ian said to come up with three more songs to add to 'D.F.O' and 'You're No Fun' and 'We Love Goo' for our EP titled *We're Masterful Johnson*. The three new songs, all written by Jammin' Jay, were: 'I Don't Want It if You Don't' (starts out with slow synthesizers like 'Forever Young' by Alphaville or that Asia song we can never remember the title of), 'Hurry! Hurry! Hurry!' (a pure pop song, a cross between Cyndi Lauper and Adam Ant about one lover waiting for another at the airport), and a song about easy money and fame called 'Desperately Seeking Pacino,' which Jammin' Jay admitted drew heavily on the early work of ABC, specifically 'Poison Arrow' from their 1982 album *Lexicon of Love* as well as from 1985's *How to Be a Zillionaire* (the lead singer of that band got Hodgkin's disease and we're hoping when he's well ABC will have a huge comeback). In just two days Jammin' Jay had written three new songs and had the instrumental tracks laid down. We marveled at his brilliance.

Masterful Johnson was the top bill at SaltBed and me and Daisy started to get really nervous. We practiced nonstop but our voices didn't seem to be able to handle the material. Ian called a special meeting and it was decided that, until we could really perform our songs, we'd lip sync. We'll record special live versions, Ian said. So that's what we did, adding a 'Hello Phoenix!' at the beginning of 'D.F.O.' Jammin' Jay rearranged a couple of the songs and added a sort of disco song called 'Trip the Light.' We'll give them something new, he said. We also recorded an acoustic version of 'You're No Fun.' Jammin' Jay coached us on how to lip sync. It's an art form like anything else, if it's done right, he said. You can't just get up there and move your lips, he said, you're not puppets. He showed us how to breathe correctly and told us we should go through all the motions of actually singing except to keep the sound locked up in our throats.

We were feeling pretty confident and agreed to work with a voice coach when it was over. Being the good guy that he is, Ian said he'd release the new recording as a special 'Live from SaltBed' recording. He said they could add the crowd noise and me and Daisy were amazed. It practically moved us to tears how nice Ian was to us. It reminded of us of how nice Rick was to us and thinking about him made us sad. We felt lucky to have in Ian someone as nice as Rick.

Stella's plane landed a few hours before the show. We'd been calling Stella all along the way, telling her what was happening with Masterful Johnson and she said she was happy for us, but we thought she was a little jealous, too. We picked Stella up on the way to our gig and the first thing she said was, Did you hear about Falco? We hadn't and Stella told us that Falco—whose real name was Johann Hoelzal—died in a car crash in the Dominican Republic while on vacation. This happened back in February, Stella said, and the details are *still* a little sketchy. The three of us loved that song 'Rock Me Amadeus.'

It just goes to show you, Daisy said. One of Daisy's greatest fears is dying a random, senseless death. She told me she had the feeling her life was going to end abruptly and violently, like Falco's. Daisy asked Stella, Was he wearing a seatbelt. Daisy always wore her seatbelt. Stella said she wasn't sure but she did know he hit a bus straight on and died at the hospital from head injuries. Was he the one driving, Daisy asked. Stella wasn't sure. Daisy got real quiet and didn't say anything else the rest of the ride.

It was good to see Stella again. Sometimes when you get so driven about something you forget to stop and think about the whole thing. Me and Daisy would be the first to admit that we partly wanted to continue with Masterful Johnson just out of spite because of Stella leaving, but really SaltBed was about the three of us, like we used to be.

We had some time to kill so the three of us milled around the Salt Mine, a camp of tents selling authentic Indian jewelry, potted cacti, beaded necklaces, vintage clothing, etc. Me and Daisy were surprised more people didn't recognize us. Stella bought one of those necklaces with a little vial of colored beads hanging from it. For luck, she said.

Besides us, the most exciting news that year was that the people at SaltBed were finally able to get a cool act that wasn't local. We don't know how they did it, but they were able to lure the Boston band Fuzzy out to Arizona to play. Fuzzy is one of the best pure power pop bands around. Me and Daisy think Hilken Mancini's and Chris Toppin's voices are right up there and once in awhile (like on the song 'Glad Again' off their excellent album *Electric Juices*) the band reminds us of Bananarama. We have been fans since we got a bootleg of a show where Fuzzy opened up for Dinosaur Jr. at some college. We like Dinosaur Jr. too but Fuzzy is the ultimate. Listen to 'Miss the Mark' and then listen to 'It Started Today' if you want to hear what a wide ranging talent they are.

So it was one of the highlights of our life to actually get to meet Fuzzy. And they were cool, really down-to-earth. We were nervous about approaching Hilken and Chris but they were sweethearts (the bassist and drummer are dreamboats, by the way) and we gave Hilken a copy of *We're Masterful Johnson* and she seemed genuinely eager to listen to it, which pumped me and Daisy up.

What pumped us up even more was when we were backstage getting ready and this short, thick man with dark hair and dark eyes came over and said 'Excuse me' in a heavy accent that made me and Daisy think of Boss Hogg from *The Dukes of Hazzard*. He introduced himself as Scott Key, an A&R guy for Sony Records. Scott Key told us he thought we were terrific, just terrific. He said we were really going to be the Next Big Thing. When the floodgates open on you two, he said, the whole world is going to love Masterful Johnson. He said he'd been sent out from L.A. especially to see us and that Sony wanted to sign us. Me and Daisy and Stella just sat there with our mouths open. Scott Key asked us if we were free to sign with Sony. We said, What did he mean, *free?* He asked if we were under contract with Cactus Records for another album. It occurred to us then that as far as we had ever talked about it with Ian, we were free to sign with Sony. We thought for sure Ian would be happy that such a big record company was interested in us. Scott Key kept saying the floodgates were going to open up on the whole world and he got me and Daisy pretty excited. He said we'd go to L.A. and shoot a video for 'D.F.O.' to play on MTV. Posters, T-shirts, hats, bumper stickers—maybe your own cartoon series, he said. It all sounded good to us. He gave us his card. I have to leave immediately after the show, he told us. He had to be in Texas the next day for the South by Southwest festival in Austin to check out a whole roster of bands like the Paranoids, Ramona the Pest, and Astro Chicken. We said we thought he had a great job and he said it was only great when he found talent like me and Daisy. Scott Key told us to call him that Monday, and that's what we planned to do.

Summers in Arizona are notoriously brutal and the first day of the SaltBed Festival was especially so. In addition to giving away free bottles of water, a misting system was set up backstage along with industrial fans that whirred like a sky full of jet airplanes. The security staff took turns hosing off the crowd from the stage and it was hard to tell who was enjoying it more.

The heat was certainly a factor in what happened. In retrospect, the Falco story probably didn't help either. Plus we'd stayed up all night excited about our recording future. Plus we were excited to see Stella again after such a long time. Also some of the bands before us played longer than they were scheduled, adding frustration to our nervousness. Jammin' Jay was nowhere to be found until right before we went on and he said Ian wasn't going to make it at all. We thought Ian had found out about Scott Key and was pissed, and we felt extreme guilt about it. Another factor—and I still blame Stella for this—was that Daisy had found Stella's Murder Book and found the page about Elliot and Hunter and Rick and, gruesome as she can be, Stella had autopsy pictures and Daisy'd ripped out the pages and had them in her back pocket. I found all this out later at the hospital and all Daisy said was, They don't belong in the book, they were real people.

Finally Jammin' Jay materialized and we took the stage with all this on our minds but we tried to give the very best performance we could. Even though it was night, people were still fanning themselves, pouring bottled water over their heads. Most of the guys were shirtless and a lot of women were in bikini tops and bras. It *looked* hot from the stage and the industrial fans the crew had set up couldn't beat back the day's heat or the heat coming from the lights overhead. So yeah, you guessed it, we were just about to hit the refrain of our first song, 'Hurry! Hurry! Hurry!' when Daisy flat passed out. Midway through spinning around, something she liked to do, she hit the stage floor. I thought she tripped and would get back up but when the crowd started craning their necks I looked over and saw she was out cold, her voice coming loud and strong through the speakers overhead. There was a moment of confusion where the festival paramedics rushed the stage while I frantically yelled for Jammin' Jay to cut the tape. The audience looked confused too but they quickly figured it out and started booing and hissing. The paramedics hauled Daisy offstage and Stella said she'd ride with her to the hospital. Jammin' Jay said, We best get out of here. The crowd seemed to be getting louder and the stage was suddenly heaped with empty water bottles, plastic cups, frisbees and anything else people could find to throw. The only thing I could equal to the feeling of sneaking away from the SaltBed Festival is when you lose your wallet and you think, it's not that big of a deal. Then you realize you have to cancel your credit cards. Then you realize you have to get a new driver's license. Then you realize you didn't cash your paycheck and will have to have another one issued. Then you realize you had over a hundred dollars in your wallet. That's how it hit me, in stages. At the hospital Stella hugged me and I said, We're ruined. It was on the radio, she said. Daisy looked pale and she drank and refilled two full glasses of water. In our minds we were both thinking what would Bananarama have done if something like this had happened to them. Surely all the times Sara and Keren went on stages in London there was at least one mechanical problem. How would they have coped?

Why doesn't Ian call, Daisy asked. We dialed the number for the studio on the phone in Daisy's room, but the answering machine came on. We hung up and the phone rang; it was Ian on his mobile phone. He told us he was in an accident and that's why he couldn't make it. His voice was changed. He was really somber and we hoped he would tell us it was going to be all right. But he didn't seem to know anything about what had happened. We asked him if he'd talked to Jammin' Jay and he said, I've got something to tell you. We thought he was going to tell us it was all over—which of course it was—but what he said really floored us. The songs Jammin' Jay quote unquote wrote are old unrecorded Phantasm songs, Ian said, and Phantasm is suing me personally and the group professionally for copyright infringement. Ian said what he was going to do when he got his hands on Jammin' Jay, but his cell phone cut out and he didn't call back.

A woman from the front desk came with some papers and asked Daisy for her autograph. Daisy dotted her *i* with a flower but the woman didn't notice. Stella sat next to Daisy and held her hand. She's going to be all right, someone out in the hall said. Stella said, This isn't anything, don't worry about it. Daisy opened her eyes and breathed in deep and then closed her eyes again. I felt faint and fell into the chair in the corner. What time is your flight back tomorrow, I asked and Stella said, I'll stay until we get out. But in the morning she was gone with a note that said, Please come visit me in California. Typical Stella.

In the morning we called Scott Key. As I tried to explain to the woman in Scott Key's office who we were, an orderly came for Daisy's breakfast tray and as he took it away I noticed the letters *SOS* traced in spilt salt.

Stella

The way you win a dead pool, if you're not familiar, is you pick a list of people you think are going to drop dead. You pick for the entire year. The one with the most right wins. Like anything. The trick is to have a couple wild cards, people that no one would ever pick. You get those by doing your homework, like reading the *National Enquirer* and those kinds of papers. But also you have to think a little bit, too. You read the regular news and think, Why is so-and-so canceling all of his appointments? How is so-and-so doing now that his wife is gone? Sometimes silence is the biggest clue. If you go a while without hearing anything about so-and-so, that's usually a good indicator.

Living in Hollywood helps, too. You hear a million rumors and all it takes is for the wildest one to be true and you move ahead of everyone else (any pick under age forty-five pays double dividends). Different dead pools have different rules; some say the obituary has to appear in at least three national newspapers to count, some prohibit two players from choosing the same celebrity, others are lotteries (names are drawn from a hat for $10 each and when a celebrity dies that ticket holder wins, clearing out the jackpot).

I'm in all the big pools: The Lee Atwater Invitational (http://stiffs.com), Chalk Outlines (http://pwl.netcom.com.~jluger/chalk-out.html), and the original dead pool, started in the '70s, The Game (http://members.aol.com/ggghostie/home.html). I had Kurt Cobain in '94 and two years ago I had Chris Farley (yeah, for a heart attack—but points are points). But I haven't been able to win it. This year my trump is Bryan Metro, the rock and roller who, my sources tell me, has fallen off the wagon in a big way. Metro canceled two shows in Tokyo last month due to 'fatigue.' So far, no other pooler has added Metro to their list.

My boyfriend, Craig, thinks I'm a sick puppy. He's just jaded about Hollywood, though. I met him when we both went to network on a pilot. The show was called *La Brea* and was about these ten friends who all worked at a restaurant called—you guessed it—La Brea, and I was to play Katy, the waitress/photographer and Craig was going to be Blaine, the pool shark/model. Craig had already been cast as Blaine and they brought me in to read opposite him and the scene was one where Blaine asks Katy to take some head shots of him and they end up falling in love. It was sort of romantic, even though the room was full of people, and I was clicking away on an imaginary camera. The audition was my one millionth in the few months I'd been living in California, and there was a weird sort of connection with me and Craig. He's not my usual type; he's more handsome than the guys I dated back in Phoenix. *I mean he's too handsome.* He's a dead ringer for Christopher Reeve, which he thinks has hurt his career. People look at me and see Superman, he sighs. But it made him perfect for the role of Blaine on *La Brea* and even though I didn't get the part, I moved in to his apartment at Highland Gardens, a '50s hotel on the corner of Vine and Outpost someone had converted to apartments. The show wasn't picked up though, so Craig had to go back to his old job doing dinner theater at the Starion, an old morgue turned into a restaurant down on Sunset Boulevard.

Since Craig is the star of the Starion, he was able to get me a job there, too. When it opened in the early '90s the dinner theater was primarily based on the works of Agatha Christie. It was my idea to do celebrity deaths (the restaurant was a morgue, after all). Monday night we do the murder of Lana Turner's mobster boyfriend, Wednesday is the drowning of Natalie Wood, Friday is a medley of automobile deaths: James Dean, Isadora Duncan and Jayne Mansfield. I suggested adding the murder of Bob Crane and a couple celebrity suicides, but management didn't think the crowd would want snapped necks or bashed brains with their linguine and clam sauce.

Due to an exceptional review in the *Los Angeles Times*, Monday night is packed with guys in suits and their elegantly dressed ladies, everyone giggling nervously as the wait staff attend to filling water glasses and taking dinner orders.

Break a leg, baby, Craig says, kissing me on the mouth.

Break a leg, I say back. I put my hand on my stomach to calm the butterflies.

The house lights go down and the crowd hushes, squinting through the low light from the candles on their tables at the red-curtained stage. Craig switches on the microphone. *Ladies and gentlemen, welcome to Monday night at the Starion. Now that your waiters and waitresses have your orders please stay seated and silent. Our presentation lasts an hour, without intermission, and we expect to hold you spellbound for that hour. If you should need your waiter or waitress, please extinguish the candle on your table and wait patiently. We hope you enjoy the show.*

Craig switches off the microphone and takes two deep breaths.

On a rainy April night in 1958, he begins again into the microphone, *the police were summoned to 730 North Bedford Drive in Beverly Hills… the home of screen star Lana Turner.*

That is my cue. The stage lights go up on Lana's gorgeous pink bedroom and I pretended to be folding laundry on the bed. I wear a white blouse and black pedal pushers with my hair up under a pink scarf. I'm barefoot, like Lana was that night. Craig's voice booms as I walk back and forth to the closet and the dresser.

Johnny Stompanato, a former bodyguard for mobman Mickey Cohen, had fallen in love with the glamorous movie star. Theirs was a passionate affair, but when Turner learned of Stompanato's underworld connections she refused to be seen in public with him. Nominated for an Oscar for her performance in Peyton Place, *Turner wouldn't allow Stompanato to escort her to the awards ceremony… so he beat her to within an inch of her life. The tension increased as Lana would phone Stompanato continuously, telling him how much she missed and loved and wanted him but wouldn't meet him anywhere other than the seclusion of an apartment. Finally… the lies and confusion came to a head.*

There's a stage knock and Lana says, 'I don't want to talk to you.'

'C'mon, baby,' Stompanato says. 'It's me.'

'We're through,' Lana yells through the door. 'Go away!'

Three more loud knocks. 'Open this motherfucker up!'

Lana hurries to the door, unlocking it.

'We're through,' Lana says, looking Stompanato straight on.

'You'll never get away from me,' Stompanato says, closing the door. Then, angrily, 'I'll cut you good, baby. No one will ever look at that pretty face again.'

Lana moves to the far end of the dresser. 'First you lied about your name—John Steele. God, it sounds like a porno name, I should've known—and now I find out you lied about your age.'

Stompanato feigns ignorance. 'What are you talkin' about?'

'That's why you left in such a hurry this afternoon, isn't it? You knew Bill Brooks recognized you, right? He told me all about you back in military school in Missouri. He told me to stay away from you,' Lana says, her voice rising.

Stompanato grabs her by the arm. 'It's too late for that now, isn't it?'

Offstage, Molly Mann, in the role of Lana's fourteen-year-old daughter Cheryl, yells, 'Mother! What's going on?'

Stompanato loosens his grip. 'You're not going to get rid of me so easy, Miss Movie star!'

'Please, Mother, can I see you for a second?' Cheryl says.

Stompanato turns to the wall, trembling with rage.

'Come in,' Lana says. Cheryl enters stage left and reaches out for her mother's hand, feeling her icy fingers. The two take a few steps in the direction opposite Stompanato.

'Why don't you just tell him to go?' Cheryl whispers. 'You're a coward, Mother.'

'You don't understand,' Lana whispers. 'I'm deathly afraid of him.'

'Don't worry. I won't leave you,' Cheryl says. 'I won't be far away.'

Cheryl exits stage right and Lana, newly confident, squares her shoulders and faces Stompanato. 'I want you to get out.'

Stompanato turns on Lana. 'You'll never get away from me! Wherever you go, I'll find you and I'll cut you good, baby. You'll never work again. And don't think I won't also get your mother and your kid.'

Lana pushes Stompanato. 'I've had just enough!'

'Cunt! You're dead!' Stompanato grabs a hanger from the closet and raises it to strike Lana just as Cheryl pounds on the door.

'Let me in! Let me talk to both of you!'

Lana swings the door open, Stompanato behind her, and Cheryl enters, walking in a straight line, as if trying to pass the sobriety test of her life. She and Stompanato come together like they're hugging.

'My God, Cheryl, what have you done?' Stompanato says, falling on his back.

Cheryl drops the knife and runs from the room as the curtain falls.

Several of the kitchen staff, who are also actors, appear in the second half, which consists of the circus surrounding the next few hours at the mansion in Beverly Hills. The cook's assistant plays Jerry Geisler, the famous lawyer who got Errol Flynn acquitted *twice* of having sex with underage girls; others play the paramedics, the doctor who can't get a pulse, the chief of police, and a reporter from a Hollywood tabloid. The show ends with Cheryl being hauled off to jail and Lana screaming, 'Bring back my baby!'

After the show Craig takes me to the Denny's on Hollywood Boulevard for grilled cheese sandwiches, our post-show ritual. I notice some fake blood dried under my fingernails so I give the waitress—Amy, a film student at UCLA—my order and go to the bathroom to wash my hands. The hot water doesn't work. I scrape at the blood with my fingernails and then I see it, up above the automatic hand dryer, scratched into a beige tile: BRYAN METRO IS DEAD.

'Beverly Hills Hotel'.

'Bryan Metro, please.'

'Room number?'

'Don't you know it?'

'Ma'am, I'm sorry but we can't connect you by name, only by room number.'

'Actually, I'm not sure that he didn't check out already. Can you tell me if he's even still there?'

'I'm sorry. I can't give out any information about our guests.'

'I just remembered: it's room six.'

'There is no room six here.'

'I said Room *sixty*. Six-oh.'

'Goodbye.'

'Beverly Hills Hotel'.

'Room 2132, please.'

'Thank you.'

'Hello?'

'Bryan?'

'Oh, I'm afraid they've rung the wrong number.'

'I'm very sorry. I hope I didn't disturb you. While I have you on the line though may I ask you a question?'

'Well, I really don't know. Who are you calling for?'

'That's what I want to ask you about. Do you know if Bryan Metro is staying there? I mean, have you seen him around the pool?'

'Who's Bryan Metro?'

'The rock star. You know, *Big Noise* and *The Vegetable King*. I'm his cousin in from South Dakota and I was supposed to meet him but I can't remember the number.'

'Did you ask the front desk?'

'They were unhelpful.'

'Well, I don't know who he is. So I don't know if he's here. Sorry.'

'That's okay. Thanks for your patience.'

'I did see Alex Trebek at the hotel bar last night.'

'Oh?'

'Yeah, he's not as smart as he thinks he is. I asked him the four states whose capital shares the same first letter as the name of the state. He was stumped. Do you know that one?'

'I guess I don't.'

'Maybe I should go on *Jeopardy!* What do you think?'

'Go for it.'

'Maybe I will.'

'Anyway, thanks a lot.'

'You're welcome.'

'Chasen's.'

'Yeah, I was in Bryan Metro's party last night and I think I left my glasses at the bar.'

'Are you sure you have the right restaurant? Bryan Metro hasn't been in here for weeks—'

'Yeah, I'm sure.'

'—and he's not allowed back as far as my manager's concerned, so it definitely wasn't last night.'

'Oh, maybe I *do* have the wrong place.'

'Okay.'

'But he was there a few weeks ago?'

'It was maybe more.'

'Before or after he was in Japan?'

'What am I, his personal assistant? How should I know.'

'Okay.'

' 'Bye.'

'Wait. Why isn't Bryan allowed at Chasen's?'

'You're his friend—you ask him.'

'Cedars-Siani.'

'Admitting, please.'

'Is this an emergency?'

'No.'

'One moment.'

'Admitting.'

'Yes, I'm calling to find out if Bryan Metro has been admitted to the hospital.'

'I'm sorry, I really can't give that information out.'

'I see.'

'Are you a reporter?'

'Uh, no, not really.'

'What do you mean not really?'

'Well, you're not allowed to talk to reporters, right?'

'Not on the record, no.'

'Are you saying you can say something off the record?'

'Well, I might be persuaded, but you can't use my name.'

'I don't know your name.'

'Right.'

'Well? Has Bryan Metro been admitted?'

'No. But we did admit someone today.'

'Yeah? Who?'

'Someone pretty famous.'

'Who?'

'Guess.'

'Uh, give me a hint.'

'You'll never guess.'

'Is it someone who knows Bryan Metro?'

'Forget Bryan Metro—he isn't here.'

'Would Bryan Metro know who this person is?'

'I would *hope* so.'

'Is it a man or a woman?'

'Man.'

'Is he famous just in Hollywood or all over the world?'

'How can anyone just be famous in Hollywood?'

'Good point.'

'Shit, here comes my boss.'

'Wait—'

'Forest Lawn Cemetery.'

'Hi. I have sort of an odd question.'

'It's a cemetery, honey. You won't offend anyone here.'

'Is Bryan Metro buried up there?'

'Metro... Metro... let me think. Is he that silent film star?'

'No, he's a musician.'

'When did he die?'

'Well, I'm not sure he did die.'

'Tell you the truth, I'm pretty new here and I don't know. The computers are down, too. Normally you can look something like that up. Do you want me to call you back when the computers are up?'

'I could call you back. I'm not really at a number where I can be reached.'

'Metro, Metro. It doesn't ring a bell. The only ones I know for sure are Gene Autry (he's in the Sheltering Hills section, Grave 1048, just in front of one of the statues), Lucille Ball (she's in the Columbarium of Radiant Dawn in the Court of Remembrance), and Scatman Crothers (he's Lincoln Terrace Plot 4545).'

'Andy Gibb's there, too.'

'Oh yeah?'

'You know who's right above him?'

'Who?'

'The dwarf who played E.T.'

'No shit. I loved that movie.'

'Well, anyway. I might call you back. When do you think the computers will be back up?'

'Who knows about these things?'

Right as I roll to a stop on Rodeo Paque turns up the stereo and says, What can beat Marlon Brando's trash?

I nod, saying, It's a score for sure.

It smells, Daisy says from the backseat.

Even though it's night, someone uses the diagonal crosswalk and I watch our reflection in the windows of Pierre Cardin.

How do they know we're not just saying it's Brando's garbage, Daisy asks.

We'll have to dig through it for something personal, I say.

I think there's fish in here, Daisy says.

Roll down the window, Paque says.

Okay, I say, who's next?

Paque pulls the yellow envelope out of the glove box and sifts through the address slips I stole from Imagistic Photo Developers, a swanky film developing place where I work on the weekends until I can get my big break.

Do you have David Hasselhoffs address, Daisy asks.

I don't think so, I say.

Too bad, she says, I'll bet he's got all kinds of cheesy stuff to steal.

Paque holds one of the slips under the glove box light. I can't read this one, she says.

What's the address, I ask.

1700 Coldwater Canyon.

Forget it. That's where Carrie Fisher lives. She's got big gates, I say.

How do you know, Paque asks.

I put my blinker on and turn left. I've been by it, I say.

Pick someone, Daisy says. This stuff really stinks.

You pick, Paque says. She holds the envelope open over her shoulder and Daisy reaches in.

Who'd you get, I ask.

It's a tie, she says. Tom Bosley and Peter Falk.

I vote for Mr. Cunningham, I say.

Where does Columbo live, Paque asks.

I turn down the radio—the B-52's—to hear the address.

1004 Roxbury Drive.

We're close to Roxbury, Daisy says.

Let's go then, Paque says.

I gotta get out of this car, Daisy says.

I suggest a quick dinner where we can sort it out, get some more loot and meet the others up at the Hollywood sign to get scored.

You like Mexican, I ask.

Sounds good, Paque says.

Any place, Daisy says.

I pull into the parking lot of El Coyote on Beverly, a Mexican restaurant whose food is notoriously bad but I can't resist showing it to Paque and Daisy. This is where Sharon Tate had her last meal, I tell them as we drift to a stop.

Who's Sharon Tate, Paque asks.

You know, I say. Charles Manson.

That's sick, Paque says. This isn't going to be a tour, is it?

I laugh. Daisy climbs out and the Hefty bag of Brando's trash sags on the backseat.

Should we go through that before or after we eat, Daisy asks.

After, Paque says, or I'll lose my appetite.

I notice a catering truck idling on the street as we push through the front doors of the El Coyote and Paque lets out a wow when she sees all the cameras and lights inside.

They're filming something, I say.

Daisy trips on a thick black cord taped to the floor. A short man in a yellow baseball cap approaches us.

Is the restaurant open, I ask.

Yeah, come in, the short man says, We're filming an MTM here and all the customers are extras. I just need you to sign this.

The short man hands us a clipboard.

What's an MTM, Daisy asks.

Made-for-TV-Movie, the short man answers.

What's it about, I ask.

The short man puffs up with importance. Charlie Manson, he says.

The three of us are seated at a brown formica-top table and someone, maybe a waitress, brings us a plate of burritos. The other tables are eating burritos too, and everyone is looking excitedly at the table under the glare of the lights. The young actress playing Sharon Tate is a dead ringer. I don't recognize any of the actors, except maybe the one playing Abigail Folger, Tate's friend. It looks like Jenny Martins, who beat me out for a network pilot about a gas station in Ohio.

The short man comes into our line of vision and standing next to him is the director, who calls out to the extras, OK, in this scene Sharon and her friends are enjoying their dinner—like you folks are—and Manson gets up and walks by their table and stares Sharon down.

The director turns to the short man. Are we set for the two shots, he asks. The table shot and the tracking shot?

All set, the short man answers.

Look at that, Paque whispers.

We all look and see the actor playing Charlie Manson, who is so into his role he sneers at us.

Manson was never in the El Coyote, I say under my breath.

Hey, the short man says, hearing me. We're taking some liberties. Are we going to have troublemakers here?

The entire restaurant is staring and Sharon looks over her shoulder impatiently.

I shake my head no.

OK, good, the short man says.

We get through the table shot in four takes. There's some easy banter between the actors about when Sharon's then-husband Roman Polanski is coming back from London and what Sharon's next project is.

The burritos are cold and the three of us do the acting job of a lifetime just pretending to eat them. We stop when the tracking shot is set up. The director tells us to take fifteen and I ask Paque and Daisy if they'd rather split and finish the scavenger hunt.

This is sort of cool, Paque admits. You'd never see something like this in Phoenix.

There's usually a cool party after the hunt is over though, I say. Daisy?

Daisy is still picking at her burrito, not taking her eyes off the actor playing Manson. He looks just like him, she says. Look how much he looks like him.

His name is probably Jim and he probably lives in Reseda, I say.

I'm certain the actress playing Abigail Folger is Jenny Martins and all I need is for her to come over and ask me how it's going. It hasn't come up, and I hope Paque and Daisy have forgotten my boasts when they dropped me off at the airport when I left Phoenix, about how big I was going to make it, but the thought of being humiliated in front of them by Jenny Martins makes me anxious. Do you want to stay or go, I ask.

Daisy quits picking at her burrito and I look at Paque, who is watching Daisy, concerned about whether or not Daisy is going to have another one of her fits. If she loses it, there's no telling in what way she'll lose it. The funniest time she lost it was when we were in high school, at the U2 concert at Sun Devil Stadium, when we saw the actor Bill Murray and Daisy screamed in his face.

We were all anxious that night because Kissel told us he could get us backstage. We overheard some woman telling her friend about seeing Charlie Sheen in the line for the men's room. And we loved Charlie Sheen. I was high-strung that night myself because we—Paque and Daisy and me—had just come from a gig as fantasy wrestlers (which was Kissel's business) and it hadn't gone so well.

The three of us were trying to get some money to go to England that summer to try to meet Bananarama. We'd tried raising money by selling No Bakes, a cookie Daisy's father invented, at the spring training games in Scottsdale, but we ate more than we sold.

So Kissel (who was my boyfriend at the time; I was seventeen and he was twenty-four) said he had this big-time client who wanted to wrestle three young girls. We didn't know anything about fantasy wrestling—we only knew it was what Kissel did. Kissel explained the levels of fantasy wrestling: competitive (where each wrestler tries to win), semicompetitive (where you wrestle for real but more just to do different moves and not necessarily to win) and fantasy matches, which is very light wrestling where women put men in different holds and the men try to get out of them.

The big-time client wanted a fantasy match and Kissel said he'd give us each $1,000 so we said we'd do it. Kissel showed us a move called body scissors—the only move he said we'd really need—where you take your legs and wrap them around a person and squeeze as tight as you can and the other person tries to break free. We also learned a couple of pinning holds, like the half-nelson, the chicken wing, and the near-side cradle, which Kissel said were popular moves in fantasy wresting as the wrestler teeters on the back of her opponent, which the opponent enjoys.

The big-time client was staying at the Ritz-Carlton and Kissel waited in the room while the three of us changed into our lacy negligees. We could hear Kissel and the big-time client talking business. Kissel pocketed the down payment and helped strip down the bed (sheets were dangerous to the wrestler).

I'm right outside the door, he said.

The match started with just Paque, who scissored the guy around the neck, his head buried deep between her legs. The guy didn't try too hard to break free, but he eventually did. He called out for Daisy and me to jump in and we circled the edge of the bed, thinking about that $1,000 all the way.

What happened, and why Kissel came running into the room, and why we were edgy the rest of the night, is that the three of us had the guy facedown on the bed, his arms and legs locked up and, while we didn't realize it, we were suffocating him. The guy kicked free, knocking Paque off the bed. I lost my balance and the guy's arms came free and in all his flailing he punched Daisy in the nose. Daisy screamed, probably more at the sight of the watery blood streaming out of her nose than the fact that she'd been hit. Kissel pounded on the door but we were all so stunned—the guy included—that no one made a move to open the door and Kissel charged in, saw the blood, and hauled off and decked the client. We tried to tell Kissel what happened but he kept punching the guy and we grabbed some hotel robes (and a towel for Daisy) and waited in Kissel's car.

Finally Kissel came out the back entrance and he was madder than shit.

The guy didn't even have the money, he said.

Daisy lay down on the backseat and her nose finally stopped bleeding. Kissel split the down payment—$500—between the three of us, not taking a share for himself.

You should get your share, Paque said.

I got my share, Kissel said.

We used some of our money that night to buy concert T-shirts.

We bought XXL's and draped them over us so that we looked like three ghosts moving through the smoky stadium. Kissel was on the lookout for the dude who was supposed to get us backstage, so he wasn't really watching Bono and the boys. The more Kissel scanned the crowd, the more nervous the three of us got. We decided to go get Cokes and that's when we saw Bill Murray. He sort of just appeared and I said, Look, and Daisy looked up and started screaming a high pitch scream. People around us laughed and Bill Murray smiled and started screaming, matching Daisy's screams pitch for pitch. Daisy was screaming so hard her nose started to bleed again and Bill Murray looked a little freaked out and his friends pulled him away and we ducked into a bathroom, cutting ahead of everyone in line.

Remember when we saw Bill Murray, I ask, trying to get Daisy's attention.

That was hilarious, Paque says.

Hey Stella, Daisy says, What exactly did Manson do to them?

The short man walks by and I wait for him to pass before I say, He didn't do anything. He had people do it. He wasn't there.

Wasn't he in love with Sharon Tate, Paque asks.

No, you're thinking of the guy who shot President Reagan, I say.

Daisy asks me to tell her exactly what happened that night and I tell her about how Sharon Tate and Roman Polanski had rented the house on Cielo Drive, about how Sharon was eight months pregnant and that Polanski was in London, working on a film, but was planning on returning for the birth of his child. So Sharon wouldn't be alone, Abigail Folger and her boyfriend Wojciech 'Voyteck' Frykowski were staying at the house. Their friend Jay Sebring, the famed hairstylist, was there that night too.

They had dinner at the El Coyote and returned to the house. Across town, Charlie Manson sent Tex Watson, Pat Krenwinkle, Susan Atkins, and Linda Kasabian out in a 1959 Ford to the house on Cielo Drive. It was around midnight and Tex cut the phone lines, which landed on the gate. Manson's group had to scale a hillside because they were afraid of being electrocuted. As they landed in the compound, a pair of headlights came at them. The women hid and Tex held up his hand. The headlights stopped and eighteen-year-old Steve Parent hopped out of the white Rambler. Parent had been up to the guest house to see William Garretson, the caretaker, who was trying to sell him a radio. Tex gave Parent four bullets at point blank range.

Didn't the people in the house hear the shots, Daisy asks.

Apparently not, I say, because Tex was able to cut a screen in the back of the house and let the others in. They rounded everyone up in the front room and Tex wrapped a rope around Jay Sebring's neck and slung it up over one of the rafters. He started fixing the other end of the rope around Sharon Tate's neck but Sebring begged that she was pregnant and Tex just shot him. Voyteck's hands had been tied with a towel and he struggled free and a fight ensued. Voyteck ran out the front door but was stabbed fifty-one times, shot and pistol-whipped on the front lawn. Abigail Folger tried to run for it but was tackled by Krenwinkle and Tex killed her just outside the house. Which just left Sharon Tate, who pled for the life of her unborn child. Tex said, Woman, I have no mercy for you and stabbed her sixteen times. They used her blood to write PIG on the front door.

That's disgusting, Paque says.

But why did Manson tell them to do it, Daisy asks.

Manson wanted to be a rock star, I explained, and the guy who owned the house was a music producer who had told Charlie he didn't have any talent. Manson didn't know the guy had rented the house out to Sharon Tate and Roman Polanski.

OK, people, the short man says, We're rolling in five.

And guess what, I say. Most people don't know that Steve McQueen was supposed to be there that night too but he got in a

68

fight with his wife and took off somewhere else.

Lucky, Paque says.

The restaurant is brought to order. A group of five appear in the door, confused by the makeshift set, and the short man shoos them out.

The director yells, Action, and the actor playing Charlie Manson stops eating, stares in the direction of Sharon Tate's table, and pushes back his chair. He is supposed to walk through the restaurant, staring at Sharon's table, which erupts in laughter as Manson strolls by. Once at the door, Manson is to stop, turn around, and narrow his eyes at Sharon and her friends.

But when he passes our table, Daisy drops her fork onto her plate and says, Don't. She puts her foot in the aisle, as if to trip him.

Cut!

The actor playing Manson says, What the fuck?

Others in the restaurant are laughing and Daisy stares Manson down until he says, Get her out of here.

The actress playing Abigail Folger is not Jenny Martins.

The short man hustles us out of the El Coyote and replaces us with the party waiting outside as Paque and Daisy and I are thrown out.

Why do they make movies about that kind of stuff, Daisy asks as I pull out onto Beverly.

People love it, Paque says.

It's late and the traffic in Beverly Hills has thinned to an occasional Mercedes or Jeep Wrangler. We pass a cop cruiser that slows next to an old woman pushing a grocery cart.

What does everybody want to do, I ask.

What happened to the trash, Paque asks.

I left it in the parking lot, Daisy says.

We decide to try and catch the rest of the scavengers and find out where the party is. The Hollywood sign comes into view, the forty-five-foot letters glowing above the darkened canyon.

Want to hear a ghost story, I ask.

Paque is fiddling with the stereo and Daisy is looking out the back window. I start to tell them about Peg Entwhistle, the actress who dove head first off the H back in the '20s, but Daisy says, We don't want to hear it, and the car is silent except for the new wave song coming over the radio. A wide dirt field full of cars and people opens up in front of us and I shut off my headlights.

Hey, I say as we get out.

Hey Stella, T.J. says. Spill out what you've got and I'll score it.

We didn't get anything, I say.

Hey hurry up, someone says, Before the cops arrive.

Paque and Daisy drift away from the crowd, peering down at the back of the sign, its wooden skeleton visible. T.J. hovers over the piles of mailboxes, license plates, Beware of Dog signs, weather vanes, potted plants, etc., tallying everything on his clipboard. And while I don't know exactly what each item is worth, I'm certain a bag of famous garbage would've beaten the whole lot, hands down.

Ms. Drew Barrymore
380 N. Martel Avenue
Los Angeles, CA 90036

Dear Drew Barrymore,

You recently had your photos developed at Imagistic Photo Developers. We want you to know how much we appreciate your business. Enclosed are coupons which are good on your next visit to Imagistic. We hope to continue to be your photomat of choice.

Also, I just wanted to say personally that I am a fan of your work. I thought you were terrific in *E. T.* And *The Wedding Singer* is one of my friends' favorite movies. I think it remarkable, too, that you've been able to overcome what you have to be the star you are today. Most people will never in their life go through what you went through by the time you were eleven. Your recovery from drug and alcohol addiction is a modern success story and I can sympathize with your having a wild mother. You should know that you really are a role model for a lot of young women today.

Anyway, just wanted to add that bit. Oh, and if it's not too much trouble I wanted to ask you something else. I saw a recent photo of you in *Entertainment Weekly* where you were at the Viper Room with Bryan Metro. I'm wondering if you can tell me anything about where he is now. I'm a huge fan and have heard some (hopefully) unfounded rumors. Any information you can provide would be appreciated. Yours sincerely,

Ms. Neve Campbell
8645 Wonderland Avenue
Los Angeles, CA 90046

Dear Neve Campbell,

You recently had your photos developed at Imagistic Photo Developers. We want you to know how much we appreciate your business. Enclosed are coupons which are good on your next visit to Imagistic. We hope to continue to be your photomat of choice.

I just wanted to add that I think you're a terrifically talented actress. I read somewhere that your first role was on a Canadian TV show called *Catwalk*, where you played a girl named Daisy in a band trying to make it big. What's funny about this is I have a friend named Daisy and we tried to start a band and make it big some years ago. Anyway, I'm a fan—I loved *Scream* and I thought *Wild Things* and *54* were good career choices. (Also, on a personal level, I know what it's like to have parents divorce when you are young. Mine did, but I hope yours are as friendly as mine are now.)

Anyway, just wanted to add that bit. Oh, and if it's not too much trouble I wanted to ask you a favor. I'm trying to track down Bryan Metro and I saw that picture in *Entertainment Weekly* of you and him at the premiere of that new Tom Hanks movie. I'm wondering if you know anything about his plans to tour, etc. I'd appreciate any information you could give me.

Yours sincerely,

Mr. David Geffen
2201 Angelo Drive
Beverly Hills, CA 90210

Dear David Geffen,

You recently had your photos developed at Imagistic Photo Developers. We want you to know how much we appreciate your business. Enclosed are coupons which are good on your next visit to Imagistic. We hope to continue to be your photomat of choice.

Also, I'm a huge fan of Bryan Metro, one of the musicians on your label. I noticed that he recently canceled two shows in Japan, the last shows of the Asian leg of his tour and I'm wondering if (hoping) the U.S. tour is still going to happen. I wanted to say too that I think it's a great thing that you are taking a chance on Bryan's comeback. He really is a talented musician and whatever problems he may have had in the '80s are hopefully behind him. After that stint in rehab his career was a wash and it really took someone brave and formidable like yourself to give Bryan a second chance (St. David Geffen!).

Anyway, just wanted to add that little bit. If you could put my name on your mailing list, I would appreciate it. And any promo stuff you have about Bryan and the tour would be great as well. Use my home address, which is below.

Yours sincerely,

Wednesday nights, Natalie Wood, are the hardest nights of the week at the Starion. Not just because the details of her drowning are sketchy—a drunken fight in the middle of the night with her husband, Robert Wagner, aboard their yacht, *Splendour*, their guest that night the actor Christopher Walken—but because my mom loved Natalie Wood in *Rebel Without a Cause* and *West Side Story*. Most families love *Miracle on 34th Street* at Christmas time for the hope it inspires, but my mom loves it because little eight-year-old Natalie 'showed so much promise and talent as an actress.' I hate the movie and won't watch it.

It's because of *Miracle on 34th Street* that I rarely call home. I made the mistake of mentioning the *La Brea* pilot, thinking I had the part wrapped up, and it was months before I could tell my mom. If only I would've got you into pictures when you were eight, she said when I finally did tell her. It's frustrating enough going on auditions and having people judge you on what you look like, how you talk, by how you carry yourself; calling home to give progress reports was a form of humiliation I had some control over.

Hard as it is, you just have to believe it's worth it. That's what Craig tells me after every Wednesday night performance. Some days I don't think it is worth it. It's hard to keep the dream of having a big house with gates and fancy cars and the adulation of everyone you meet in front of you at all times. But when Craig reminds me how it's worth it, I believe him. He would know. His father was a successful Broadway actor in the '60s who made the jump to Hollywood. He starred in *The Dennis Hartwell Story*, a popular movie in the early 1970s. Craig was just born when the movie came out but he remembers how famous actors were always coming over to his house in the Hollywood Hills (which Craig's mother set fire to in a jealous rage over one of his father's co-stars). His father hosted a cocktail hour every day of the week, which lasted from four in the afternoon until whenever. There's a picture of Craig sitting on a young Clint Eastwood's lap at a table full of gifts wrapped in shiny paper.

Craig's father didn't want him to be an actor and even though his mother begged his father to get him small parts in his father's movies, he refused. So in high school Craig secretly went on auditions and got a small part in a summer beach movie. When his father found out he showed up at the set, drunk, and disrupted the scene Craig was supposed to be in. The director threw Craig and his father off the set and Craig had to drive his father home. No son of mine is going to become an actor, he yelled at the passing cars. Craig only told me this story once, and I never bring it up. He couldn't know at the time that his father was just protecting him, that his father had sunk into the shadows of Hollywood, which came out when Craig's father was arrested in a hotel room with another actor and a few grams of cocaine. The actor was Craig's age. Craig changed his last name and wasn't there when his father passed away from emphysema in a VA hospital.

Wednesday nights give me that same feeling of alienation. When we get to the part where Natalie and Robert Wagner and Christopher Walken return to the boat from their dinner on Catalina Island, the house lights go down and the sound of the ocean comes over the speakers. People in the audience usually stop eating and the candles on their tables flicker like a misshapen constellation. Craig and I fight as Wagner and Wood, and then the theater is silent except for the electronic undulation of waves. The script calls for me to count to ten and then scream. Before I get to five-one-thousand I begin to tremble, the solitary feeling of loneliness engulfing me. The silence is shattered by my scream, the thump and splash that follows breaking my trance.

Ms. Jennie Garth
12055 Contour Drive
Van Nuys, CA 91423

Dear Jennie Garth,

You recently had your photos developed at Imagistic Photo Developers. We want you to know how much we appreciate your business. Enclosed are coupons which are good on your next visit to Imagistic. We hope to continue to be your photomat of choice.

Also I wanted to tell you what a fan I am of yours, on and off the screen. Your involvement with PETA is something I admire as I am an animal lover, too. (I'm trying to take it to the level where you're at, but I enjoy a hamburger now and again.) I admire your career as well. Like you I'm from Phoenix (well, I know you're not *from* Phoenix, but you lived there) and I moved to L.A. to become an actress. I hope I have half the career you've had (I've seen every episode of *90210*).

Anyway, just wanted to add that personal bit. Oh, and to ask a question. I saw in the *L.A. Times* that Bryan Metro played at the last PETA benefit, a couple of months ago, and I'm wondering if you still hear from him. I'm a huge fan of his and have heard some rumors that I hope aren't true. I'd like to get any information about his whereabouts. Any small thing you know might be helpful. Thanks.

Yours sincerely,

Ms. Alyssa Milano
12632 Woodbridge St.
Studio City, CA 91604

Dear Alyssa Milano,

You recently had your photos developed at Imagistic Photo Developers. We want you to know how much we appreciate your business. Enclosed are coupons which are good on your next visit to Imagistic. We hope to continue to be your photomat of choice.

Also I wanted to add a little personal note about what a fan of yours I am. I think you are terrifically talented and I think *Fear* really shows your acting range. I'm also a fan of your music career, which I guess not a lot of people know about. I recently found your debut album, *Alyssa*, at a used record store on Sunset. They also had a copy of *Locked Inside a Dream* that you'd autographed to someone named Jackie Land. (They wanted too much for the autographed copy or I would've bought it.) Anyway, I'm a fan of yours and I'm also a fan of Bryan Metro. Not a lot of people who love Bryan's music know that he co-wrote the song 'Straight to the Top' from your second album, *Look in My Heart*. Anyway, I'm wondering if you're still in contact with Bryan. As a fan I'm concerned about the recent rumors and about his canceling those dates in Japan. I know it's a long shot but I thought I'd put a line or two in about him in case you know his whereabouts. Anything you can say would be appreciated.
Yours sincerely,

Mr. William Rose
5067 Latigo Canyon Road
Malibu, CA 90265

Dear Axl Rose,

You recently had your photos developed at Imagistic Photo Developers. We want you to know how much we appreciate your business. Enclosed are coupons which are good on your next visit to Imagistic. We hope to continue to be your photomat of choice.

Also, I can't resist telling you what a fan I am of your music. It's been quite awhile since the world has heard anything from Guns N' Roses. I hope you're working on something new with the band.

Anyway, accept our apologies for the negatives. Oh—I wanted to ask you something: I read an article in *Entertainment Weekly* that said you were with Bryan Metro in Japan. The article even said that you and Bryan were working on some new material together (though it didn't say whether it was for a new Bryan Metro album or a new Guns N' Roses album). I'm wondering a) if this is true and b) if you know anything about what Bryan is up to now. I'm a huge fan of his and after those cancellations in Japan I'm concerned (as a fan). Did Bryan see any doctors in Japan? Is he in the states now?

Sorry to go on so long but any information you can give would be appreciated.

Yours sincerely,

SWEET PEA: Anyone here?

MAX FACTOR: Yo, Sweet Pea, what's up?

FABULOUS PERSON: Hi, Sweet Pea.

SWEET PEA: Have any of you heard anything about Bryan Metro?

FABULOUS PERSON: You mean the singer?

SWEET PEA: Yeah.

MAX FACTOR: He just canceled those shows in Japan. I heard he was dead.

SWEET PEA: Yeah, that's what I'm trying to find out. Where did you hear it?

MAX FACTOR: Here.

FABULOUS PERSON: I think I hate Bryan Metro. Doesn't he sing that song 'The Pain Purples Me Too'?

SWEET PEA: That's him.

MAX FACTOR: I only know this one thing about him. He used to hang out with the guys from House of Pain, remember them? One of the guys from the band, Danny Boy, dated the porn star Savannah (she also 'dated' Billy Idol, Pauly Shore, and both Slash and Axl from Guns N' Roses) and she was staying in his house while the band was on tour. She and Bryan were coming back from a wild night and Savannah was racing her white Corvette up the winding roads of Universal City when she slammed into a fence. She hit her head, cut her face and broke her nose. And she was supposed to go do a $5,000-a-night gig at this place in upstate New York. Bryan wasn't hurt and he helped Savannah get back to the house, where she called her manager, saying she should be taken to the hospital. Metro passed out in front of the TV, figuring the ambulance was on the way and that everything was taken care of, right? Well, the ambulance *did* come later, after Metro found Savannah on the garage floor with a flower-shaped hole in her head. Unfortunately when she put the gun to her head, it kicked and she was still alive (barely). Metro rode in the ambulance.

FABULOUS PERSON: That's awful. What happened?

MAX FACTOR: Her parents pulled the plug.

SWEET PEA: Yeah, I read about that somewhere. That was a while ago.

FABULOUS PERSON: Who just logged in?

WHAT-UP-CHUCK: Here I am. What are we talking about?

SWEET PEA: Bryan Metro.

WHAT-UP-CHUCK: He rocks, of course.

SWEET PEA: I'm trying to find out why he canceled those shows in Japan.

WHAT-UP-CHUCK: My friend works at Geffen, his label, and he said the official reason was fatigue but that Metro got into trouble with the Japanese police.

SWEET PEA: What kind of trouble?

WHAT-UP-CHUCK: Some underage kids in his hotel room.

MAX FACTOR: Cool.

FABULOUS PERSON: My God, what a cliché. Can't these rock stars be more original?

WHAT-UP-CHUCK: Rock is all about getting p**sy.

FABULOUS PERSON: If you're a man, maybe.

SWEET PEA: WUC: Does your friend at Geffen know anything else?

WHAT-UP-CHUCK: Like what?

SWEET PEA: Like if Metro is still alive.

WHAT-UP-CHUCK: Shit, is he dead?

SWEET PEA: That's what I'm trying to find out.

WHAT-UP-CHUCK: I'll try to call my friend on his cell phone. Excuse me.

SWEET PEA: Thanks.

MAX FACTOR: Hey, Sweet Pea. Why are you so interested?

SWEET PEA: I'm a fan.

FABULOUS PERSON: Where do you live, Sweet Pea?

SWEET PEA: In Hollywood.

MAX FACTOR: Ever see any stars?

SWEET PEA: Yeah, I work in a photo lab in Beverly Hills.

MAX FACTOR: Who did you see recently?

SWEET PEA: Last weekend Tommy Lee came in.

MAX FACTOR. He has the biggest schlong in Hollywood.

FABULOUS PERSON: You're gross, Max Factor. 4Sweet Pea: Why do you work in a photo lab?

SWEET PEA: Well, I only work there on the weekends. I'm trying to be an actress.

MAX FACTOR: Have you been in anything I might've seen?

SWEET PEA: NO. I do dinner theater in Hollywood.

FABULOUS PERSON: What play?

SWEET PEA: It's a series of plays about celebrity deaths.

MAX FACTOR: Like who?

SWEET PEA: Well, on Friday nights we do a car crash-themed play about Jayne Mansfield.

MAX FACTOR: Who's that?

FABULOUS PERSON: She was a movie star from the '50s.

SWEET PEA: She wasn't really a movie star. She was sort of like Anna Nicole Smith. She referred to herself as a 'starlet in training.' The play we do is the night she was killed, in New Orleans, on the way back from a gig in Biloxi, Mississippi. The whole play is set in the limousine. I play Jayne and my boyfriend plays her lawyer friend, Sam Brody. Extras from the restaurant play Jayne's three kids.

MAX FACTOR: Why did the limo crash?

SWEET PEA: The driver came around a corner on U.S. 90, just outside of New Orleans, and ran into the back of a truck that had one of those mosquito fogging machines on it. The truck was stopped and the road was narrow, so...

FABULOUS PERSON: Was the driver speeding, like Princess Di?

SWEET PEA: NO, the top of the limo was shaved off. The car looked like a convertible.

MAX FACTOR: Did everyone die?

SWEET PEA: NO. The children lived. People think Jayne was decapitated but really it was just the wig she was wearing. It flew up on the hood of the car.

FABULOUS PERSON: Who was the actress who had her scarf caught in the back wheel of her car?

MAX FACTOR: I never heard that one.

SWEET PEA: Isadora Duncan. She wasn't an actress; she was a dancer.

WHAT-UP-CHUCK: Hold on, Sweet Pea. I'm trying some different numbers.

SWEET PEA: Thanks, WUC.

FABULOUS PERSON: Goodnight people.

MAX FACTOR: Goodnight, Fabulous Person.

SWEET PEA: 'Bye.

MAX FACTOR: NOW that the children are out of the room, what's all this Bryan Metro stuff?

SWEET PEA: It's for a dead pool.

MAX FACTOR: I'm in a dead pool!

SWEET PEA: Which one?

MAX FACTOR: It's one at my school. This guy in my chemistry class runs it.

SWEET PEA: I have a feeling you should add Metro to your list, if you can.

MAX FACTOR: Man, I've had Don Knotts for the last two years. I thought he was going to win it for me.

SWEET PEA: Yeah, I got Don Knotts.

MAX FACTOR: Any other friendly tips?

SWEET PEA: Sorry.

MAX FACTOR: That would be something if Bryan Metro *was*

dead. It would be like having River Phoenix back in '93. Or Kurt Cobain in '94.

SWEET PEA: I had Cobain.

MAX FACTOR: How did you guess that one?

SWEET PEA: Dead pool rule of thumb: When a rock star turns 27, put him on your list.

MAX FACTOR: How old is Bryan Metro?

SWEET PEA: 43.

WHAT-UP-CHUCK: Don't count your money yet, Sweet Pea. My friend says Bryan Metro is alive and well.

SWEET PEA: Does he know where he is?

WHAT-UP-CHUCK: L.A. He's resting before the American tour. My friend said he was at a party two nights ago and Metro was there. It was for the new Brad Pitt movie. He said Metro looked like shit and that David Geffen had him put in a limo and sent home.

SWEET PEA: Does Metro have a place in L.A.?

WHAT-UP-CHUCK: Sorry, didn't ask.

SWEET PEA: Is there any way I can call your friend and ask him some questions?

WHAT-UP-CHUCK: No can do. If they find out he's talking, he could get fired. There's been some stories floating around and Metro thinks its people at his label leaking stories about him because they want to dump him.

MAX FACTOR: There goes the pool.

SWEET PEA: Thanks, WUC.

WHAT-UP-CHUCK: No problem.

Ms. Tiffani-Amber Thiessen
3253 Wrightwood Court
North Hollywood, CA 91604

Dear Tiffani-Amber Thiessen,
You recently had your photos developed at Imagistic Photo Developers. We want you to know how much we appreciate your business. Enclosed are coupons which are good on your next visit to Imagistic. We hope to continue to be your photomat of choice.

Also, I wanted to tell you that I thought *Saved by the Bell* was a pretty good show, and that I liked your work on *90210*, or *Melrose*, I can't remember which now. Somewhere I saw a picture of you as a child, when you modeled for the Peaches and Cream Barbie doll. I saw you once in person too, out in front of Mann's Chinese Theater. You were with what looked like your brothers (one about eighteen, the other in his mid-twenties) and you were goofing around putting your hands in the cement hands of movie stars. You look like a really nice person.

Anyway, just supposed to be sending these coupons. Oh—and I wanted to ask you a question. You gave an interview to *YM* magazine last month and the interviewer asked you a question about what you liked to do with your free time and you answered that you liked to travel and the interviewer asked you a question about where you liked to go and you said Hawaii. It came out that you liked to stay at the Hilton and I don't know if you know this but that's where Bryan Metro stays when he goes to Hawaii (which I hear he likes to go to a lot) and I'm wondering if you were ever there when he was there. I'm a fan of his and am concerned about the rumors that are going around. I know it's a long shot but if you can provide any information about what Bryan's up to now, it would be appreciated.
Yours sincerely,

Mr. Michael Ovitz
1357 N. Rockingham Avenue
Los Angeles, CA 90049

Dear Michael Ovitz,

You recently had your photos developed at Imagistic Photo Developers. We want you to know how much we appreciate your business. Enclosed are coupons which are good on your next visit to Imagistic. We hope to continue to be your photomat of choice.

Also, I understand that you are Bryan Metro's new agent. I'm wondering if it's possible for you to forward the enclosed letter to him. Bryan doesn't know me but I am a huge fan of his and I'd like to get in touch with him. I don't know if you have a policy against forwarding mail—some places do, I know—but I would appreciate it if you would make an exception in this case. I'm not sure how else to reach him as I'm told the president of his fan club has gone missing somewhere in Costa Rica and mail sent to the P.O. gets returned. Please, Mr. Ovitz, forward this letter to Bryan Metro.

Yours sincerely,

P.S. I'm also enclosing my head shot. I'm an up-and-coming actress and would love to be represented by you.

I set my alarm to wake up at five. Craig rolls away from me as I sit on the edge of the bed. It feels like night. I am confused as to whether I've actually been to sleep and if so, that I've closed my eyes long enough to dream. I smell like the cigarette I allowed myself on the ride home, the long drive up Sunset after dropping Paque and Daisy off.

I eat a bowl of Applejacks in the glow of the computer screen. I chew quietly but each crunch sounds like a rockslide in my head. Milk drips over the bowl and onto the magazines fanned out under the chair. *Variety, People, Entertainment Weekly, Rolling Stone, Spin, Details, Maxim, GQ, Esquire, Vanity Fair*—even the *National Enquirer*, the *Star* and the *Globe*. Nothing. No mention of Bryan Metro, not even an article in the monthlies about the canceled shows. The silence makes me suspicious.

The agenda this morning is to check in with my dead pools, hit the Bryan Metro homepages (official and unofficial), check the online versions of *Entertainment Weekly* as well as the *San Francisco Chronicle*, the *Washington Post*, the *Wall Street Journal*, and the *New York Times*. I'm debating whether or not to hire a clipping service as I retrieve the *Los Angeles Times* from outside the front door when the headline screams out: VIDEOTAPE SHOWS SEAN FEAR IN HOTEL ROOM WITH MINOR. Before it registers that Sean Fear is Craig's best friend—it can't be that Sean Fear, can it?—that Craig and Sean were roommates when they both first moved to Hollywood, that Sean's fiancée, Heidi, is actually a good friend of mine, that Craig and I last saw Sean and Heidi—when? dinner at Succor on Melrose?—before any of that registers the phone rings. Dazed, I walk back into the bedroom. Craig is sitting up in bed saying, You're fucking kidding me, right? and I offer him the paper as proof but he pushes it away without reading it and just like that we're driving through the deserted Hollywood streets, to the Chateau Marmont, where Sean Fear, the popular actor of such films as *Night Game, Renters*, and *Knollwood*, is hiding out.

I know from the one other time I've been to the Chateau—when I first moved to Hollywood I sought out bungalow 3, where they found John Belushi on his side in bed, all the blood drained from one half of his body and collected in the other—that the Chateau Marmont is not the most secure hideout in town. I know this because the one other time I was there I simply strolled through the front door, past the draped lobby and front desk and walked back to the pool without seeing a soul. This time Craig and I take the same route but the guys from Hootie & the Blowfish are playing frisbee in the narrow courtyard while a couple girls look on from the shaded patio. Inside, the lobby is lit by the early sun and the dark greens and reds and yellows of the couches and carpet make the lobby look like that room at your grandparents' house that no one ever sits in. The place smells like someone is baking lemon pies.

There's no one at the front desk but Craig knows the room number so he punches the floor on the elevator and the door starts to close but a hand catches it, startling me, and the actor Christopher Walken gets in and presses his floor. Even though it's early morning, Walken is sweating and he seems tired. He starts to lean against the elevator wall but catches himself and then stares at me. I don't look but can feel him staring and when he exits the elevator I think how much he looks like Gerald, the waiter who plays him at the Starion.

Craig clicks open the door to Sean's room. Heidi has on sunglasses and is on the bed, flipping through a copy of *The Paris Review*. Sean comes out of the bathroom once he hears that it's us. This is the Jim Morrison suite, Heidi says nonchalantly and starts giggling.

Hey, Craig says to Sean.

Sean nods. His big screen smile is gone and his eyes scan the floor.

Hey, he says. Thanks for coming.

We're just standing, not saying anything. Heidi has a smile plastered on her face and she looks up from *The Paris Review* and says, Now you have another play for the Starion.

Sean winces. Heidi, please don't, he says.

Did Jim Morrison really stay here, I ask, trying to ease the tension in the room.

It's the Jim Morrison suite all right, Heidi says. She lifts her sunglasses and I see that her eyes are swollen from crying. Legends only, she says.

Sean doesn't say anything. Craig asks about the tape and Sean recounts what he'd already confessed to Heidi, that the tape was real, that it happened in New York. She didn't even give me a chance to buy the tape from her, Sean says, incredulous. Heidi replaces *The Paris Review* in the night stand and pulls out a prescription bottle and dry swallows two blue tablets.

Did you know she was underage, Craig asks.

Sean shakes his head no. She isn't underage anymore, he says. That much I know.

When did you find out she sold the tape, I ask.

I woke up to the sound of the mob of reporters outside my gate, Sean says.

I smuggled him out in the trunk, Heidi says proudly.

Do you know for sure it was the girl who sold the tape, I ask.

Sean thinks. I'm assuming, he says.

Well, Craig says. What now?

I'm to lay low, Sean says. Stay out of sight.

Why don't you take a vacation, Craig suggests.

We are, Sean says. We're leaving tonight for Greece.

Do you need anything while you're gone, Craig asks. Someone to look after the house?

Sean smiles. I think it's well looked after as is, he says.

I laugh and even Heidi cracks a smile.

But there is one thing, Sean says. We left so fast this morning that Heidi forgot her purse at the house. And it has all of her identification in it.

I can't stand the thought of going back up there, Heidi says.

Sean looks at us. Is there any way I can ask you to fight through the madness up there to retrieve Heidi's purse, he asks. I'd offer you money but I know that would just insult you.

Craig, loving the challenge, says, No problem.

Sean gives Craig the keys to Heidi's car and goes over how to deactivate the alarm on the house. I excuse myself and go to the bathroom. Someone has carved I LIKED MYSELF BETTER BEFORE I BECAME WHO I AM on the windowsill and I run my fingers along the smooth grooves of the letters.

Craig and Sean were in this Saturday afternoon movie called *Nimble*, about two would-be thieves trying to pull off the score of a lifetime. Craig played a guy named Anderson, a beach bum whose parents were killed when he was small and Sean played Pluto, an ex-con who had relocated to California so he 'could see the sun' after all his time in prison. Craig has a tape of *Nimble* and sometimes I pop it in if I'm bored. It's an awful movie—Sean's studio leaves it off his official bio—but one of those awful movies that you take pleasure in watching every once in a while.

As Craig navigates Mulholland and Sean's house comes into sight, I'm reminded of the scene in the movie where Anderson and Pluto manage to sneak past the security guard at the gallery where the jewels they've been hired to steal are kept and, with trembling fingers, open the safe only to find it empty because as we ease up to Sean's gate, there isn't a soul around.

How weird, Craig says.

Once we're through the gate Craig clicks the garage opener and the garage door opens slowly like a heavy eyelid. We pull in next to Sean's Mercedes and the garage fills with the smell of exhaust.

The air conditioner blasts throughout the house and I stand in the modern kitchen and hug myself. The phone rings, startling me, and I hear Sean's voice on the answering machine. His mother leaves a worried message and when she hangs up the phone rings again and it's Sean's publicist, wanting to know where he is. She leaves three or four numbers where she can be reached and I scribble them down in case Sean wants to call her back before he leaves.

Found it, Craig says. He's got Heidi's purse slung around his shoulder.

Is everything in there, I ask.

Craig opens the purse. Yep, driver's license, credit cards, and passport.

The phone rings again. This time it's Sean's sister calling from Phoenix. Craig tries to pick it up but she hangs up before he can get to the phone.

I go to the refrigerator and swing open the double doors. The bright light hurts my eyes and I squint at a pitcher of orange juice that has an island of mold floating along the top.

They eat out a lot, Craig says when I point it out to him. He switches on the small TV in the kitchen and scans the channels. I'll bet it's on CNN, he says. Let's wait for the entertainment news and see.

We sit at the kitchen table and listen to the drone of the newscast. It's ten after the hour, which means we only have to wait ten minutes for the entertainment news but Craig seems to be concentrating on the little screen with the same intensity he uses to memorize lines. A memory I've been fighting back since I saw the paper this morning surfaces, the time Craig told me about how he felt jealous of Sean's success. It was the first time in our relationship where he was vulnerable to me and he very honestly described his bitterness at having to do dinner theater at the Starion while Sean got roles in bigger and bigger films. Craig was confused as to why it wasn't happening for him too, especially since they'd started out together. What makes one person go way up and not the other one, he asked me. I remember telling him I thought a great deal of it was luck. I haven't even been in movies like *Nimble*, so I should be feeling the same sort of frustration, but then again there's something hopeful about not yet having to play a down-and-out thief in a movie that wasn't released in theaters but went straight to video.

So when I come back from turning down the air conditioning I'm not entirely surprised to overhear Craig picking up the latest call in the kitchen.

He's staying at the Chateau Marmont, Craig says into the receiver. But he's leaving tonight for Greece. Yeah, you're welcome.

I pause in the hall and when I walk back into the kitchen Craig is watching the TV again. Is it on yet, I ask.

It's coming up, he says expectantly.

In Hollywood movies take forever to make but a good rumor can circulate as fast as it's told so the scene back at the Chateau was, in some respects, predictable. By the time we got there, the police had been called to hold off the reporters who had been ferried by the vans lined up outside the hotel, their satellites aimed at the sky, ready to beam the first salacious tidbit anyone could dig up into homes all around the world.

Craig and I scale along the outside of the mob—men in suits so early in the morning and on a Saturday was a curious sight—and find the back gate. The cop posted there is telling a reporter to get lost, that he is trespassing, and is about to tell the same thing to us when Craig says, We're guests of the hotel.

So am I, the reporter says.

Get lost, the cop yells and the reporter backs off. He turns to us and says, I'm not in the mood for tricks, so you better be who you say you are.

We were here earlier, Craig says. We just ran an errand and now we need to get back in.

The cop calls out to another cop, who appears from inside the grounds and Craig and I are escorted to the front desk. We tell the woman at the desk who we are and she says, I'm sorry, but they've left the hotel.

We're really his friends, Craig says. He looks out the windows at the cops yelling at the reporters and an amused smile comes across his face. It's okay, he tells the woman, we're his friends.

I'm sorry, she repeats, but they left about a half an hour before all this started.

Did they say where they were going, I ask.

The woman shrugs.

Maybe they left us a note in the room, Craig suggests.

I can't let you in their room, the woman says as if we ought to know better.

But we have their car, Craig says. I can't believe they'd leave.

The elevator opens and I'm thinking, Maybe the key to their room is on Heidi's key ring and I'm about to pull Craig away from the desk to ask him, when I glance up at the curious figure peering out the window at the cops and crowd, a figure that seems instantly recognizable from the countless photos I've stared at over and over. Bryan Metro stalks over to the front desk, his hair slicked back and held in place by a pair of Ray Bans, and asks the woman, What's going on out there?

ACT ONE
Scene 1

EXT. HIGHLAND GARDENS. NIGHT. *We See* STELLA *quietly get out of bed, already fully dressed. She slips out of the house without waking* CRAIG.

Scene 2

EXT. HIGHLAND GARDENS PARKING LOT. NIGHT. STELLA *pulls out into the night traffic.*

Scene 3

EXT. CHATEAU MARMONT. NIGHT. STELLA *parks along a side street.*

Scene 4

EXT. CHATEAU MARMONT POOL. NIGHT. *We see* STELLA *spying around a corner on* BRYAN METRO, *who is laid out on a chaise lounge, the pure white light coming from the pool reflected in his mirrored sunglasses,* BRYAN METRO *is in jeans and a T-shirt and appears to be sleeping. There is no one else around. The traffic on Sunset Boulevard can be heard,* STELLA *walks stealthily towards* BRYAN METRO, *stopping in front of his chair.*

> BRYAN METRO
> (*without taking off his sunglasses*)
> What's up, man? I don't need anything.

> STELLA
> (*in awe, almost whispering*)
> I thought you were dead.

93

BRYAN METRO
(*mildly alarmed, raises his sunglasses but then sees he's in no danger*)
It's L.A., man. Everyone here is dead.

STELLA
Are you hiding out from someone?

BRYAN METRO
You got a lot of questions for a cabana boy—, er, girl.

STELLA
I don't work here.

BRYAN METRO
(*pauses*)
Are you a reporter?

STELLA *sits down tentatively in the chair next to* BRYAN METRO'S, *as if he's a mirage that may disappear.*

STELLA
No.

BRYAN METRO
Cool, man.

STELLA
Why did you cancel those shows in Japan?

BRYAN METRO
Why do you want to know?

STELLA
(*thinks*)
I guess it doesn't matter now.

BRYAN METRO
(*not really hearing her*)
Fuckin' Chinks.

STELLA
I don't think Japanese people are called Chinks. Those are
the Chinese.

BRYAN METRO
Whatever, man. Fuckin' Japs, then. Okay?

STELLA
Why did you say you would play shows in Japan if you hate
the Japanese?

BRYAN METRO
I don't hate them, man. They hate *me*.

STELLA
Is this about the maid at the Hilton claiming that you
raped her?

BRYAN METRO
(*sits up, shocked*)
Who told you that? That fuckin' Roger, I told him to keep
his mouth—

STELLA
(*cutting him off, laughing*)
I heard it on the Internet.

BRYAN METRO
Yeah, well.

STELLA
Is it true?

BRYAN METRO
(*automatically*)
Next question.

STELLA *goes to the edge of the pool and kicks off her sandals, touching her toes to the water. She is still somewhat fascinated by* BRYAN METRO, *having spent so much time thinking about him. She can't believe she's talking to him and is trying to remain calm.*

BRYAN METRO
Wanna go to a party?

Scene 5

INT. PRIVATE PARTY AT NAMELESS CLUB. NIGHT. BRYAN METRO AND STELLA *are stuffed in a booth with* FAMOUS ACTORS AND ACTRESSES *from popular film and television. Candle-light is the only light and everyone is chain smoking, talking rapidly. The music, the newest song from the hottest band, is playing too loud and people have to scream to be heard,* BRYAN METRO *offers* STELLA *a cigarette and even though she doesn't smoke, she takes one. The* FAMOUS ACTOR *sitting across from her lights it and* STELLA BLOWS SMOKE ACROSS THE TABLE.

BRYAN METRO
(*yelling*)
... so I told them to fuck off. Right, man?

FAMOUS FILM ACTOR #1
(*yelling*)
That's fuckin' right, Bryan. Scumbags.

FAMOUS TELEVISION ACTRESS #1
(*yelling*)
Bryan, where've you been? We haven't seen you in forever.

BRYAN METRO
(*yelling*)
Camped out. Stella here got me out.

STELLA *waves and smiles awkwardly.*

FAMOUS FILM ACTRESS #2
(*yelling, to Stella*)
Are you in the business?

STELLA
(*yelling*)
Yeah, sort of. Trying to be. (*She nods her head rapidly.*)

Someone has complained that the music is too loud and it notches down to a decent level.

FAMOUS FILM ACTRESS #2
(*to Stella*)
What have you done?

STELLA

Mostly I do theater. At the Starion. (*No one says anything.*) With
Craig Copeland.

FAMOUS TELEVISION ACTOR #2

(*laughing*)

I worked with that dude on *La Brea*. What a no-talent fuck.

Everyone at the table laughs, STELLA laughs too.

FAMOUS FILM ACTRESS WHO STOPS BY THE TABLE:

Bryyyyyyyyyannnnnnnn! (*squeals*) Where have you been rascal?
I've been soooooooooo worried about you.

BRYAN METRO

(*nonchalantly*)

Hey, baby. I've been around.

FAMOUS FILM ACTRESS WHO STOPS BY TABLE

(*shamelessly showboating*)

Why don't you come around to the Four Seasons? I'm there for a
week.

BRYAN METRO

(*salutes her with two fingers*)

Roger, dodger.

*The FAMOUS FILM ACTRESS WHO STOPPED BY TABLE
saunters off. The others at the table make scandalous comments about her.
BRYAN METRO reaches under the table and puts his hand on STELLA'S
inner thigh, which startles her but she lets him as she's been drinking and is
comfortably relaxed in the booth.*

Scene 6

EXT. PACIFIC COAST HIGHWAY. NIGHT. STELLA *is sticking her head out the window of a black limousine, puking,* BRYAN METRO *is alternately laughing and trying to remember the words to 'Billie Jean' by Michael Jackson.*

BRYAN METRO
(*drunkenly singing*)

She was more like a beauty queen... than popped-cherry
ice cream—

STELLA
(*pulls her head inside the car*)
Maybe the driver should pull over. There's puke all down the side
of the car.

BRYAN METRO
(*continues to sing*)
I told her my name was Super Queen ... and she said ...

STELLA
(*her head down, eyes closed*)
Bryan.

BRYAN METRO
(*singing loudly*)
I said I am the one, but the kid has got a gun ...

STELLA
(*yells*)
Bryan!

BRYAN METRO

What, baby?

STELLA

Tell the driver to pull the car over.

The driver pulls over and STELLA *stumbles out of the limo.* BRYAN
METRO *follows.*

BRYAN METRO

(*singing in a high-pitched voice, trying to imitate Michael Jackson*)
Hee, hee, hee—

STELLA *leans on the trunk and vomits,* BRYAN METRO *comes up
behind her and slips his fingers under her skirt,* STELLA *passes out.*

ACT TWO

Scene 1

INT. BRYAN METRO'S SUITE AT THE CHATEAU MARMONT. EARLY MORNING. The floor is littered with pornographic magazines. Hustler, Playboy, Oui, Penthouse, Barely Legal, *etc. The night table is heaped high with bloody tissues. The phone is off the hook,* STELLA *is in bed, asleep. Her eye is swollen, she has bite marks on her cheek, and her lip is split. Next to an unopened bottle of champagne are needles, a rubber hose, and a small balloon of heroin. Through the bathroom door we see* BRYAN METRO *curled up on the floor, next to the toilet.* STELLA'S *eyes open and she stares for a long time without blinking, then closes her eyes again.*

Scene 2

INT. BRYAN METRO'S SUITE AT *THE* CHATEAU MARMONT. EARLY MORNING. *There's a knock at the door. The knocking continues and neither* STELLA *nor* BRYAN METRO *gets up from the bed.* CHAZ, BRYAN METRO'S *dealer, opens the door.*

CHAZ

(holding his nose)

Jesus.

CHAZ *hears a noise in the hall and checks it out, paranoid.* ROGER, BRYAN METRO'S *manager, walks in.* ROGER *is wearing an expensive Italian suit and we get the impression that he expects* BRYAN METRO *to be ready to make an appointment.—*

ROGER

Hey, Chaz. What's our Boy Wonder up to now?

CHAZ

(*pointing at the bed*)

Not a lot, apparently.

ROGER *goes around to* BRYAN METRO'S *side of the bed.*

ROGER

(*shaking* BRYAN METRO)

Wake up, wake up, wake up, wake up, wake up,
wake up.

BRYAN METRO *opens his eyes, squints.*

BRYAN METRO

What, man?

ROGER

What, man, what? Tell me you didn't forget our meeting today.
Tell me you didn't forget.

BRYAN METRO

I didn't forget, man. I didn't forget.

ROGER

Then tell me who it is we're meeting. Who are we meeting today,
Bryan?

BRYAN METRO

Man, I told you I didn't forget. Just give me a sec.

ROGER

(*impatiently*)

Who are we meeting today, Bryan? Who?

BRYAN METRO
(*sighing*)
I give up, man. Who are we meeting?

CHAZ *laughs.*

ROGER
Multiple choice: a) the president of the United States,
b) Pope John Paul II, c) your dead parents, God rest their
souls, or d) the fucking people who are financing your
pathetic attempt at a comeback.

BRYAN METRO
(*staring at the ceiling*)
Wait man, don't tell me. D?

ROGER
(*rips covers back*)
Ding, ding, ding.

STELLA, *who is nude, reaches for the covers. She's just becoming aware of other people in the room.*

CHAZ
Hey, Bryan. Who's the chickadee?

BRYAN METRO
Don't touch her, man. Not this one.

CHAZ
(*holding up his hands*)
Easy, Tex. Easy.

ROGER
(*sighs heavily*)

Bryan, is this another cleanup operation?

BRYAN METRO
(*sits up in bed*)

No, man. It's cool. We're together.

ROGER *grabs* BRYAN METRO *and throws him out of bed.* STELLA *jumps up and screams.*

STELLA
Bryan! Bryan!

CHAZ *holds* STELLA *back.*

CHAZ
Easy, easy.

ROGER *slaps* BRYAN METRO *around.*

ROGER
When I tell you to fuckin' be ready, you be ready. You hear? You're not going to fuck this up. This is your last chance. *Comprende?* You want David Geffen to see you like this?

BRYAN METRO, *who is covering his head, nods,* ROGER *picks up some random clothes from the floor and throws them at* BRYAN METRO, *who puts them on.*

CHAZ
(*to Roger*)

What should I do with the girl?

STELLA *struggles with* CHAZ.

BRYAN METRO
Leave her alone.

ROGER
(glaring at BRYAN METRO, then to STELLA)

*Honey, if I were you, I wouldn't be here when this
loser gets back. (He pulls out some bills.) I don't want to
read about this in the National Enquirer either. Got it? (He throws the money
down on the bed. Turns to BRYAN METRO.) Ready?
ROGER pushes BRYAN METRO towards the door, CHAZ*

*throws STELLA down on the bed and smirks, ROGER, BRYAN METRO,
and CHAZ leave, STELLA climbs back into bed. The money falls off the bed
and into the general litter of the room.*

Scene 3

INT. BRYAN METRO'S SUITE AT THE CHATEAU MAR-
MONT. EARLY MORNING. *The mess in the room has increased,*
BRYAN METRO *and* STELLA *are in bed, awake.*

BRYAN METRO
(without inflection or interest)
I thought you were going for a swim.

STELLA
I am.

BRYAN METRO
When?

STELLA
Are you trying to get rid of me?

105

BRYAN METRO
No, baby.

STELLA
Besides, I already went for a swim once today.

BRYAN METRO
That was yesterday, baby.

STELLA
(*uncovers her eyes, looks around*)
Are you sure?

BRYAN METRO
Pretty positive.

STELLA
What day is it?

BRYAN METRO
I don't know. It's definitely after Monday, though. It might
be Friday.

STELLA
Well, I'm going for a swim.

STELLA *doesn't budge from the bed.*

BRYAN METRO
Okay, baby.

Scene 4

EXT. CHATEAU MARMONT POOL. NIGHT. STELLA *is bouncing up and down on her toes at the edge of the pool, as if she is going to dive. She has a determined look on her face. Behind her, a party is raging in one of the cabanas.*

Scene 5

INT. BRYAN METRO'S SUITE AT THE CHATEAU MARMONT. NIGHT, STELLA *walks in with a robe on. Her hair is dry and she clearly has not been in the pool,* BRYAN METRO *is sitting on the bed, the rubber hose around his arm, the end in his teeth. He's about to inject himself with heroin.*

> BRYAN METRO
> (*through gritted teeth*)
> How was the water, baby?

> STELLA
> Nice.

Scene 6

EXT. CHATEAU MARMONT POOL. MORNING. STELLA *bounces on her toes again at the edge of the pool. The party from the night before is still going on. She bounces and bounces.*

Scene 7

FADE IN. INT. BRYAN METRO'S SUITE AT THE CHATEAU MARMONT. *The room is completely cluttered and the camera pans around, BRYAN METRO and STELLA are in bed, asleep.*

FADE OUT.

Daisy

D ear Sara and Keren,
    I wanted to bring you up to date about what has happened since my last letter, the one I wrote about everything that happened and how we ended up in California. (I got this address from www.bananarama.com. I hope this is the right address, and if not please forward on to Sara and Keren.)

Paque and I always thought the sun shone every day in California, but it rained our first day in Hollywood. The hour or so flight from Phoenix to L.A. was like walking from a sunny day into a darkened room. Stella, who I told you about in my last letter, picked us up from the airport and we gave her Alan Hood's address on Sunset Boulevard. Paque and I were curious to see where we'd be living—if only temporarily—and got sort of a kick out of telling our friends in Phoenix we'd be living on the famous Sunset Boulevard.

But we had it wrong. Or really Alan told us it was Sunset Boulevard—he gave the address as 21047 Sunset Boulevard. We drove for a while without seeing any numbers, and then we saw 16501 on one of the old-time McDonald's, the ones that look like the drive-ins from the '50s. The next thing we saw was Von's supermarket, 19988. We crossed Hollywood Boulevard where it bisected Sunset and we saw the house, 21047, a smallish white adobe with yellowing patches of grass along a narrow sidewalk. This is 21047 Beaumont Avenue, Stella said. Are you sure it's the right house? Paque looked back up Sunset and I looked the other way, where you could see Sunset dead-end into a three-post fence with red reflectors nailed to the graying wood.

Alan Hood himself opened the door and we introduced ourselves. Alan shook our hands and invited us in. Even though it was late in the day, he looked like he'd just gotten out of bed. His thick brown hair was misshapen; he ran his fingers through it, piling it high on his head and squinted with his small blue eyes. Stella said,

110

Didn't you write for that television show *La Brea?* and Alan was very pleased she knew his name.

A great show, Alan said.

Stella said, Yeah, my boyfriend was on it. Craig Copeland.

This is the kind of stuff that drives Paque and I crazy, about how Stella tries to horn in on everything.

Yeah, Alan said. You could tell he didn't remember Craig.

The house was bigger than it looked from the street, which had to do with the fact that there wasn't much in the way of furniture. The front room had the most windows but was furnished with only a desk and a computer. Some framed movie posters leaned in the corner near the fireplace, which looked like it hadn't ever been used. The desk was littered with papers and somewhere underneath the mess a phone started to ring. Leave it, Alan said.

He gave us the tour: the master bedroom, which housed film editing equipment and a small mattress. Several CD racks stood like sentries against the far wall, swollen with plastic cases. Alan showed us where we'd be staying, a room sort of what I imagined a dorm room in college would look like: two beds against opposite walls, two small dressers and a closet. A window between the beds looked out on Sunset and we could see the Von's from where we stood.

Stella helped us unload our bags and said, He seems like a nice guy. I'm sorry you couldn't stay with me, she said, but it's already too crowded with me and Craig.

No sweat, Paque said. Paque didn't want Stella getting her meathooks into our film or into Alan Hood. I felt bad for Stella myself. She'd had a rough time since moving to L. A. I would run into her mom in Phoenix and she would always shake her head when I asked about Stella.

We were anxious to find out more about *Plastic Fantastic II*, the film Alan promised to make with us, so Alan took us to lunch at Deep Dish on Vine and told us there was a slight delay because of some financing that hadn't come through. He explained about his cable-access dating show, *Who Fancies Me?* which he was about to sell for big money, money he was going to use to finance *Plastic Fantastic II.*

How much longer, Paque asked, disappointed.

Not long, Alan said, but in the meantime how about being on the show?

Paque asked him what that meant and he told us how the show worked: contestants came on the show and asked 'Who fancies me?' and whoever from the crowd did came up (up to five at the most) and the contestants asked them questions until they've narrowed it down to two. Once it was narrowed down, the two final contestants duked it out verbally in front of the contestant, essentially fighting over her or him.

The second person is always a ringer from the staff, Alan said. How would you like to come down and be on the show until we can start shooting the film, he asked.

Shouldn't we be learning our lines for the film, Paque asked. Alan said he was going to write the script as we shot it so there really wasn't anything to memorize per se. It's more spontaneous that way, he explained. So Paque and I said we'd be on *Who Fancies Me?*

It might be fun, Paque said.

And it *was* fun. I mean, I was too shy to get up there but Paque wasn't. We talked to the contestants, who were chosen randomly from a clutter of postcards Alan kept in a box in a cramped office behind the set, which was in this old church right down Sunset from our house. It looked like they still had services there on Sundays. The set was just a stage with a plump red couch on one side (where the contestant sat, patiently awaiting that person who fancied him or her) and on the other side were four recliners of various colors and sizes. If you walked behind the stage you saw the stuffing coming out of most of the recliners.

The contestants, John Blake from Pasadena and Rolf Weddenstein from La Jolla, were OK guys. They were both in college and looked pretty much like hipsters. Alan explained the rules but Rolf said, It's cool, dude, I watch the show, which made John pipe up, Me too. Alan pointed Paque out, so they would know she was not really a potential idol worshiper and Rolf was perceptibly bummed out, which Paque saw and she gave him a kiss on the cheek for good luck.

I was in charge of letting in the studio audience. Alan explained to me that since one of the worshipers from one of the first episodes went on to become a VJ on MTV, the audiences had been packed with wannabes and a couple times he found out after the fact that scouts were posing as twenty-somethings in the crowd. So keep your eyes out, Alan said. Today we're shooting two guys, so don't let any men in, he told me. When do you shoot the women, I asked. Alan pointed at his watch. Men in the morning, he said, and women after lunch.

Sure enough outside the church there was a line of women all the way down the street and around the corner. You never saw so many miniskirts. I found out later I was supposed to actually *choose* thirty people, not just let in the first thirty. Alan said it didn't really matter but that people would quit lining up if they weren't one of the first thirty, and I said next time I'd do it right.

The show used two cameras and both cameramen had on oversized T-shirts that read WHO FANCIES ME? The crowd filed in, sitting in the risers. Overhead a stereo played KROQ, a new song from Jewel.

It feels like an assembly, from back in high school, Paque said.

Alan—his hair slicked back and his face so white his eyebrows looked like two clouds floating in space—welcomed the audience and 'those viewing from the safety of their homes' and then introduced John Blake, who came out center stage and looked right into the camera. John gave his name and what kind of mate he was looking for ('a caring person with a good heart who enjoys the outdoors and laughs easily'). He paused dramatically, like all contestants are supposed to, and then asked the crowd, Who fancies me? Everyone applauded and there was whistling too.

Alan was right about needing ringers. Three chairs filled up pretty quickly, the girls preening for the camera in between smiles to their friends in the audience.

Is there anyone else who fancies John, Alan asked the audience.

A timid girl with glasses was pushed to the stage by her group of friends and you could tell she didn't want to go up but the camera focused on her and so she sort of had to. Alan winked at Paque, who was sitting in the front row, and Paque sauntered onto the stage, to the delight of the crowd.

The camera panned down the row of girls as each said her name and Alan handed John an oversized envelope, white with a red bow, which contained the questions John would ask to narrow down his admirers.

John opened the bow dramatically and read the first question: After a date would you tell a guy to call you to make sure you got home safely, or ask him to nudge you for breakfast in the morning?

The crowd whooped rabidly.

Each of the girls answered the question and the first girl, the one called Katrina, was the first casualty.

The girl with the glasses looked like she was going to cry as John read the second question: Size matters—true or false?

The camera panned down the row and the girls each answered. Paque was the funniest because the two before her answered false and she looked at them like they were crazy and answered, True. The crowd clapped and whistled, as if on cue.

The girl with the glasses bolted from the stage and disappeared behind the curtain to the exit. Alan deadpanned a stare into the camera and everyone laughed. Well, he said, and then there were three. He turned to the stage, Okay, John, let's hear the next—

Before Alan could finish an alarm sounded and the stage lights went down while a siren flashed. You know what that means, Alan said, turning to the stage, It's time to fight for your man!

The alarm stopped and the stage lights came back up and the portion of the show where the remaining girls verbally sparred over the contestant began when John, on cue, said, Who fancies me most?

Girl #1: I do.

Girl #2: I do more.

Paque: I do too.

Alan: Tell John what you love most about him girls.

Girl #1: I love his dark eyes and long fingers. (*The crowd oohs.*)

Girl #2 (*looking at the camera, big smile*): I love how his mind works. (*The crowd boos. John gives a thumbs down*)

Paque (*playfully*): I like what I see. (*The crowd erupts in applause.*)

It went on like that—finally it was just Paque and the second girl and they went at it. John, choose me and you won't be sorry. John, let me show you what love's about. John, choose your soul mate. John, I'll take you to heaven and back.

Paque's job was to whip the other girl into a frenzy, which she did with flair, and John knew he couldn't choose Paque anyway so it was really an entertainment about what Paque could get the other girl to say.

John, choose me and you can do anything you want, she said, and Paque said, He's yours then. The crowd stood and clapped wildly and the other girl looked confused for a moment but then John stood up and she went to him and they hugged like they were family. Offstage, Paque stood with her arms folded across her chest, smiling. I thought she did a quality acting job and Alan even said so later, after some of the guys from the crowd tried to give Paque a consolation prize.

Fortunately, *Who Fancies Me?* was sold shortly thereafter because doing it for a week straight was boring.

I have to sign off now because Stella (the one I told you about) is taking us on our first celebrity scavenger hunt. I'll let you know...

Daisy

Dear Sara and Keren,

Paque is out with Alan so I thought now would be the right moment to drop you a line to fill you in. Please thank whoever it was in your office who sent the photo and newsletter. I tacked it up on the back of the door in our room, to give us inspiration.

When I said above that Paque is out with Alan I mean that they are at Von's, which is just up the street, getting some groceries. I didn't want to give the impression that Paque and Alan were out on the town together, or that they were together in some vague California way. Paque and I haven't had boyfriends in God knows how long. My last boyfriend, Daryll, didn't last long (I don't want to go into that now).

I did meet this guy though. Remember I told you about the scavenger hunt? The hunt was pretty much a bust but afterwards there was this party thrown by a guy named T.J. He works as a professional housesitter, which I think is one of those jobs that you could only find in L.A. But apparendy there's a real demand, so T.J. doesn't have a place of his own and, as he puts it, 'lives around.'

The party was in Brentwood, at this enormous Spanish-style house that T.J. said belonged to one of O.J. Simpson's lawyers, who was a friend of T.J.'s family. What I liked about T.J. was the way he cracked himself up. He would be in the middle of telling you a story and he'd say, Can you believe that? God, that's funny. And then he'd laugh in such a way that you'd laugh too, whether it was funny or not. (Also, did I mention, he's really, really, really cute.)

There were only about ten or fifteen people and we hung out around the oblong pool in the back yard, sipping cold Budweisers. The trees hanging over the pool made the backyard seem really dark and T.J. lit the tiki torches pitched in the mound of lava rocks behind the diving board. Paque told Stella that we had to be back at a decent hour because the next day was the first day of filming and Alan had scheduled an early shoot. But I was happy where I was. T.J. was showing off for me, doing stunts off the end of the diving board. Others stripped down to their underwear and a competition started, who could make the biggest splash, who could jump the highest, the furthest, etc. I dipped my legs in the shallow end with Paque and Stella. Stella was telling us about this guy she met who thinks Kurt Cobain is still alive and that his suicide was a fake but I tuned her out, imagining instead that T.J. was my boyfriend and that we lived in the Spanish-style house. Paque and I have talked about it before and basically we decided that while we're trying to establish ourselves we're not allowed to have boyfriends. We want boyfriends, but all of our friends who have boyfriends have to spend all their free time with them. Pretty soon you'd see less and less of them and then they'd get married and you wouldn't see them at all.

We want to do all that, someday. I just don't see how you could put anybody through being second fiddle to your dreams. I don't know if you know Madonna personally but you probably know her story, about how she moved to New York from Detroit with basically no money. She wanted to be famous no matter what and she ended up sleeping in her band's rehearsal space. After that she moved up to a bedroom smaller than you would get if you committed a crime and were put in prison. She lived off two dollars a day. *In New York City*. Paque and I have been to New York City and you can't do anything for two dollars a day. I always think of Madonna homeless, sleeping on a mattress, whenever I get down about how hard it is to get a break. You have to want it more, is all.

Plus, to be honest, I feel responsible for ruining the start we got back in Phoenix. I suffer from anxiety, and that day at the SaltBed Fest was the most anxious I've ever been. Everything was really going our way until my accident. There aren't any second chances either, we learned that. We weren't so surprised that Scott Key from Sony wouldn't take our call, but a couple weeks after that even Ian wouldn't talk to us because of an article that came out in the *Arizona Republic*. But the reporter twisted what we said all around. In the article it sounded like Paque and I blamed Ian for what happened. And they had a good time about Jammin' Jay, too. The reporter made Ian out to be some sort of faker for putting out our record even though we didn't sing every track on it. Paque and I tried to call Ian to tell him that we didn't blame him, that it was our fault for not practicing as hard as we could, but all we ever got was his answering machine.

That's why when Alan called from Hollywood with an offer to make a short film, Paque and I said yes right away. Alan had read about the film my brother made, *Plastic Fantastic*, in an interview Paque and I did with *Phoenix* Magazine. We've never even seen the movie (Chuck was supposed to send us a copy) and Alan admitted that he hadn't seen it either but he thought making a movie would be a 'great way to turn around what happened in Phoenix.' When someone extends you a hand like that, you should take it, right?

T.J. and I ended up kissing in the bathroom, his wet trunks pressed up against me. It was nice to kiss someone. I worried that he would want to do more, but someone knocked on the bathroom door and T.J. smiled. We're caught, he laughed. God, isn't that funny?

Paque said it was time to get back and I rolled the window down and let the wind blow my hair as Stella drove us back to Alan's, who was already in bed. T.J. asked for my number, which was the biggest compliment I'd had in as long as I could remember, but I took his number instead. Paque and I crept into our room, trying not to make any noise, and I put the scrap of paper with the carefully printed numbers under my pillow.

In the morning, T.J.'s number was gone. I tore my sheets apart but couldn't find it. I even suspected Paque of taking it, but didn't say anything. The whole thing felt like a dream and it put me in a very bad mood, but honestly I'd forgotten all about it once Paque and I arrived on the set for our first day of shooting.

Our movie is not called *Plastic Fantastic II* but *World Gone Water*, and Paque plays Angie Boulevard, a nymphomaniac patient in an avant-garde behavioral rehabilitation center run by Dr. Hatch (who is played by Jesse Armstrong, the guy who plays the father on that show about the twins who have mind powers). I play Jane Ramsey, 'Dr. Hatch's fetching assistant.' The rest of the cast is Brian Del'Acorte, who plays a fellow patient nicknamed X-Rated (you can probably guess why) and Robert Anaconda as Caleb Stone, a guy from Arizona who transferred into the program from prison (where he spent time because he raped someone).

It's sort of an updated *A Clockwork Orange*, Alan told us.

Alan explained that we would shoot all the interior shots first and then do the exterior shots, which was confusing to me. I thought that movies were made just the way you see them on the screen. By that I mean, if at the beginning of a movie a friend says a sad good-bye to someone at the airport and then at the end of the movie the friend says a warm hello, that final scene isn't possible without everything that's happened in the middle. But Alan said it's too expensive to set up shots so that once everything is set in a particular locale, you shoot every scene that takes place there. Which makes being an actor that much harder, I thought.

Fortunately, Alan said, most of the movie takes place inside the behavioral center.

I noticed that most of the crew was from *Who Fancies Me?* The makeup and wardrobe girl, Cindy, recognized Paque and the two of them chatted it up while Cindy made me up in a white labcoat and pulled my hair back into a ponytail. I don't usually wear makeup—I'm lucky enough to have fair skin—but Cindy insisted that because of the lights I would have to wear a special kind of base to prevent glare. The base made me very uncomfortable. It felt like I had cement skin. I tried smiling and my cheeks felt like they were breaking through a brick wall.

We only shot one scene that first day, which is actually the first scene in the movie. It's a scene with me, Dr. Hatch and Caleb Stone. Caleb has just come to the facility and Dr. Hatch is giving him an entrance interview. I only have one line in the scene: We respect honesty here, Mr. Stone. But Alan said there's a lot of subtle stuff going on in the scene, namely that Jane is secretly falling for Caleb, a sort of 'rebel without a cause' type. So there were several takes of cutaway shots to me where I'm supposed to 'smile with my eyes.'

Everyone, including Paque, who wanted to get to her first scene, was annoyed with me because I wasn't giving a good enough performance. When I felt like I was 'smiling with my eyes,' Alan said I looked like 'a mentally unstable child staring at a piece of candy.' I told Alan that yelling at me didn't help and he said he was sorry, but Jesse Armstrong—Dr. Hatch—sighed every time I blew it and Alan had to yell cut.

Finally, Alan called for a break. Paque and I wanted to go outside, maybe take a walk around the block, but Cindy said she'd have to redo my makeup and Alan said to just stay inside. So Paque and I went into the bathroom while Alan and the others huddled around a tiny screen to watch what we'd done so far.

Paque washed her hands in the sink, not saying anything.

I'm trying, I said, the words echoing off the bathroom walls.

I know, Paque said. But you just have to concentrate. You have to forget that you're Daisy and pretend that you're Jane Ramsey. I think that's the problem. You aren't pretending to be someone else. If you don't believe that you're Dr. Hatch's assistant, then the audience isn't going to believe it. It's sort of like Robin Williams. You know how every Robin Williams movie makes you conscious of the fact that it's Robin Williams—except for *Dead Poets Society* and *Good Will Hunting*—where at a certain point in the movie he breaks out of his character and does that thing with his lip and his voice gets crazy and he starts shaking his head and you say, Look, it's Robin Williams. He becomes a stand-up comic in the middle of the movie. Compare that, she said, with the character in *Good Will Hunting*, where the last time you think about Robin Williams is when you see his name in the credits. After that, you believe that that psychiatrist is a real person, that he has a practice in Boston, and that you could fly there right now and be his patient. That's the difference.

I see what you mean, I said.

So what's Jane Ramsey's favorite color, Paque asked.

Blue, I said.

What's her favorite kind of food?

Mexican.

If she found a hundred dollars on the ground would she keep it or try to find out if someone dropped it?

She'd keep it.

And if she secretly liked a patient but didn't want her boss to find out, would she try to let the patient know in a subtle way, or would she be obvious about it?

Subtle.

Then let's see it, Paque said. I gave her a hug and Cindy knocked on the door and said, Okay let's do it.

Alan was grimacing and the others settled in, figuring it was going to take all week to get the scene.

I'm proud to say I got it right in one take, which gave me a boost of self-confidence. When one thing goes right, it seems like everything is going right. (I found T.J.'s number, which had snaked itself inside my pillow case.) I'm riding that wave for now.

Daisy

Dear Sara and Keren,

Alan got a new client today. Annette Laudin. She's from London, but I'm not sure you would know who she is. She's recently famous, as they say. Annette read the article in *Variety* about Alan and how he took on Paque and me. *She flew* from New York to meet him. I asked Paque if she knew who Annette was but she said she didn't, that Alan told her later that she used to be queen of the socialites in Manhattan, but that that was all just an experiment by these two women who had taken Annette away from her boutique job and decided to make her famous.

How did they make her famous, I asked.

Apparently one of the women was a publicist and the other one was a socialite, Paque said. The story reminded me of that movie *Trading Places*, where the two old men fuck someone's life up for a dollar.

These two women, the publicist and the socialite, decided to take Annette and dress her up in designer clothes. Betsey Johnson, Prada, Versace, DKNY, etc. They put her up in their houses in the Hamptons, making sure she arrived at all the parties in limos. At these parties they made sure Annette was photographed with any celebrity in the room. And the next day they called up their friends at the New York magazines and gave them nice little stories about Annette, what she was up to, what she said about so-and-so (only nice things, though).

And it worked. Annette was a 'must-have' on every party list. She made friends with all the other famous people in New York—even Donald Trump. The daughter of some billionaire, one of Annette's new friends, asked her to be a bridesmaid in her wedding. But the weekend of the wedding, the daughter of the billionaire discovered that her husband-to-be was in love with Annette and the wedding, hours away, was canceled.

The next party Annette showed up for, she was turned away

from the door by the very two women who had made her. You're an ugly bitch, they screamed at her.

I agreed with Paque that this was awful but in the back of my mind the story made me worry about our future. Alan had used his friends at *Variety* and *Entertainment Weekly* and the *L.A. Times* to print stories about *World Gone Water*, like those girls did to make Annette famous. I felt like we were Alan's experiment. I started to think about what would happen to Paque and me after the movie came out. A certain number of people would hate it on principle, because these two no-names from nowhere were given attention that they, or someone they knew, deserved. A certain number of people would love it for the same reason. And maybe it would lead to parts in other films, and maybe we'd go on late-night talk shows and talk about what it was like to make it big. But I couldn't fight the feeling that on the other side, no matter how hard it was to get famous, it was somehow *harder* once you did become famous. You had to watch out who you were seen talking to. You had to be careful where you went. You had to treat your body like a car you loved more than your own life.

These thoughts circled around in my head as Paque and I sat for what Alan called 'some pre-publicity publicity.' Filming was suspended for a day to capitalize on an article that Alan 'placed' in *Daily Variety* about *World Gone Water*. The article reported that Julia Roberts and Elizabeth Hurley originally expressed interest in the roles of Jane Ramsey and Angie Boulevard but that 'director Hood selected two fresh faces from obscurity to play the roles of seducer and nymphomaniac.'

We woke the morning of that article to the sound of the phone in the living room ringing every few minutes. The answering machine took the calls. Paque and I stood and listened as agents, publicists, personal trainers, nutritionists, personal assistants and even someone from Paramount Pictures left messages offering their services. It gave me goosebumps, but scared me at the same time.

Hello, Hollywood, Paque said.

Alan said, Forget those people for now. He hauled us off to a house in Woodland Hills where Paque and I spent the day in the pool while a photographer friend of Alan's—John Henry—told us to hold our breath under water for as long as we could (and to make sure our eyes were open). John Henry took some shots from a ladder he'd constructed on his diving board. Then he stripped down to his boxers and switched cameras and jumped in. He told us just to swim towards the camera slowly. He went under and we chased him around the pool until our fingers and toes were waterlogged.

John Henry had a TV the size of one whole wall and Paque and I watched a *Road Rules* marathon while Alan went over the photographs, selecting the best one.

That night Alan took us to a party for the all-girl issue of *R*O*C*K* magazine at Shampu.

It's time to show you off to L.A., Alan said.

Paque and I still had the outfits that we bought for SaltBed, so we wore them to the party. I miss Ian, Paque said as we got ready. Just hearing his name—and standing there in the mirror in the outfit he paid for—made me tremble.

I wonder how he's doing, I said.

Maybe we could give him a call later, Paque said.

His phone is disconnected though, I reminded her. I passed her the bottle of Keri lotion and she smoothed some on her legs.

I think I'm sunburned, she said.

Alan appeared in the doorway dressed all in black and Paque let out a low whistle. Ready to dazzle, he asked. He smiled, and I think it was the first time I'd seen him smile since we met him. I took the chance to ask him something that had been bothering me.

Is it right to do what we're doing, I asked.

Paque stopped lotioning her legs.

What are we doing, Alan asked patiently.

You know, I said, the way you said in the article that Julia Roberts and Elizabeth Hurley wanted to be in *World Gone Water*, and the posters of Paque and I in the pool that are going to go up all over town. I mean, it's sort of like lying, isn't it?

Alan unbuttoned the top button of his black jacket and sat down on Paque's bed. Well, he began, it's sort of like this. In Hollywood, everything is about illusion and expectation. How many movies do you think get made every year?

I looked at Paque but we couldn't guess.

Too many, Alan said. And let's face it—I'm an unknown in this arena; I haven't made a movie before. But I believe in second chances. Everyone who needs one should have one. Including you two. So the only thing that can launch this second chance is to get as many people as we can to want you to have a second chance. Does that come close to making sense?

I see what you mean, I said. I guess it just feels … dishonest.

Robbing banks is dishonest, Alan smiled. We're not robbing banks.

Not yet, Paque said. Which made me laugh.

Alan laughed too but then got serious again and said, And I should probably tell you that there isn't even going to be a movie. The plan is to shoot a few scenes and put them on the Internet. Then we'll start returning those phone calls on the answering machine. And hopefully by this time next year you'll be filming a movie with Tarantino or Scorsese or Oliver Stone or whoever.

Paque fished through her purse for her lip gloss. You know, we tried to manipulate the public before and got burned, she said.

That was my fault, I said.

Paque stopped smearing peach gloss on her lips and said, It wasn't your fault.

126

You were in the hands of amateurs in Phoenix, Alan said. Besides, this is Hollywood. It's different. Didn't you read in *Entertainment Weekly* about the actress who was supposed to be eighteen but was really thirty-two? She lied and she doesn't have to worry about running out of work ever again.

Alan convinced us that what we were doing was making an advertisement for ourselves, like a résumé, and that made me feel better about the whole thing.

The limousine Alan rented for the evening picked us up right at seven and we navigated the streets in style, though passing so many limos made it feel less special. We came to a stop at a red light and we had limos on either side of us.

Alan told us not to talk specifically about *World Gone Water*, especially to any reporters. That includes photographers, he said.

At Shampu it felt like people knew who we were. The volume of the conversations seemed to increase as we walked in, Paque and I each looping our arms through Alan's. Silver and gold confetti littered the floor, and Paque's tennis shoes were caked in it by the time we made our way to one of the plush sofas next to a wall-sized poster of Sarah McLachlan on the cover of *R*O*C*K*, looking glum and alluring in the way rock stars sometimes do.

Look, Paque said right as Sarah McLachlan walked by.

Weird, I said.

Alan went to get us drinks and Paque and I scanned the crowd for people we recognized: Chloë Sevigny, Matthew Broderick, Courtney Love, Anjelica Huston, David Geffen, Natalie Merchant, Shania Twain, Charlie Sheen, Denis Leary, Janeane Garafalo, Ben Stiller, Fiona Apple, and Abra Moore. Bruce Springsteen was talking to Gloria Estefan when someone bumped him and he spilled his drink on her shoes.

Look, she's dancing, Paque joked.

Alan made his way back through the crowd, dodging a very

wasted Bryan Metro, who someone pointed in the direction of the men's room. We should work the room, he said.

Paque and I sipped our vodka tonics while we strolled with Alan, who introduced us to Sarah McLachlan, whose skin was so white she appeared to glow. Paque and I told her how much we loved her music and she seemed genuinely flattered.

We posed for pictures with Jennifer Love Hewitt, Melissa Etheridge, and Vince Vaughn, who asked Paque for her number.

I started to feel a little ill, remembering that I hadn't eaten any dinner. A plate of hors d'oeuvres floated by on the arm of this really cute guy and Paque and I stopped him and ate three or four of the little cheese things wrapped in bacon. We followed that with some cold peas with chevre and melba toast with salmon and brie.

Hey look, Paque said. She pointed out Hilken Mancini and Chris Toppin from Fuzzy.

We broke free of Alan, who was chatting up Marilyn Manson, and went over to Hilken and Chris, who remembered us from SaltBed.

Sorry about what happened, Hilken said. That must've been really terrible.

Yeah, it was embarrassing, I said.

The worst part was that we were being scouted by Sony Records, Paque said. Do you guys know Scott Key?

Hilken shook her head no and looked at Chris.

Never heard of him, Chris said.

Matt Dillon leaned in and told Hilken and Chris how much he liked their new album, *Hurray For Everything*. He said a friend gave it to him and it was the only CD he played in his Jeep. We were all sort of mesmerized by how handsome Matt Dillon was and after he walked away it took a minute for us to realize he was gone.

What are you guys doing now, Chris asked.

We told her that we were shooting a movie, which felt like a lie and we liked them too much to lie so I said, It's really a short film.

Wait, I think I read about this, Hilken said. Julia Roberts wanted to be in it, right?

Right, Paque said.

Alan dragged us over for another photo and we waved goodbye to Hilken and Chris. My eyes started to burn from squinting at the flashbulbs so I excused myself and slipped into the bathroom, which was entirely marble. My shoes clicked as I shut the door to the stall. The attendant whistled something I vaguely recognized. On the back of the stall door someone had Magic Markered THE WORLD IS FULL OF VANITY AND MALICE in slanted letters that made me feel like I was losing my balance, or maybe it was the vodka, or my empty stomach, or the flashbulbs exploding like tiny crashes around the room but when I walked out of the bathroom the last thing I saw was Bill Murray and I passed out cold.

It was pretty embarrassing.

Daisy

Dear Sara and Keren,

I'm enclosing one of the *World Gone Water* posters. What do you think? I think it looks peaceful, the way the deep blue water sort of envelops us (we aren't really that white!) and the way our hair fans out behind us. Even though you can't really tell, we're both extremely out of breath. Also, Paque's face is air-brushed (she has a mole high on her right cheek). Doesn't it look like we're staring right at you?

You can't go anywhere in L.A. without seeing the poster. Which is kind of funny considering what Alan said about it not even being a real movie. Paque and I ran around with Alan the other day—just doing errands—and we saw the poster all over. On the side of a 7-Eleven on Pico, stapled to telephone polls along Vine, plastered in the window of the Trax-n-Wax on Hollywood (Alan knows the owner), even one someone had ripped down and put in the back window of their car in the parking lot of a bar in no man's land called the Liquid Kitty. Alan said there were a few you could see from the Santa Monica Freeway, and some in Malibu. Paque and I said we'd like to go to Malibu but Alan said, Maybe after we're done shooting. Paque and I discussed it and decided we'd give Stella a call and maybe the three of us would take a drive. We intentionally haven't called Stella because we know she's desperate to break into the movies and we don't want her horning in on our deal. Paque is still very pissed about Stella leaving us back in Phoenix, but I'm wishy-washy on the subject. There was no answer at Stella's though.

We shot another scene as well. It's in the can, as they say in Hollywood. (I just thought of a question: Why didn't Bananarama ever make any movies? You know, the way Madonna did. Your videos are so good it makes sense that you could've made a movie.)

Annette Laupin has joined the cast, too. Paque and I were a little miffed at first but we really like Annette. She's a cool chick. She seems like she's stuck up but she's funnier than shit and you can tell she's been through a lot. She said she doesn't have any desire to be a movie star—she told us not to say anything, but she felt Alan probably wasn't the right person to help her rehabilitate her image; she thinks she might move back to New York after 'an extended vacation' and that that might be enough—but that Alan asked her to play the part of Natalie Stone, Caleb Stone's sister, and Annette thought it would be a kick. That's the kind of chick she is. Like I said, pretty cool.

We haven't had a scene with Annette yet. The scene we filmed was another scene at the rehabilitation center. A group session scene featuring Caleb and Angie Boulevard, who act out a sequence as husband and wife where Angie has to confess that she has cheated on Caleb, monitored closely by Dr. Hatch and my character, Jane. The scene was pretty intense. Robert Anaconda, who plays Caleb, must be a method actor, or must have studied method acting anyway. His reaction was not the normal reaction you would expect if a husband finds out his wife has been unfaithful: He basically accepts it as part of human nature, and it's shocking in a quiet way (that's the best way I can describe it). When Angie Boulevard becomes confused by Caleb's reaction (Paque is very convincing), Jane, who you'll remember is having an affair with Caleb, challenges his views. My role is really psychologically challenging and I stayed up the night before rehearsing with Alan, who read Caleb's lines. The trick to my part, as I might have mentioned before, is that no one knows about Jane and Caleb, but Jane takes the wild theories Caleb espouses in group session personally—for obvious reasons.

Paque and I hung around through lunch to watch Annette film her scene. Alan fussed quite a bit over her appearance—she wore a beautiful white gown—giving Cindy the make-up girl a lot of specific instructions. The scene as Alan explained it was that Natalie, or Talie, had been stood up by her cotillion date and called Caleb (who Alan filled us in was out of rehab by then). Caleb shows up in jeans and a shirt but Talie, as is part of her character, doesn't care what other people think and they go in and dance one dance and then leave.

The rehabilitation center was quickly transformed into a dance floor. The boom guy and the cameraman hung a disco ball above the four-by-four tiled floor. The cameras moved in and Annette and Robert Anaconda did a run-through without the music. The script called for Caleb to console Talie about being stood up, but Alan changed it on the spot to a conversation about their first loves. It was amazing to see Alan work—he dashed out the dialogue in about five minutes.

The film rolled and Annette and Robert Anaconda swayed slowly back and forth, staying within the tiles (which were their markers—Paque and I learned about that when we filmed *Plastic Fantastic* for my brother, Chuck, in New York). Annette and Robert Anaconda had an instantly easy rapport and I felt a little embarrassed because they seemed like lovers. I thought we were going to have to spend all day shooting but when the scene was finished and the music stopped and the lights came up, Alan was crying.

That's it for today, he said.

It was a pretty awkward moment. Annette and Robert Anaconda went off somewhere and Paque and I had to hang around and wait for Alan, who just sat and stared into space until finally he got up and said, C'mon, let's go. We rode home in silence.

Oh, hey, you can check out the scenes we've done so far. They're on the Internet at www.worldgonewater.com. You have to have a special video thing in your computer and you have to have speakers. Alan showed it to us the other day and I think it looks pretty cool. It looks like a scene from an actual movie. When Alan first brought it up on the screen Paque said, I bet we'll sound like robots. But we didn't.

The phone continued to ring with interest in the movie and with offers for Paque and me. Alan said it was too early yet to start calling people back. The hype has to reach just the right level, he said, before we can really capitalize. Alan said so far the people who had called were 'little fish' and that we had to wait for the right bite. It won't be much longer now, he told us. These things take on a life of their own.

We know something about that, Paque said with not a little hint of irony in her voice.

I know even more than she does. I never told Paque about my father—the one time she asked I said he lived in Minneapolis, which is true, but I didn't tell her why. I'm always curious about rumors, about which ones make it to full-blown gossip and which ones turn out to be true (so few rarely do). In the short time we've been here it seems to me that Hollywood is full of rumors. Everyone starts a conversation with, I heard this, or, I heard that. Everyone is hearing things. I overheard a woman in Von's talking about how she heard that one of Michael Jackson's kids was 'on death's door.' The woman she was talking to didn't even know Michael Jackson had kids, and the other woman assured her that he did.

I was just a kid—ten—when I heard the rumor about my father. Funny, now that I remember it, it was in a grocery store, too. I was with my mom and my brother and my mom ran into one of our neighbors. I forget their name now. My mom stopped to talk to them and my brother and I got bored so we ran over to the cereal aisle. Chuck loved Cap'n Crunch (he ate it breakfast, lunch, and dinner) and I wanted Lucky Charms but my mom always made us agree on a cereal (consequently I hate Cap'n Crunch). Chuck and I raced back to our mom, who had moved down the aisle and as we raced past the neighbors, I heard the man say, He's as gay as the day is long. Naturally I didn't know who he was talking about, or even what the phrase meant. And I forgot it until a few weeks later when Linda Pegg came up to me at recess and said in front of everyone, Your dad's a homo, you're dad's a homo. The others started saying, Homo, homo, homo. None of them knew what it meant—not even Linda Pegg—but they kept on until I started crying. I left the playground and ran home. I asked my mom what 'homo' meant, and she started to say something about how it means you're not like everyone else but she gave up and just started crying. That's when my mom moved Chuck and me to Phoenix. My father sent birthday cards for a while after that but pretty soon we just didn't hear anything anymore. Sometimes I wonder what he's up to and secretly I hope that he'll read something in the press about the movie and try to get in touch with me. I can't ask my mom. I don't know why I know that, I just do. And Chuck doesn't care. He says he can't even remember what our father looks like. Wouldn't know him if he passed him in the street, he always says. I told Chuck he probably looks a lot like us and Chuck said, Yeah, so what?

I thought about calling Chuck the other night. Paque and I were bored, and not tired, and we were flipping through the channels and we saw ourselves on TV. On C-Span2 (it's an egghead cable channel that usually has very boring programs on). We were just going from one channel to the other, talking about how many more scenes we would have to shoot before we could accept an offer for a real movie, when Paque's face lit up the screen. She was clicking so fast she didn't even see it.

Go back, I said.

Paque clicked it back and there we were in New York, the time we went to go see Paul Newman with Chuck. Chuck raised his hand and Paque said, God, this was embarrassing.

What's it doing on TV, I asked.

Sometimes they put stuff like that on TV, she said.

I imagine you're both used to seeing yourself on the screen but I have to say it was thrilling to come across ourselves randomly on the television like that. It made me feel like we were famous. And it made me miss Chuck. You always miss someone when you think about them, and seeing Chuck on TV like that made me miss him even worse. I wanted to call him and tell him to come out to Hollywood— he would love all of it—but not knowing exactly what was happening day to day made me hesitate. But I did call and left a message on his answering machine that I missed him much.

I hope you can take the time to write back. I'd appreciate any sort of advice you could give about what Paque's and my next move should be.

Daisy

Dear Sara and Keren,

You've probably had times when you realized something unknown was moving against the balance of things. Like when Siobhan left the group to be in Shakespear's Sister. There might have been a change of energy in the recording studio once Siobhan made up her mind, or maybe she skipped out on an interview, or was constantly late for shooting a video, etc. Once she left Bananarama you both could probably pinpoint the exact moment— in retrospect—that that conclusion was foregone.

Paque and I had that feeling one morning—last Wednesday to be precise—when Alan woke up early and disappeared. We had overslept and panicked when we couldn't find Alan (he keeps his bedroom door locked so we pounded on it, but knew he wasn't in there), especially since the interview Alan had arranged with *L.A. MovieNews* was that morning. By the time Paque and I realized Alan really wasn't home, the *MovieNews* people were knocking on the front door.

Just let them knock, I said, and they'll come back later.

Nonsense, Paque said, let's do the interview. Paque was frustrated at the pace of the *World Gone Water* shoot. The clips had been on the Internet for more than a week and Alan hadn't started returning the calls on the answering machine like he promised he would. Paque asked him when he planned on calling them back but Alan would just mutter something about 'critical mass' and then he'd go in his room and lock the door.

So Paque and I would spend our days answering the growing cluster of fan mail on our website, which was fun for a while. Guys were writing in and asking us our favorite color and what was our favorite food and all kinds of crazy questions. There were a couple gross ones too, but because it's over the computer it was sort of easy and okay to find those ones funny, too.

Then we got the letter in the mail from the toy company. Paque read it over and said, They want to make dolls of us. I took the letter and saw the bright pink logo. What should we do, I asked her. The letter said that if we agreed to the contract we'd receive $25,000 within a month of signing, against future sales of the dolls.

I wonder if we can help design them, Paque said. You know, what kinds of clothes they wear. Stuff like that.

Does it say anything about that in the contract, I asked.

There were a lot of things in the contract that we didn't understand, but we didn't see anything about us being involved with the manufacture of the dolls.

We signed the contracts. Paque wrote *Let us help with the outfits* at the bottom of each copy and we walked the envelope over to the mailbox on the corner so Alan wouldn't find out.

We did the *MovieNews* interview, too. We let them in and they set up in the front room. I don't think we knew what we were going to say—at least I didn't—and I just sort of followed Paque's lead. She's quick and I guess she decided that she was going to give them the most scandalous interview they'd ever printed. Before I knew it, I was going along with what she said.

They asked us what life has been like in Hollywood for us and that opened it up. Paque said, Well, you know, it's been a little bit rock and roll. (Which I thought was a great answer.) For instance, take the other night, she said. Me and Daisy were hanging out with the guys from Counting Crows, we were getting cones at that great ice cream place on Olympic, and we run into Jack Nicholson, who is also getting cones with his girlfriend and his daughter. Jack invites us all to go with him to the La Brea Tar Pits—his daughter wants to look for dinosaurs—so we all follow Jack's Mercedes to Wilshire and we park and get out and the guys from Counting Crows keep telling Jack how much they liked *Chinatown*. Jack is very gracious and his girlfriend and his daughter go to the fence to look at the pits and Jack tells us about this great party at Dennis Hopper's house, which we go to sans Counting Crows. We never meet Dennis, and we didn't see Jack, but we met Gary Busey, who was walking around with Buddy Holly glasses on singing 'Peggy Sue.' We tell them about Ashley Judd, who asked us if we wanted to go on a beer run—apparently she only drank lite beer and Dennis didn't have anything that wasn't imported—and we said, Sure, we'll go. Gary Busey came along too and he did this really funny thing with the Coke display in the grocery store, but then they wouldn't sell to us and we got kicked out.

Paque looked at me and I was biting the inside of my cheek so hard I could taste blood. Yeah, I said, but the night before was even cooler. Jerry Seinfeld had a party at the hangar where he keeps his Porsche collection. It was a really society affair. A champagne and caviar party. We ended up laying in the grass at the end of a runway at three in the morning with Seinfeld and Michael Richards, the guy who played Kramer.

The *MovieNews* people were making notes and hurried to flip over the cassette in the tape recorder when it snapped off.

Paque gave them the best one though. She told them about going to Hollywood Park, the horse track, with Magic Johnson, who we supposedly met at Dennis Hopper's party. Paque described us going to the winning horse's stable after the race because Magic knew the owners. The house was full of people in tuxedos and gowns, mostly moneymen from Los Angeles, along with some Arab sheiks (I thought that was a nice touch myself). Someone rang a bell, Paque said, and we all went out to the stable, where Hallelu-jah, the horse who'd just won at Hollywood Park, was frolicking with Little Lady, the mare who'd won the Preakness and the Ken-tucky Derby the year before. Everyone gathered at the fence—even the ladies in gowns—and these two models came out in bikinis. All the men hooted and hollered and the models tried to settle the horses down. A guy who looked like a ranch hand came out and steadied Hallelujah. The models crawled under the horse like you would get under a car and cupped the horse's balls. Hallelujah danced around a little bit but the ranch hand had a hold of his reins and petted his nose as the models massaged him. The horse's thingie came out just like a ladder on a fire truck and everyone clapped and whistled. Little Lady came sniffing around and the two models and the ranch hand helped Hallelujah mount her. Once he was inside her, everyone lifted their glass. The two guys standing next to me and Daisy shook hands. There was a china bowl in the hall on the way out where you could win a trip to all three Triple Crown races by naming the soon-to-be horse.

Paque and I told them some other stuff that wasn't true, like that *World Gone Water* was going to be a five-hour epic movie that incorporated elements of sci-fi, animation, the Western, rock-u-mentary, and French period pieces. Alan didn't think that was very funny when he returned but *L.A. MovieNews* didn't end up using our interview after all (the bit about the horse showed up in a gossip column the next day though).

Paque demanded to know where Alan was and why he messed up the interview. She screamed at him that he was fucking things up royally and chased him to his room. He slammed the door in her face without saying anything and she kicked it over and over and I held my hands to my ears.

Let's call Stella, she said. We'll tell her to come pick us up.

I called Stella's number and Craig (her boyfriend) answered. He told me Stella wasn't there and that he hadn't seen her in a couple days. He said he thought she was with Paque and me and that now he was really worried. We called the photomat where Stella worked and they said she didn't work there anymore.

I was so frazzled that I ran out to get a couple of hot apple pies from the McDonald's on Sunset, and by the time I walked there and back, Paque had cooled down and was sitting at the kitchen table with Alan, who looked like his entire family had been killed in a plane crash.

I have something to tell you, Alan said. I pulled out a chair at the kitchen table and set the McDonald's bag down next to a completed script with the words *World Gone Water* typed on the front. Some big investors picked up on the movie, Alan said, and they want to back a full-length movie.

Great, I said but the look on Paque's face told me it was not great.

It's not that simple, Alan said. These guys have conditions attached to their investment.

I looked across the table at Paque, who I noticed was smoking Alan's Marlboros. She sat with a dazed look on her face. I nervously opened the McDonald's bag and unsheathed one of the apple pies.

How is it hard, I asked.

One of the conditions is that I have to use two actresses that they want, Alan said.

I swallowed the gooey filling and said, So you're replacing us. Just like that.

Alan winced as he ran his fingers through his hair. It isn't like that, he said. I don't want to have to do it but I have to play by the rules if the movie is to get made.

I thought you said it wasn't even going to be a movie, I argued. You said we weren't going to make a real movie.

We weren't, Alan said. But this story is important to me—it's my story—and I'd like to see it get made.

Why do we need these guys then, I asked. We can do it without them.

They have enough money to get it done and I don't, Alan said, leaning back. It's that simple.

So what are we supposed to do, I asked.

We'll have a project together, I promise, Alan said. I'll develop something especially for you two. He tried to get Paque's attention but she was staring at the floor.

Who are these actresses anyway, I asked.

You wouldn't know who they are, Alan said. They're nobodies.

Like us, Paque said.

I started crying and excused myself from the table. Paque came into the bedroom behind me. She ripped down the *World Gone Water* poster taped to our closet door and for the first time that I could ever remember, Paque cried.

Alan knocked on the door and Paque screamed, Go away, but Alan knocked again and said, Daisy, your mom's on the phone.

Tell her I'll call her back, I said.

Should I ask my mom to get us plane tickets home, I asked Paque. She'd stopped crying and was studying the weeds growing outside the window and said, I don't think that's necessary.

Okay, I said.

Alan's car was gone and I called my mom back and when she asked how it was going I said, Everything's fine.

That night I had a dream Paque and I were back at SaltBed and that we were on stage singing while Alan was in the audience. My mom was in the audience, along with my brother Chuck and everyone I'd ever known in my life. People were screaming out requests for Masterful Johnson tunes and we sang them perfect, every one the crowd asked for and in the morning I woke up exhausted, as if I'd spent the night giving every ounce of energy I had.

Daisy

Dear Sara and Keren,

When you need someone, you can't count on anybody. Stella is either avoiding us (she's probably mad because of all the publicity Paque and I have been getting), or she finally got an acting gig and is somewhere on location. Those are the only two answers Paque and I will accept. We really needed her after Alan dumped us. Neither one of us wanted to say it but we realized we didn't have anyone we could call.

Then I remembered T.J. I paged him and he agreed to pick us up.

Should we pack up our stuff, I asked.

There isn't anything that can't be replaced if we don't come back, Paque said.

T.J. picked us up in a cinnamon-colored convertible BMW, which turned out to belong to the actress Jennifer Grey, who T.J. was house-sitting for. She really lives in New York, but is renting out here because of her TV show, T.J. said.

Paque sat up front and I closed my eyes and let the wind whip around me. Whatever romantic feeling I thought I had for T.J. disappeared when I saw him again. Behind the wheel of the car, checking both ways for traffic, he seemed like just another guy to hang out with. I sensed from his coolness that he felt the same way. The clean scent of the new leather seats comforted me and I imagined it was the day before we got dumped, before we knew anything about how quickly something certain turns into something completely unknown.

Paque and I decided not to say anything to T.J. about what had happened. We told him we just wanted to get out of the house for a bit.

It sounded like an emergency, T.J. said.

It wasn't, Paque said.

Have you seen Stella, T.J. asked. She owes me some money.

Neither Paque or I said anything.

Well, T.J. said, I'm sure she'll pay me when I see her.

T.J. drove us back to Jennifer Grey's house in the Hollywood Hills, a cute little yellow house nestled safely behind a sprawl of lilac bushes. T.J. carefully pulled the BMW into the garage and you got the feeling that he probably wasn't supposed to be driving it.

Guess who used to rent this house, T.J. asked.

Who, I asked.

Barbra Streisand, he said.

It looks a little small for Barbra Streisand, Paque said.

T.J. stopped and collected a few empty beer bottles lined up on the pathway between the garage and the house.

Who is Jennifer Grey anyway, I asked.

She was the sister in *Ferris Bueller's Day Off*, T.J. said.

Think *Dirty Dancing*, Paque said.

What TV show is she on, I asked.

It's a new one where she plays herself, T.J. said, and the storylines are based on her real life.

Are they going to use the one where she and Matthew Broderick accidentally killed those people in Sweden or Norway or wherever it was, Paque asked sarcastically.

From what Paque said I knew then who they were talking about. I remembered reading in one of Stella's notebooks about the crash, about how Matthew Broderick had pulled out on the wrong side in his Volvo, right into an oncoming car. Stella's information had it that it was an accident, and that Matthew Broderick didn't have to go to jail. Anyway, I think that's what happened. I only remember it because I thought it was weird that they were playing brother and sister in the film but they were really boyfriend/girlfriend.

Paque opened the side door and was startled by a man in a blue silk shirt and boxers rummaging through the pantry. His skin was

143

tight and tan and his hair was bleached white. Oh, hello, he said with a British accent.

This is Jason, T.J. said. He's with the production.

Paque and I introduced ourselves and Jason said, You're in that movie. He snapped his fingers trying to come up with the title.

World Gone Water, Paque said.

That's it, Jason said. He pulled down a box of strawberry Pop-Tarts and opened one of the shiny packages with his teeth. If you've got call for a mechanized go-cart driver, I race professionally, he said.

Paque said, I don't think there's any go-carts in the movie.

Jason's jaw bounced up and down as he chewed. That's too bad, he said between bites, I'm really good. He disappeared out the sliding glass door in the kitchen and Paque and I went to the window above the sink and watched him rejoin a small group out by the pool. A woman in a red robe sat in a lawn chair under an umbrella, reading *Entertainment Weekly* while an enormous man waded in the shallow end of the pool with a camera perched on his shoulder. A second man stayed dry at a soundboard at the edge of the pool.

That's Earl, T.J. said. He gives me money to let him film porno at the houses I stay at.

What happens if the person sees their house in a porno, Paque asked.

That hasn't happened yet, T.J. said. He rapped his knuckles on the wooden kitchen counter.

The refrigerator is covered with photos of a woman and a chocolate Labrador. Is this Jennifer Grey, I asked.

Yep, T.J. said, help yourself to anything in the fridge.

It doesn't look like Ferris's sister, I said. I leaned in to study one of the photos.

She had a nose job, T.J. said.

I thought she had a cute nose, Paque said.

It definitely looks better now, T.J. said.

It's wild, I said, it really doesn't look anything like her.

T.J. looked at the photo. Yeah, when I got the gig and I came up to the house I couldn't believe it was really her. Don't get me wrong— she's beautiful, maybe more so. But when you think of Jennifer Grey you think of Baby in *Dirty Dancing* or Jeanie Bueller. I think it's been hard for her to get work because people don't recognize her.

Only in Hollywood can you be tossed to the bottom of the heap by improving your looks with plastic surgery, Paque said bitterly.

T.J. offered to let us stay at Jennifer Grey's—Jason and the woman in the red robe, Maria, were staying there as well. We thanked T.J. and told him we'd stay the night, and he didn't make any sort of joke about us owing him big, which we appreciated.

T.J. ran out for Kentucky Fried Chicken and I took the opportunity to talk to Paque. I want to go home, I said. There's nothing here for us now.

You might be right, Paque said. But what harm is there if we hang around to see if Alan makes good on his promise to find something for us.

I looked out the window at the scene in the pool. Alan's going to be tied up with that movie for at least a year, I reasoned.

Maybe we'll get bit parts, Paque said.

That's part of the problem, too, I said. We're only good for bit parts. We're not actresses. I don't even want to be an actress, do you?

Paque didn't answer.

Sure, I jumped at the idea when Alan called, I said, but that was because I was desperate to get away from the humiliation in Phoenix. I'm not even sure I can ever go back to Phoenix, but things can't be as crazy as they were. Plus, I'm afraid we're going to get involved in something that's going to humiliate us even more.

Humiliation is sometimes the easiest way to become famous, Paque said smartly.

It seems like we've tried everything, I said.

Yeah, Paque sighed. She looked out the window at Jason and Maria, who were toweling off. But it's precisely because we've tried everything that we should probably stick it out just a little bit longer. Why come as far as we've come—and you have to admit we've been lucky along the way, even if the end result has been unlucky—and not go all the way? We can always go back to Phoenix. And if we humiliate ourselves, as you put it, here in Hollywood we'll either get a book deal or a TV show at worst, and then we can decide whether or not we want to walk away.

I don't know, I said.

Why don't you call Chuck and see what he thinks, Paque suggested.

I've been trying to reach him actually, I said. But I can't find him.

Paque stayed up watching television and smoking pot with the others. I took one of the spare bedrooms, the smaller one at the end of the hall with the thick white shag carpet and the twin bed. It smelled like no one had ever been in the room and dust motes rose when I switched on the bedside lamp. It seemed to me there wasn't anything to be happy about. The last thing that really made me happy was making the record for Ian. If you would've told me we were going to blow that one the way we did, I would've bet against you. Plus Paque and I really love music. All those nights we stayed up late designing album covers and picking who we wanted to be in our videos seems like a waste of energy now. I started to think about second chances. Jennifer Grey got one, but she had to play her last trump to get it. I mean, what would she sell after she sold her life to the TV show?

I decided Paque was right, that we should ride this one out as far as it would go. And if it went badly, we would walk out of Hollywood and not look back.

Daisy

Dear Sara and Keren,

I'm sorry to be sending you a letter again so soon after the last one, but you're not going to believe what's going on now. Paque and I camped out at T.J.'s for a couple of days, listening to Jason and Maria's stories about trying to make it in Hollywood—you never heard such terrible stories. Jason once pitched a tent on a director's lawn, was beaten up (not by the director), and thrown off the property. He pitched his tent again and the director gave him the part. And Maria told this disgusting story about what she had to do to just to get to *read* for a part. It all but convinced me that you have to have a check on your ambition. There has to be some things that you're not willing to do. Though I agreed with Paque that being famous is the loftiest of goals, more ambitious than being president. You can pretty much divide the world up into people who are famous and people who are not (otherwise known as People Who Wish They Were Famous).

What's behind wanting to be famous, Maria asked.

Don't give me that need-for-attention horseshit, Paque said, or that it's insecurity. It's about freedom. It's what money used to represent. But now anyone can get rich.

Exactly, Jason said.

I thought for me it was setting out to get something and getting it, but didn't say so. That's why I didn't hesitate when Alan asked us to do what we did. That and because I was still smarting from what Alan did, which pointed up how out of our control Paque's and my situation had become.

We actually saw it on Jennifer Grey's TV before Alan told us anything about it. Paque and I stayed up late talking. I said I was having a hard time dealing with the guilt I felt about what happened at SaltBed. I was sure Paque blamed me and I knew I was risking making her mad by bringing it up. We were sitting cross-legged on the L-shaped sofa— T.J. was asleep in the recliner—and Paque said, It's my fault. It was me who convinced everyone that it was a good idea to lip sync. I told Ian and Jammin' Jay that you agreed with me, she said, even though I knew you wanted to skip SaltBed.

There's no way we could've had our voices in shape for SaltBed, I said. Things were happening too fast around us for us to be able to make the right decision.

Paque said, Yeah, but you were right, we should've skipped the festival.

I smiled. It probably would've heightened expectations, I laughed.

Paque laughed and looked away and that's when we both heard the guy from CNN say our names. It was like someone had our heads on a string and had pulled tight. The *World Gone Water* poster flashed on the screen too quick for us to really catch it and then the story, whatever it was, was over.

What was that, Paque asked.

She flipped to E!, the cable entertainment station, and we didn't have to wait long to hear the story.

At first, the story didn't seem to involve us and we were beginning to think we'd imagined seeing the poster. The woman on E!—that dipshit I can't stand—talked about how Arnold Schwarzenegger escaped near death while appearing in a cameo role for an indie film, apparently some sort of favor to the director. The ceiling of the sound stage collapsed during the filming and there was a picture of Schwarzenegger striding out of the building with soot on his face and his shirt ripped, just like an action hero from any one of his films. He mugged for the local news camera but looked a little shaken.

Then it happened again. The *World Gone Water* poster appeared and the E! woman said, There are unconfirmed reports tonight that the much-hyped film *World Gone Water* was filming in another part of the soundstage. A call to Alan Hood, that film's director, went unanswered.

Paque grabbed the phone. Pick up, pick up, pick up, she said after the answering machine beeped.

Alan picked up and before Paque could ask anything he said, Where are you?

We'd only been gone two days but seeing Alan made it feel like we'd been gone for a year. He was so nervous he drove ten miles under the posted speed limit.

I tried to call you last night when it happened, he said. I thought you were at your friend Stella's. Her boyfriend told me Stella was at the Chateau Marmont and I figured you were there so I went over.

A pickup truck came up behind us, the headlights shining like daylight through the back window.

Did you see Stella, Paque asked.

They didn't have anyone named Stella registered there, Alan said. I thought you guys were fucking around with me. I called the boyfriend again, but he hung up on me.

Alan pulled to the side of the road and asked Paque to drive. They switched seats and Paque pulled out into traffic, gunning it.

I wondered where Stella was.

So, Paque asked, is it true.

Alan adjusted his glasses. It's true, he said.

Are they dead, I blurted out.

Jesus, no, Alan said. He turned around in his seat and glared at me. They're in the hospital, he said.

How bad are they hurt, Paque asked.

Broken legs and broken arms, Alan said. We weren't even filming, just having a preliminary meeting. The ceiling didn't fall on them but it knocked over a camera and some of the set. They got caught underneath.

One of my favorite songs came over the radio and I wanted to ask Paque to turn it up—I wanted the song to drown out the image of those poor girls in hospital beds, their once perfect bodies cracked and sewn together—but I didn't. It's funny how fast you can go from hating someone (Paque and I were calling them the Bitches) to feeling sorry for them.

The phone won't stop, Alan went on. It just keeps ringing and ringing and ringing.

So what happens now, I asked.

Alan stared straight ahead, pretending to think it over, as if he had just came up with the idea on the spot: I need to ask you a big favor, he said, The biggest.

I think I knew what he was going to ask before he asked it. Anyway, I wasn't surprised when he proposed his plan.

I need you to make a public appearance, Alan said. They all think it's you who are hurt and if they see that you're okay, that'll buy me some time.

Time to do what, I started to ask, but Paque slammed on the brakes and we skidded into a Mobil parking lot. I bounced back against the seat and Paque yelled, You've got a lot of nerve. You bring us out to California with all these promises and then you kick us off the film and now you want us to pretend we're still in it to save *your* ass? Fuck you. Why should we?

Paque was so mad she frightened me. I hadn't seen her that mad since Stella told her she was moving to California.

Calm down, Alan said. All you have to do is go with me to this benefit tomorrow night—some dance thing—pose for a couple pictures and you're done. What you get out of it is you can tell whoever will listen that you're quitting the picture. You can even say what you want about me, I don't care. That'll start the phone ringing. You'll have enough offers to keep you in pictures for ten years.

Alan looked at each of us, pleading, and I said, I'll do it.

Paque looked at me incredulously, but then she realized what I did—that it was the only way to get ourselves away from Alan and the whole mess.

150

Okay, she said.

Alan looked touched, as if he was surprised he had persuaded us.

The benefit—a star-studded evening put on by Chase Dance Theater for the Multiple Sclerosis Foundation—was held in the auditorium of Hollywood High. A train of black limousines waited to pull up to the red carpet that gaped from the auditorium entrance like a thirsty tongue, drawing celebrities inside in groups of two or three. Our limo idled and Alan said, Remember, no interviews. Just wave and smile.

When the door to our limo opened, Paque and I stepped out into the warm evening. A single flashbulb went off and I looked in its direction. Up ahead, Will Smith and his wife were posing for pictures. The one flashbulb drew attention our way and Will Smith looked over his shoulder as the paparazzi moved towards us.

This way, someone shouted.

Over here!

One here!

Look!

Paque!

Daisy!

Were you hurt in the accident?

Is anything broken?

Were you scared?

What was going through your mind?

This way!

Over here!

Alan, Paque and I linked arms and smiled, ignoring the questions. Where usually ignoring reporters' questions only makes them ask more, no one pressed the issue—it was enough to take our pictures, I guess.

It was a relief to get inside the auditorium. Something funny: We all had to take our shoes off because a special dance floor had been assembled and the floor was 'sensitive.' They had a guy in a tuxedo who exchanged your shoes for a little red ticket.

Besides Matt Damon and Ben Affleck, who were skating in their socks in the hall, Paque and I noticed how uneasy some of the celebrities were around one another. After the handshakes and the cheek kisses everyone took their seats and it seemed like the first day of class, like no one knew anyone. The dance company was waiting for the sun to set so we all just sat and shifted in our chairs. Pierce Brosnan sat next to Alan and I kept asking Alan pointless questions about the performance and the architecture of Hollywood High just so I could sneak a look at James Bond, who Paque and I agree is one of the handsomest men alive. You just know he would make a good boyfriend and/or husband. Alan, in contrast, wouldn't.

Watching the first dance number, a funny piece called 'Con Queso,' I remembered the ballet I put on in the kitchen when I was five for my mother and father. The ballet was called 'Up and Up and Up' and was about a little girl who met a magician (played by my brother, Chuck) who gave her the power to fly. (I repaid Chuck by appearing in his Batman and Robin costume drama. How he talked the principal into letting him chase the Joker—who had me in tow—from classroom to classroom I'll never know. That's just Chuck. I remember one fifth-grader was so scared she peed herself and her mom had to come pick her up.)

The rest of the numbers—'Red Delicious,' 'Untitled #1,' and 'Lemons for Loveliness'—were breathtaking. My mother had me keep one of those books you write in that asks your height and weight and age and what you want to be when you grow up. I wrote 'dancer' every year through sixth grade. It was my dream to become a ballerina, though now that seems like a dream only a child could have.

Daisy

Dear Sara and Keren,

Paque and I demanded that Alan take us to the hospital to see the actresses. He hesitated, saying it was too gruesome, but when we insisted he relented. Based on his hesitation, I imagined body parts here and there but the truth was Alan didn't want Paque and I to know that one of the actresses who replaced us was Annette Laupin. She and the other actress, Portia (like the car) D'Angeles, shared a room, but they were so bound up in traction that they couldn't communicate with each other. Identical breakfasts of eggs, toast, and orange juice sat perched on the stand between the beds.

Hospital rooms make Paque nauseous—she spent a lot of time in them when her parents died. She doesn't ever talk about it but when she was with me in the hospital in Phoenix, I could tell she wanted to bolt.

Alan waited in the hall and Paque and I set the pink and blue teddy bears we bought in the hospital gift shop next to the breakfasts. Annette opened her watery eyes and smiled when she saw us.

I'm on goofballs, she said.

Paque and I laughed.

Does it hurt much, I asked.

Only when I think about it, she said.

Portia tried to lift her head but struggled under the effort and gave up.

Alan thinks you're going to sue him, Paque said loud enough for Alan to hear. Alan pretended like he wasn't listening, but he was.

Annette grimaced. I can't do anything until I can walk, she said.

I wanted to apologize for the things Paque and I had said about Annette and Portia, but they wouldn't have known what I was talking about. Of course we didn't know it was them when Paque and I called them the Bitches. We were just mad; no one could blame us. Still, seeing the two of them strung up and cocooned in so much plaster made me sorry for the things I'd said before.

There didn't seem to be anything to say. Portia called for the nurse to give her some more painkillers—the nurse refused—and Paque and I just stood there.

Well, Paque said.

Annette filtered back into consciousness and said, Thanks for stopping by.

Paque and I said we'd stop by again, wondering if we really would, but didn't discuss it in the elevator. Alan kept quiet, too. When the elevator doors opened, Paque and I saw someone from our past who startled us: Fred Meyers, the reporter from the *Arizona Republic*.

Well, well, Meyers said. Just who I was looking for. He seemed older, and swaggered towards us like he was going to prove to his buddies that he could pick us up in a bar.

Hi, Fred, Paque said, What are doing here of all places?

I'm with the *Los Angeles Times* now, he grinned.

Congratulations, Paque said.

You're Alan Hood, right, Meyers asked.

Alan and Meyers shook hands. Nice to meet you, Alan mumbled.

A pale young girl in a wheelchair pushed by a nurse passed in front of us. I smiled at the girl, who was trying to grasp a balloon someone had tied to the wheelchair.

So, are you just here for a check-up, Meyers asked. He reached for his notebook.

Uh, yeah, Alan said. Just wanted to make sure nothing was broken.

Is anything?

Nope, Alan said.

Meyers scribbled something in this notebook and at that moment I noticed that he was slicking his hair back now. It scared me that I didn't notice at first and I nervously laughed, What's with the hair?

Meyers seemed taken aback. He ran his hand along the slicked down side of his head. What, he asked.

Paque laughed.

Anyway, Meyers said, I'd like to get an interview for the paper. Can we do it now? Just a couple of questions?

Hey, buddy, how would you like a scoop, Alan asked. Daisy and Paque are quitting the film. How's that for news?

Meyers looked at us and we nodded.

Why are you quitting, he wanted to know.

Because I'm the worst filmmaker in the history of Hollywood, Alan said. Make sure you spell the first name right. A-L-A-N.

Meyers waited for the punchline but Alan didn't say any more.

We're fielding other offers now, Paque said confidently. We want to work with Spielberg, or Frances Ford Coppola.

Or Penny Marshall, I said.

Okay girls, Alan said, let's go. He turned to Meyers, Better print that story quick. There might be a press conference later today. A scoop like this can make a reporter's career.

Meyers looked indignant but didn't argue. I'll call for a follow-up, he said.

Alan herded us out of the hospital and nobody said anything on the ride back to Alan's.

Since I'm sure you read about it in the papers—someone Alan knew called up to say it was in the London *Sunday Times*, too—you know that Meyers did call us up and that we gave him the real story. I don't think Paque and I knew that we were going to rat Alan out. We *were* pretty pissed off with him, but he had this way of making you feel sorry for him even though you really despised him and what he'd done.

But that didn't matter. Meyers had dirt on us. He tracked down some guy who said he hired us to come to his hotel room and that he ended up getting beat up and robbed (this isn't what it sounds like; Paque and I used to be fantasy wrestlers—just once, really—and this guy tried to kill us). The guy even had pictures, which could only have been taken by someone hiding in a closet.

Paque and I got on separate phones and told Meyers what really happened in that hotel room, but he wasn't interested.

I want to know what's going on with *World Gone Water*, he said.

We're not doing it anymore, Paque said. We told you that already.

What if I said I didn't think you were anywhere near that set the night the ceiling caved in, Meyers asked.

I'd wonder who told you that, Paque said. I couldn't tell if she was as nervous as I was, but if she was you couldn't hear it in her voice.

What if a certain porn actress said she was with you the night of the accident, Meyers asked. He paused to see if we were going to respond. What if someone else said they were sure you'd been replaced.

Stop it, I yelled. If you know all this why are you asking us? What difference does it make? We told you that we're not doing the film any more, we told you that we're not even … affiliated … with Alan Hood Productions.

Paque tried to shush me but I was delirious.

You know, Fred, you should think about your life, I continued. Remember how concerned you were for us back in Phoenix, remember how you protected us from the reporters who were trying to eat us alive. Well, now you're one of those vultures. Are you happy now that you're a vulture? Yeah, sure, it's all true. You want to know the truth. The truth is that we were replaced, and we weren't there that night, and that those two girls are in the hospital with broken bones. I fail to see how that's even a story. How did this become a story?

Hey, I just—Meyers started to defend himself.

You just what, I said. You're just doing your job? Isn't there real news in the world? Doesn't anybody care about anything that's real, that's not phoney baloney make-believe and put up with cardboard walls? I'm hanging up, and don't call back.

I gripped the phone to give it a good slam and the last thing I heard was Meyers answering my question: Not in Hollywood.

That's how the real story got in the papers. I called my mom to arrange a flight back to Phoenix and she put two tickets at the Southwest Airlines counter.

But we couldn't get to them. By the time the story broke—Fred Meyers didn't break it; it was in *Daily Variety*—we had our suitcases packed. Alan's bedroom door was locked and we weren't even going to say goodbye. We weren't going to say anything to anyone. Except for Stella. We wanted to say goodbye to Stella. I did especially because I didn't know what was going to happen once the plane landed in Phoenix. I couldn't remember the last time Paque and I had a conversation about anything that wasn't related to trying to make it. And since we didn't make it—and since I didn't want to make it—it seemed realistic that Paque and I saying goodbye to Stella might be the last time the three of us stood in the same room together.

It started with the afternoon edition of the papers. HOLLYWOOD OUTRAGED AT STUNT. PLOT TO CONCEAL INJURIES TO ACTRESSES ABHORRED BY THE BIZ. FELLOW ACTORS EXPRESSING SYMPATHY. DISTRICT ATTORNEY TO FILE RECKLESS ENDANGERMENT CHARGES AGAINST HOOD. Paque and I imagined a mob scene if we showed our faces at the airport.

Imagine anyone in Hollywood being outraged by anything, Paque said.

Craig told Paque that Stella had moved into the Chateau Marmont with Bryan Metro. Why would she do that, Paque asked, but Craig had already hung up.

Should we stop by and see Stella, I asked.

Paque thought for a moment. Who knows what's going on over there, she murmured.

I could guess what Paque was thinking. On the one hand what if Stella had some great advice on what to do about our situation, but then again, on the other hand, what if she was living it up with Bryan Metro? Paque wouldn't be able to bear the sight of that.

We should say goodbye, I said.

Paque didn't disagree but just shrugged her shoulders, so it was decided.

On our way out to the curb to wait for the cab we noticed a pink box on the front steps. Paque tore off the top and sifted through the plastic peanuts, pulling out the prototypes for the Paque and Daisy dolls.

Which one is you and which one is me, I asked.

Paque held them up. The dolls were long and slender and looked the same, except one had light hair and one had dark. It's hard to tell, she said.

Where's the money, I asked.

Paque read the letter. 'A check for the amount due on signature of the contract follows this package in 6-8 weeks,' she said.

Fairy dust, I said.

In the cab a woman on the radio was saying how disgusting the whole episode was and that she thought Paque and I should be held responsible. She went on and on about taking responsibility for one's actions, etc. She called Paque and I frauds. Actually she said scam artists. The woman on the radio said she only heard of such things in the movies, not in real life. She said what Paque and I did might make a good movie, but it wasn't acceptable in real life.

It might make a good movie, I thought, but I wouldn't want to star in it.

When the cab let us off at the Chateau the place seemed

deserted. The trees in the courtyard shook with the wind and you could hear a dog barking off somewhere. The woman behind the desk let Paque use the phone to call Stella up in Bryan Metro's room and in the elevator Paque said, She sounded terrible.

As we walked down the hall my mind bounced back and forth between going back to Phoenix or staying in L.A. You can't go there but you can't stay here, is what I thought. I thought maybe I'd go to New York and stay with Chuck, maybe try to get into college. The idea of me in school, hitting the books, was so much of a fantasy that it depressed me further and I started taking deep breaths to keep from fainting.

Stella answered the door wearing a long white dress shirt and dark sunglasses. The shirt had what looked like a wine stain down the left sleeve. God, I'm glad you're here, she said and hugged us both. She smelled like she hadn't showered in a week.

We heard voices inside and I was stunned into silence when my eyes focused on my brother, Chuck, standing with Bryan Metro and David Geffen out on the balcony. Chuck turned around and saw me and I felt instant relief. There you are, he said and put his arms around me. I went limp against his body. I felt like I could sleep for a year.

I've been trying to call you, I said.

I know, Chuck said, I was worried about you so I came out to find you. Craig told me he thought you'd be here. Are you okay?

I started to cry and Chuck hugged me tighter.

It's OK, Chuck whispered. I think we've figured this out.

Stella excused herself and went to the bathroom and for the first time I noticed the sea of litter on the floor. Paque was out on the balcony introducing herself to David Geffen, who was talking on a cell phone as he shook her hand. He put his hand on her shoulder as if to say, Hold on a minute, and I started to ask Chuck what was going on when Bryan Metro came in off the balcony and said, This is so great.

I could feel Paque getting excited as Bryan Metro and David Geffen hatched their scheme involving us. Stella would be involved, too. They'd do the whole story, Phoenix and everything. Bryan would do the soundtrack and Geffen would get Spielberg to direct. Can we sing on the soundtrack, Paque wanted to know and David Geffen shook his head no. Absolutely not, he said. Chuck had worked it out so that he would be the second unit director, which Paque and I didn't know anything about, and Stella came out of the bathroom and everyone was staring at us, waiting. Paque looked at me and all my anxiety came back. You could see how much it meant to everyone in the room—to Stella, to Paque, to my own brother. The sunglasses Stella was wearing reminded me of a long time ago, when it was the three of us, out by Stella's parents' pool, leafing through magazines of celebrities at parties and movie premieres, celebrities smiling out at you in a way that let you know that their life was just fantastic, that every day was like their birthday and that their worst day was nothing like your worst day. We spent hours by the pool talking 'What if,' which over time became 'When,' but I don't think we had any idea of what it would take to have a life where every day was like your birthday.

Geffen's cell phone rang but he didn't make a move to answer it. What would you say if someone offered you a chance like that? The phrase 'make it big' floated through the room—it seemed like everyone was saying it at once—and so I guess you probably know what we said.

Daisy

Typical of the Times: Growing Up
in the Culture of Spectacle

For my wife

Introduction

We're So Famous was my first published novel, but it is not the first
novel I wrote. I originally attempted to emulate my hero F. Scott
Fitzgerald, attracted to and influenced as I was by his narratives
about sad young men, a thread I'd pick up later for my trilogy about
Charlie Martens. But when my first novel failed to sell, I cast about
for another theme that interested me, and didn't have to ruminate
long before recognizing my intense interest in the culture of celebrity. It seems naive to claim that back in the late 1990s, celebrity
culture was a relatively new phenomenon, but fame for fame's sake
seemed new and curious to me—previously those who wanted to
become famous aspired to be athletes or actors or musicians or
models—and so it was the perfect subject for a novel in that moment
in time before the Internet truly became the enabler it is for any and
all attention seekers. (As proof of how pre-Internet this novel was,
I remember a late-night trip to the record store to confirm the spelling of the name of one of the singers in Bananarama, at the behest
of the copy editor.)

As I contemplated the afterword for this new edition, I tried to
transport myself back to that time and place in my life when I was
obsessed with and amazed by fame, to create a little sketch meant

to provide the context in which the novel was written. Instead a torrent of words issued forth over the course of a month, and so the afterword became *Typical of the Times, Growing up in the Culture of Spectacle*. When I was finished, it was apparent not only why I wrote *We're So Famous*, but also that it was a book I was destined to write.

—Jaime Clarke

That vanessa williams thing was right around the time of the mcdonald's massacre you couldn't turn on a television without hearing about those poor innocents just eating lunch and then a circumstance occurs like earlier when the teenage sears security guard shooed away the kids gathered around the in-store video game console and the younge but over the years it will become apparent that unlike other places you've lived everything about phoenix was master-planned except the freeway to los angeles which ends in a pile of concrete and slumbering construction vehicles a block from the house on the west side your father and younger brother rented in advance you and your youngest brother and mother staying behind in rapid city for reasons you may never know like all the childhood questions that just remain questions like why did everyone mail away for those free gum balls made out of a new kind of sugar and you suspect the answers are unsatisfying as answers anyway and so you don't bother two bryan adams concerts in one summer is the result yes you dreamed at the first concert in rapid city of meeting a girl and had no idea that months later at your second time through the set list that you'd be holding hands with a girl who would ultimately get you kicked out of phoenix veterans memorial coliseum but you think the move to the empty upper deck is for something more than hand-holding and not for smoking cigarettes which security would spot pretty quickly yes you had broken up with your first phoenix girlfriend on her birthday while lying in the dark on the phone unaware that your chronic nosebleeding wasn't tears on your cheek all those afternoons going over to the first girlfriend's trailer across from your new school how many new schools you didn't care to remember the first girlfriend's mother was always home and let you hold hands on the couch while watching television but you weren't allowed down the hall except to use the bathroom and only when the first girlfriend was firmly stationed in the front room or sometimes the kitchen the first girlfriend's friend who lived in the trailer park had one of those arms that wasn't all the way an arm more than the def leppard drummer after he crashed his corvette into a brick wall but still not like everyone else and you didn't care if people stared but she did yes you broke up with the first girlfriend for the reasons time immemorial that men break up with women but you didn't yet understand that until you did that one afternoon when the girl-who-would-ultimately-get-you-kicked-out-of-the-bryan-adams-concert's sister stalked into the bathroom and poured cold water on you both in the shower parents that both work is a thing you have in common including an overwhelming interest in sexual exploration her lost fake fingernail found in your boxers at the rest stop on her family's trip to california you imagined you were daniel and she agreed she could be ali from the karate kid when you snapped pictures at the same golf n' stuff as in the movie her grandmother made you sleep on her couch in indio and the curios and doilies were unnerving and you asked to bunk in with her older brother much later the grandmother's house is confused in your mind with that of the actor ray milland when you learn he died in indio madonna sings her new song like a virgin at the video music awards wearing a wedding dress and a bustier vh1 debuted a couple of hours after the def leppard drummer crashed his corvette come to think of it the time the girl was inconsolable when her five-year-old stepbrother was killed run over in the street is the prevailing memory of that time also the eighth-grade graduation trip to disneyland purchased by selling tom-wat door-to-door because a lot of kids will never graduate high school the teacups and the hotel with piss-stained elevators and strawberry hill and california coolers after curfew because the basketball coach is on watch california coolers with the basketball coach that one time he drove the starting five from the basketball team to magic mountain you sandwiched between the center cradling a barrel of unwrapped smarties double lollies and the team's point guard nursing the wine cooler so his allergy to alcohol didn't flare or the time with the limo driven by the basketball coach his side job for the actual graduation stumbling out of the limo for more wine coolers spotted by someone who knew the girl's mother the girl's mother telling your mother in the checkout line at the alpha beta but the time the girlfriend was inconsolable is the prevailing memory that was when everything was new and burnished for memory keeping moving to phoenix the day before classes start a new kid yet again after being new again and again and again memories in boxes the kids in south dakota didn't seem to know anything about what happened to john lennon that made all the teachers at your school in north dakota hang their heads or all those hostages they let go or when another someone tried to impress that actress months later or when kiss came on without makeup or fractured fairy tales or the bloodhound gang and vice versa the kids in williston were left void of knowledge of the girl from somewhere in the east being invited to russia after she wrote a letter to yuri andropov which made you start writing letters to celebrities to see if they'd write back though they mostly sent signed pictures of themselves or the handful of videos on the new music channel or michael jackson's thriller video or what happened to michael making that pepsi commercial or the first woman on the supreme court or when that famous actress fell off the boat and died or the first test tube baby it all happened after none of it connected in your mind at least important to remember all the new names easier to make friends if you seemed like you were always there call out someone's name make them feel known so that you can be too first calling attention to yourself in some way that wasn't too obvious was always the next step not like ozzy and the dove or lawn chair larry in montana it was reading the most books and winning lunch with your teacher the batman skit the previous year performed with the assent of your second-grade teacher the jar of ash from mount saint helens you swept from your driveway the nude poster you claimed to have of the actress who played daisy on the dukes of hazzard in north dakota it was lighting fires with the neighbor kids learning hey jude on the piano as a favor to your neighbor who was mad like your teachers about the john lennon thing the variety show like the mandrells' you proposed to emcee in the gym to impress the girl who tantalized you by giving you a pocket radio and telling you to listen to dr demento at the same moment she was lying in bed listening in south dakota it was finger-printing the teacher's assistant you were in love with making your parents drive you to the local bottling company for enough carbon-ated water to make strawberry soda as a science experiment for your class racking up the high score on pac-man and dig dug and centipede and donkey kong at the arcade showing the older kids how to seesaw a comb across your hand to quickly toggle the but-tons for defender marathon sessions of space invaders and breakout on the atari at home waiting for your parents to come home from work writing the hardy boys–inspired novel you bragged about writing to your teacher who called you on it and who agreed to type it up and send it to publishers who all rejected it which burned more when that kid published his star wars quiz book the music teacher knew you were lying when you said you went to a country music convention at the civic center and that you'd gotten up on stage and sang a conway twitty song made you sing a song in front of the class to see if you could sing dating the seventh grader at the junior high your sixth-grade teacher passing notes to her one neigh-bor to another you and your younger brother each play a song on the piano on television your piano teacher arranging it your name glowing from the television as you play silver bells it seems like magic learning the moonwalk to go with the beaded glove you and your friend billy fashioned for the purpose of walking around rush-more mall getting stares writing and directing your own version of the tv show whiz kids with the av equipment from the junior high after seeing wargames a hundred times and the milwaukee 414s on the cover of newsweek also because the world stopped for the final episode of m*a*s*h you still can't think of it without welling up when you think of hawkeye's inability to say good-bye he only had to say it once change is sometimes change but sometimes it isn't in phoenix the first order of business is getting out of the gifted and talented program really just a place to hide away the restless and hyperactive kids the bus would come for you in north dakota in the middle of the school day to transport you to the high school where the gifted program was high school kids throwing snowballs hard at you at recess the new kid new again but just on thursdays locking the gifted classroom door on the way out with the teacher's purse and keys inside does the trick in phoenix as does the unrevealed fact that the eighth grade in phoenix is a repeat of the seventh grade in rapid city which means coasting academically speaking everyone thinking you're some kind of genius but you only care about being freed to reinvent yourself shedding all the computer nonsense in favor of sports and music a pantomime of the guitar solo in let's go crazy you standing on a chair the yardstick quivering in your hand like prince's ax wins unanimous approval from all who witness it and naturally you form an air band with some newly made friends from the basketball team for which you're a starting guard by virtue of being tall the air band you call phantasm after the horror movie you watched with the team on a friday night at the basketball coach's house sworn to secrecy about the booze the basketball coach a former phoenix police officer but something funny about the story never really know for sure but don't care as long as he keeps offering discounts on limos from his family limo company it always seems cool when the basketball coach shows up as the limo driver means he'll buy for you too like the night everyone had their wits scared away from watching phantasm which rumor had it was directed by a teenager and then you want to make a movie too but after the band which wins the school talent show handily you lip-synching the words to open arms and don't stop so convincingly that you incur a fan club among sixth-grade girls who start turning out for the home basketball games and then again in the bleachers during softball season phantasm is asked to headline the next parent-teacher dinner and the keyboardist drummer and lead guitarist agree with your suggestion of performing a couple of bryan adams songs run to you and heaven make the cut the whole band shops for stage clothes at the millers outpost at westridge mall keeping the receipts and tucking the tags in so everything can be returned the following day there are perks to celebrity you come to know when you follow some girls into the bathroom as a joke and even though you get hauled into the principal's office nothing happens you sell the box of lunch tickets the printer dropped and no one wants to believe it's really you doing it you toilet-paper the gym teacher's car and he knows it's you and your friends but nothing happens you break curfew at the hotel in anaheim on the graduation trip to disneyland and again nothing happens not just the basketball coach watching your back but other teachers too except for your homeroom teacher who notices and you can tell she's unamused at all the free passes but then you rise through the ranks of spellers and represent your school at the state competition lasting a few rounds before going out on the word yawl which you spell with an o instead of an a but even that defeat is treated like a victory and back at school there are congratulations aplenty someone jokingly asks if you're on the recording for we are the world and you laugh but there's also menace in the joke and you think careful careful careful you don't really understand backlash until that spring when new coke debuts and even though the soda delivers everything it promises there's such a stink about it that they bring back the old coke and there's a rumor that the guy who came up with the idea was fired and you think about that maybe more than you should when you're selected as the valedictorian speaker and over the summer as you think ahead to your freshman year the summer of repeated viewings of back to the future and miami vice reruns if only to stay out of the crushing heat waiting for the sun to set to walk the neighborhood with your boom box playing van halen's 1984 crashing party lines for however many cents a minute at night the summer all the girls dressed like madonna consternation that the like a virgin tour wasn't coming to phoenix the rumor that madonna had a revolving bed onstage while she was singing or maybe it was prince another tour that wasn't coming to phoenix though it didn't matter because you had to be seventeen to go everyone wondering why wild sexual rumors as guesses the kid who had a copy of purple rain on betamax the kid who asked where's the beef so much people started avoiding him that was the summer of live aid the kids starving in ethiopia phil collins playing the london show and then flying to america on the concorde for the other show the same day jack nicholson everywhere that day too everyone cooing over a band called u2 taking the job at the fish and chips down the street from your future high school slinging monsterburgers dixie dogs fish sandwiches fries with everything using the money to catch weird science your new favorite movie replacing st elmo's fire your other favorite movie but tied with the breakfast club and better off dead then the rock hudson jokes but no jokes about ryan white the kid born the same year as you whom they wouldn't let go to school because he had aids from a blood transfusion parents of other kids and teachers scared out of their minds john cougar and michael jackson and elton john and kareem abdul-jabbar became his friends alyssa milano gave him a kiss ryan white proved you could get aids if you weren't a homosexual which some people seemed to fear more than aids but he was just a little boy another innocent in a circumstance like the girl who wrote the letter and

172

went to russia then died in a small plane crash somewhere back east right before you start high school and you think how can someone get all the way to russia and back only to die in a small plane crash in america it doesn't make any sense but it recalls the not-too-distant past in rapid city when your entire sixth-grade class wrote letters to lyle alzado the l.a. raiders football player your teacher knew from when she tutored him in college no answer to the letters which didn't upset you except you thought maybe your teacher one of your favorites was embarrassed that someone she once knew and helped had turned his back on her now that he was famous like madonna had to her own flesh and blood the year of madonna really desperately seeking susan marrying sean penn sean penn firing at swarming paparazzi in helicopters waiting in the parking lot of a 7-eleven to ambush someone safe but sympathetic who could buy you the penthouse magazine with madonna on the cover the photos not as good as the ones you'd seen in rapid city on rodeo weekend the dumpsters full of magazines you'd never heard of a hierarchy quickly developed oui penthouse playboy penetration the difference maker in your mind but not just yours madonna is the first celebrity you've seen fully nude and even after you've high-tailed it out of the 7-eleven parking lot you can't believe what you're seeing like the time someone on the basketball team had a vhs copy of faces of death or the film you needed a permission slip to see in junior high the choose your own adventure about how babies are born everyone says michael jackson now owns all the songs written by the beatles which is confusing the question about whether or not your grade-school popularity will transfer with you to high school is answered pretty quickly as you become an anonymous freshman face in the small mexican town on the outskirts of phoenix the high school mostly mexican too but white kids bused in from everywhere until the mexicans are a minority again those mexicans you get to know through your after-school job at the fish and chips some of them even recognizing you from over the summer especially those you began to favor with free food including the security guard a local you've cultivated the saxophone that has lain dormant since the seventh grade reawakens in your first-period band class marching season that fall playing halftime at home and away games riding the bus hassled at work for needing friday nights off the busiest of the week don't you know but band is your entrée into the world of upperclassmen who take a liking to you like others in south dakota and north dakota and montana did previously and you don't try to analyze it just say yes to hanging out with them at their houses late into the night drinking their parents' alcohol or to the midnight showing of the rocky horror picture show some of the upperclassmen are in the drama club too throwing toast and rice at the screen after your shift at the fish and chips has ended then driving around until all hours of the night looking for alleged parties sometimes in other school districts someone knows someone who is having a party or not breaking into the resorts ringing camelback mountain to use the pool if all else fails that fall you adopt wholeheartedly the fashions of sonny crockett which gets you noticed in good and bad ways but mostly good when it comes to girls and the blonde whose locker is on your row and who doesn't wear a bra finally gives in to your badgering her for a date when you ask her to the ac/dc concert your colleague at the fish and chips who spent the summer drawing in pencil the scene of the seven dwarfs all puffing from the same bong offers to drive for a ticket to the concert he'll even throw in a bottle of southern comfort but he hits on the blonde all night annoying the hell out of you but it doesn't really matter because she's gone by the encore falling in with some older friends she knows from you don't want to know where but you have better luck with the junior who is the section leader of the flutes your first high school girlfriend and she takes some guff for dating a freshman but any who know you are okay with it same for whoever nominates you for homecoming prince you feel like it's a lock everyone saying it's going to be you but then it's not and not even really close a local kid whose friends apparently all voted for him wins and you file that lesson away all music must come with warning labels now if the lyrics are graphic you watch huddled around the television in the classroom as the challenger explodes upon liftoff there's an atomic meltdown at chernobyl a place you don't really know where that is campaign season and your friends suggest you run for sophomore class president make your mark for jaime clarke on your signs and out of your mouth and when the lopsided victory is yours there's yet another lesson about which is coveted more the beauty contest for homecoming prince or the academic honor of being class president the difference between duckie and blane even on the makeshift stage at thomas mall before it is demolished strutting with the other teenage models booked through the dubious agency you joined with your friend the surfer who orders his clothes from the international male catalog the agency books you for a commercial for an italian restaurant says bring your saxophone you never know if the commercial runs never pay for anything the only money exchanging hands is yours for head shots dressing up in various costumes against various backdrops your vanity from the time the girl in the water park in south dakota thought you were corey hart and other instances like that and maybe even the lost homecoming prince election driving you to believe but you tell no one and your surfer friend is equally mum there's a lot of talk about who is going to be participating in hands across america the guy from st elsewhere coming to phoenix to be part of the chain the idea something ferris bueller might come up with like yours to take the senior girl you meet playing in the orchestra pit of the high school production of the hobbit on a one-day trip to disneyland limo to and from the airport courtesy of your old friend the basketball coach airline ticket courtesy of your fish and chips fortune you can't believe when

175

she says yes but then the day is overwhelmed with the gesture the spontaneity second-guessed with questions about if you do things like this all the time and you say no even though you know you do and when you're not you spend too much time daydreaming grand schemes that you desire with all your heart to come true you always the star of the show another self-aggrandizer like that fake jimmy swaggart who gets wal-mart to pull rolling stone magazine from its shelves or all those celebrities in the antidrug stop the madness video including old friend and noncorrespondent lyle alzado the world is full of attention seekers it seems sean penn punching a musician at a club in los angeles eg or anyone on entertainment tonight or a current affair which becomes obsessed with the preppy murderer in new york only because he's handsome but new york city is as far away as the moon from the hot and humid summer you spend working and scheming about your sophomore year at a loss when not actually in school an environment you thrive in the endless possibilities not true of the summer or school vacations which are all just work boredom work sophomore year starts off with the inxs concert at the mesa amphitheatre the pastel-colored crowd sweating in the summer that won't end and when it's over some of the crowd follows the limo you and your friends rented to ferry you to and from the party thinking maybe you're the band but your friend sticks his head out of the window and the jig is up and the cars fall back everyone laughing but some annoyed not to have teased the ruse further to at least see if any girls were in the trailing cars no one can answer the question about whether or not max headroom is a real person or not the freshman sax player in your section agreeing to become your girlfriend which is mostly ceremonial since she's a mormon and can't date until she's sixteen and even then only in groups of other mormons is the word but it hardly matters your relationship mostly revolves around band practice and traveling to away games and band competitions you going to her

176

parents' house after school but before your shift at the fish and chips to shoot pool and listen to music or watch movies while her mother lurks somewhere her mormon friends like you and vice versa the good crowd from school the kids all the teachers like even the security guard who catches you and your girlfriend and some other friends off campus during school hours your idea all the way not realizing residents in the small town would look out their windows and call campus security but them not realizing you have campus security in your back pocket feeding them and their families for free at the fish and chips your girlfriend panicking her reputation surely taking the biggest hit but the security guard recognizes you and gives everyone a ride to the edge of the football field as the bell for the next class rings he'll say he couldn't find anyone and you'll continue to repay the favor for as long as you work at the fish and chips wishing you had the same influence over the security guard at a rival high school when he finds you hiding in the men's room while your friend and fellow student council officer searches the campus for her boyfriend to confront him about cheating the security guard seems pleased to drag you to the principal's office the principal yelling about calling the police charging you with trespassing and as your friend arrives in the clutches of a second security guard you remember that a girl from a party you found yourself at over the summer is on the student council at the rival high school and you claim to be her cousin from south dakota the security guard not buying it but the principal seeing a way out of the mess that threatens to turn an otherwise ordinary day into a vortex of procedure and you pretend to cower under a tongue-lashing the security guard escorting you both to the parking lot a tale that becomes as legendary as the flames shooting from your saxophone at halftime of the homecoming game your section leader rigging camping stoves in his and yours passing a lighter at a key moment on the field everyone astonished even the band teacher who is both angry and awed by the pyrotechnics you didn't consider that he could get in trouble with the school but you and your section leader disappear the camping stoves and no one asks you about it you try for another piece of legend when in your official capacity as assistant to one of the chemistry teachers during your free period you leak some test answers not knowing that there are two sets of answers so when the girls you're trying to impress answer their test with the exact sequence of answers for the test they're not taking you get busted and your free period is converted to detention for the rest of the semester said detention held in the band room and run by the band teacher who lets you practice or leave early the papers full of oliver north and his secretary fawn hall and iran-contra the term plausible deniability floating through conversations a term you like there's a rumor rob lowe is dating the secretary and also a rumor about richard gere the heavy metal group judas priest is ordered to stand trial over two teens in nevada who shot each other on a playground one of them dying instantly the other maimed and living a few more years their parents think they did it because of subliminal messages in judas priest's music the mormon car salesman elected governor without a majority cancels martin luther king jr day calling it an illegal holiday also calling black children pickaninnies and telling black people they don't need a holiday they need jobs oh and the time he told a jewish delegation that america was a christian nation and boy did those japanese businessmen's eyes get round when they found out how many golf courses arizona had and the retribution is sure but slow playing out for months and years to come the kid in your class who disappears for long stretches of time is liberace's protégé and the proximity of celebrity at your tiny high school in a tiny town on the outskirts of phoenix is unbelievable there's a rumor his hands are insured for millions no one really seems to know him one kid calls him a fag like liberace and the protégé punches the kid with his million-dollar fists the protégé presents an interesting shot

178

at political redemption after the disastrous first semester of your reign as sophomore class president not outwardly disastrous but a failure in your eyes the homecoming float the largest piece of legislation on each class's agenda your idea to get a corporate sponsor met with confusion and more confusion when said corporate sponsor is the local mcdonald's so that the sophomore class offering is a floating advertisement for mcdonald's during construction in the jv quarterback's backyard everyone working diligently to re-create the golden arches out of chicken wire and crepe paper you're amazed both at how bad the idea is and how readily everyone was willing to undertake it the spring class fund-raiser is a chance to erase those memories and after approaching the protégé with the idea you present the protégé in concert as your class fund-raiser some officers had no idea about the protégé and some don't know who liberace is but once again everyone just goes along and so the concert is booked the lone apple macintosh that constitutes the school's computer lab is used to create the promotional flyer ads are taken out in the local papers the protégé has a piano delivered to the school auditorium he's contractually obligated to use only a certain brand of piano and the night of the concert you pace with the protégé backstage as the auditorium fills to half its capacity the protégé says i can fill radio city music hall but not a high school auditorium and you give a nervous laugh but he's not really kidding much later you'll think about this over and over and over but then you go on with the show by parting the stage curtains and introducing the protégé whose playing mesmerizes the audience the success of the fund-raiser inspires you to fill a notebook with the names of bands you intend to contact via letter about playing at your high school raising even more money ac dc yes u2 of course quiet riot and duran duran and depeche mode and then a list of bands possibly looking for a way to expand their audience but the absence of congratulations on arranging the concert with liberace's protégé is disappointing it's like the concert never happened except for those in the audience no students really by the way just adults who enjoyed liberace's music and absent the accolades the whole thing feels hollow unappreciation leads to some bitterness and the sudden realization that your friends will be graduating leaving you among your fellow sophomores most of them not your friends most of them resentful of your friendship with upperclassmen or indifferent but regardless there's no way to come back into the fold and your one other friend from grade school the one who went to private school appears as a lifeline and the private-school friend arranges a shadow day where you follow him around campus and attend class with him the private school is an all-boys catholic school which is full of non-catholics since it's one of the only private schools in phoenix and is generally regarded as the best the words college prep in its name the giveaway the private school sits on central avenue the dividing point between east phoenix where the haves live and west phoenix where the have-nots like you live the school is populated mostly with the haves which suits you just fine though in your heart you know you'll never really be friends with any of them and that your friends will be have-nots like your private-school friend but that's okay because you really just want the association not to have to pretend that you're a have though you and your private-school friend angle to get a pair of fake rolexes from mexico and hoover up all the polo shirts at the used-clothing store after your application is accepted for the fall why you failed to mention either your shadow day or your application to your girlfriend balloons as a glaring cruelty when she learns about it from someone else the confrontation one of the terrible moments of your life up to that point you have no answer fumbling with an excuse that you didn't think you'd be accepted though you never doubted that for a minute looking good on paper will become an obsession your girlfriend is never fully assuaged even though you promise you never thought of it as a betrayal and you craft a good joke about dating a mormon girl while attending a catholic school which gets you both past it also you remind her about your newly minted driver's license which means no more hitching rides to her house after school meaning you can visit more often which you promise to do and mean it at the time you utter it not realizing the true freedom a license and the used ford mustang ii your parents give you bestow the preacher on the sunday-morning tv show loses his job because he drugged and raped his secretary along with another preacher which completely validates and supports everything you think about religion same again when the other preacher gets caught with a prostitute months later and same again but this time about politics when the photo of the senator running for president and the model on his lap is everywhere everything is just a cloak for attracting people's attention sometimes sexual attending the baptist church with your private-school friend a megachurch down the street from the private school mostly to use the phenomenal exercise and sports facilities in an effort to curb the toll nightly meals at the fish and chips are taking on your body surprised to see the rocker alice cooper in the front pew with his family his daughter's baptism on the agenda of the program in your lap you really don't have any idea who alice cooper is but know he's someone famous who lives in phoenix but he just looks like a father and a husband in church after watching your friends graduate and leave high school behind forever you move a little farther west into a neighborhood being terrorized by a rapist the starlight rapist is the name named for the neighborhood but it sounds like an album and no one goes out after dark only men are walking dogs suddenly you and your private-school friend go for jogs because you highly doubt that anything will happen to you and you both openly hope to catch the pervert roaming the streets talking tough about the violence you're capable of everyone listening to the new u2 album the first few bars of the first song everywhere like weather someone initiates a recall of the mormon car salesman governor and then the news becomes just about that the story advancing incrementally sometimes without any new facts just everyone's anger and embarrassment especially when the governor digs in and doubles down like politicians always seem to just like the senator with the girl on his lap did when everyone said he was finished they're always the last to know you trade the ford mustang ii in on a midnight blue volkswagen rabbit a wolfsburg edition which just means the color and seat covers are different but feels important for the start of your new school akin to owning a nagel painting your parents are upset because the mustang ii was almost paid off but you can't go to a fancy prep school in a mustang ii you and your private-school friend get vanity plates too yours is my hare and his is beemer for obvious reasons your junior year starts and it's like moving again nothing that happened before really happened or is relevant and everything is in the now saying the private school's name perks every listener's ears and for maybe the first time in your life you feel the benefit of exclusivity membership in a club you want to belong to but know you probably don't and never will your grades were good enough to get in but only because the public school was easy and probably only really because your teachers wrote stellar recommendations but the private school is hard harder than you anticipated and then because you live on the west side of phoenix and not the east you don't really enjoy the social aspect of your new peer group certainly not the company of the girls who attend the all-girls private school adjacent to yours no one has heard of the area where you live and because you didn't go to any of the same middle or junior schools as the other students and because your family doesn't know any of the other families you're marked as an outsider from day one and you take note of the fact knowing it'll come into play for the rest of your life but rather than be daunted by it you just let it go you aren't even sure what it is you hoped to gain by becoming friends with rich kids you don't need a loan for chrissakes and they have no idea how or why they're rich they just enjoy the designation even the son of one of the phoenix 40 a list of the rich and powerful in town who offers to sell you some cocaine at lunch somewhere in texas a baby falls through the tiny opening of an abandoned well and for two days the television documents the rescue the baby miraculously okay when she's pulled free your english teacher the one who kisses the ass of the kid whose father is a famous golfer and the other kid whose father is a state politician and has a terribly lame joke about meeting his wife she was a stockbroker and he was looking to invest and the joke is he went in looking for stocks and came out with a bond assigns the great gatsby and you devour it thinking it's a book about you astonished by the similarities between your story and jay gatsby's and you become convinced that your girlfriend is daisy at least narratively and you adopt the attitude that your love for each other is doomed especially as you seem to be spending less and less time together owing to your commute downtown and then your racing back west to work your paycheck suddenly suffering the heavy tax of keeping up appearances at the private school but also because you frankly spend time cruising the east side of phoenix a part of town previously unknown to you exploring the roads lined with expensive homes even wending to the top of camelback mountain where the priciest homes of all are perched and also the biltmore area with its boutique shops and exclusive restaurants and the difference between this world and yours solidifies all of it bifurcated by the private school that resides geographically between the two and maybe not just geographically just like the two eggs in gatsby though you start to think less of jay gatsby and more about f scott fitzgerald famous and rich and then broke and forgotten in the same lifetime but immortal in death and that seems more desirable than money something to really strive for but the how is too hard to parse and you drop it until you're watching the credits roll on the midnight showing of less than zero and see that the movie which you consider powerful for its examination of the importance of loyal friendships is based on a novel and later you do a little sniffing around the phoenix public library and learn that the author is more like fitzgerald than not and maybe that's the blueprint you read the author's second book which isn't as well received as the first just like fitzgerald and it's about the doings of kids at a college in the woods of vermont and you truthfully can't make much of it but the striking difference between the author photos of the first two books is something to note the party scenes in the book exceed anything you experience hanging out with your graduated high school friends in their new digs in tempe the college town built up around arizona state university one friend living in a dorm with beer bottle caps pressed into the ceiling of the hall so many they gleam like a metallic rainbow and the other moving into a newly built pink stucco apartment complex across the street from campus for students only miles better than the other apartment complexes which are really just old cinder-block motels repainted and repainted all with crumbling swimming pools ringed with coeds catching rays it's quickly clear that all the cool kids will be living at the new complex the rental application asks for fraternity affiliation so rival frat members aren't accidentally booked into the same four-person apartment the complex deciding who will live with whom the only drawback but no one seems to mind for access to the sand volleyball court and the sparkling pool but really for the weekend parties so legendary that kids at your new private school have heard of them the apartments are identically furnished so that while the locations of the parties are different each weekend the parties have the feel of having picked up where the other ones left off all of the faces nameless to you and to everyone you think but no one cares you first hear about the u2 concerts at sun devil stadium at one of these parties and the notion that the tickets are only five dollars seems like drunken rambling but radio stations all over town start broadcasting that the band will play two shows on consecutive days to film a documentary and to ensure the stadium is full both nights all tickets are only five dollars word is celebrities from hollywood are driving through the desert in their limos to attend and you and your private-school friend score some tickets excited at the prospect even if the seats are terrible all the way up toward the top of the bowl some kids have tickets for both nights which you find slightly annoying but you also wish you could go both times but when you're actually at the show you're distracted by the murder of the owner of the fish and chips two nights prior someone knocking on his door while he was sitting down to dinner in his apartment the owner always lived frugally even though his chain of fish and chips was successful and mostly all-cash operations and while the apartment where he lived was in a better part of town he was still shot point blank through the chest when he opened the door his dinner still cooling on the table and in the days after leading up to christmas it becomes known that the killer was after the sack of silver coins commemorating the fish and chips' fortieth anniversary the owner kept in his closet the local pawn shops are put on alert and just like in the movies the killer tries to pawn the coins and is arrested and revealed to be the investigator hired by the insurance company the fish and chips owner had applied to for better rates the recall election of the car salesman governor is set and your private-school classmate's dad who is a congressman agrees to run though before the election can happen the car salesman governor is indicted for this and that and removed as governor you actually like the classmate he was the kid who sat in front of you on your shadow day way back when and he actually spoke to you unlike the others and you identified him as an all-right guy right off though you never really became friends with him or the kid running for student government who gave his campaign speech in the gymnasium and listed one of his hobbies as being an avid beaver hunter and everyone shrieked ending the kid's candidacy and earning him a week's suspension but also a bit of legend which far outweighed the punishment though not so for the senior who appeared on camera during a news investigation about boondockers in the desert kids gathering with illegally purloined alcohol and then scattering drunk and whatever else behind the wheels of their cars the senior agreeing to be interviewed on camera and telling the reporter that nothing could stop them from partying which although it was probably true did abruptly end his studies at the private school when he was expelled as not representative of the school's student body you have more pressing concerns though as you realize your relationship with your high school girlfriend has completely crumbled you never see each other there aren't enough hours but also maybe you're just a little more interested in your reincarnation as a private-school student the part-time job at the law firm down the street from the private school another piece of the new puzzle the idea of quitting the filthy fish and chips job the ultimate goal but for now you must work both especially since you traded in the new volkswagen you've hardly made any payments on for a red nissan pulsar nx with t-tops and a vanity plate that reads o2b yng taking on an outrageous monthly car payment but appearances are becoming more important every day exhausting as it can be the two lives being lived simultaneously and so you initiate the breakup with your high school girlfriend in a cowardly way by writing a letter and asking her to meet you a month later to give everyone time to think about everything and when the month is over you're kind of surprised that she shows up at the time and place you suggested but the surprise quickly turns to chagrin when you realize she's rightly been simmering for a month and pulls out her own letter and reads it to you cataloging all your sins and drops it at your feet you knowing you deserve every word but the devastation is sudden and uncontrollable and you can barely remember driving the freeway back home your old friend who looks like anthony michael hall attempting to flag you down from his front yard as you turn onto your street but you don't want him to see you that way not knowing it's your last chance to talk with him never knowing what he wanted to say to you that day or why he shot himself months later his parents quietly moving back to colorado you are excused from classes to attend a seminar on teen suicide held at the convention center and your friend thinks it's a great ruse for getting out of class and tags along so the experience becomes a goof and not the chance to heal or at least to be a little less bewildered your private-school friend has a friend who lives in rancho palos verdes outside of los angeles and you both bomb through the desert to the cool foggy shores of the rich suburb your friend's friend is a nationally ranked motocross racer who tours the country on his sponsor's dime which is in your mind pretty legendary except you don't care anything about motocross but traveling here and there to perform before adoring crowds as a teenager engenders some jealousy but the motocross racer is a cool guy and he takes you and your private-school friend to a couple of parties sneaks you into the local yacht club though you get caught and escorted out the ocean air filling your desert-dried lungs hey there's a nude beach nearby the moto-cross friend says and you park above overlooking the beach but it's the opposite of what you hoped for just families frolicking in the surf without any clothes a bummer for sure but you're perked up by the motocross racer's saying that lyle alzado lives in his neighbor-hood and as you pass in front of the palatial white estate behind a tall iron gate the distance between where you are and where you've been feels oceanic and it makes you a little sad to think of your sixth-grade self penning the unanswered fan letter and you think maybe it would be funny to ring the doorbell and bring it up with alzado who has retired from football to become an actor but who will really become famous a few years later when he dies from a brain tumor he claims was brought on by his steroid use but you don't that fall your history teacher wants everyone to volunteer for a political campaign during the current election cycle the incumbent democratic candidate for senator's office across the street from campus the obvious choice but just to be contrary you answer an ad for the republican challenger someone you've never heard of a financial planner of some kind who hasn't a prayer of winning and when you report to the financial planner's house in the gated biltmore estates you learn the campaign team is just you and the financial planner's son who has dropped out of the university of arizona and put his band's music on hold to work on his father's campaign the mission that day is to put up campaign billboards but the posthole digger is impotent against the hard desert floor and you don't get one sign up the incumbent wins by a couple of hundred thousand votes and you feel no way about it not like you did in the mock vote for president in the fourth grade when you were sure carter would win and woke up to the complete opposite the credit for working on the financial planner's campaign can't offset the reality of your college algebra teacher holding you after to tell you that you are failing and might not graduate in the spring you beg for another chance and he says there are two jaime clarkes which one will show up and you promise the right one even though he never does and you're ultimately busted down to a lower-level math class that you almost don't pass though you get an a in your christian service class which has you volunteering at the children's crisis nursery where kids are taken when the police remove them from their homes for whatever reason the popular volunteer spot is the state mental institution the stories of all the loonies acted out back on campus to slack jaws and disbelief and mocking laughter but you know you won't last a day there and so the children's crisis nursery it is just playing with kids during your shift and they're just kids and love having fun and it's sad only when you remember the high chain-link fence around the building and the orders not to let any parents who might be wailing outside in to see their kids the investigator for the insurance company who murdered the owner of the fish and chips goes on trial and the schedule is arranged so that you and your private-school friend can attend along with some other employees the murderer looks like someone's grandfather the windowless courtroom antiseptic and overly acoustic and simply boring there's no doubt the guy did it the procedure is just to string together the narrative in a cohesive way so that everyone can put the matter behind them before christmas the year punctuated by news that one of the popular wrestlers back at your old public school has asked your ex-girlfriend out to the christmas formal and blind with jealousy you undertake a successful campaign to win her back which is a win you needed everyone needs a win it seems not just your new private-school friend who is living in his own apartment off the freeway hiding from his deranged father but also the woman and her young daughter living in the economy housing next door to the new fish and chips location you transfer to when you and your private-school friend have a falling out over your going back with your high school girlfriend the private-school friend annoyed to lose you as part of a recent foursome with two vietnamese girls you've been spending quality time with you just as a wingman but you put the kibosh on the whole thing which sends your private-school friend to the moon and you don't speak ever again necessitating the transfer to the new location where you get your new private-school friend a job the new private-school friend's deranged father learns he's working there and shows up waving a gun on the sidewalk you roll the metal window guards down and cower by the fry cookers waiting for the police who come and your new private-school friend watches while his father is placed in the back of a squad car the woman and her young daughter ask you about it later they weren't home when it happened and you shrug even though you were for a moment fearful and change the subject and ask them if they have their christmas tree yet and the mother says it's either the tree or something to put under it which guts you and you play santa and buy a big tree with lots of ornaments and tinsel and surprise the woman and her daughter who seem embarrassed and then you are too when the tree won't fit easily into the tiny apartment the awkwardness increased when the little girl shows off the christmas tree hanging on the wall made from toilet paper tubes and cotton balls the last time you see either of them because they quit coming around a serial killer everyone describes as handsome is executed in florida you and your high school girlfriend easily fall back into the old routine of never seeing each other especially as you start spending more and more of your free time with your old public-school friends out in tempe hatching a plan to move in with them in the summer after your high school graduation a plan you're up front about with your high school girlfriend but it's theoretical and besides she's never been to your house or met your parents so what does it really matter the relationship is kept within the confines of the school you no longer attend and her front room which you frequent less and less and church dances different from the rave you attend at an old warehouse in downtown phoenix with adults you don't know your college friend procuring the address the streets dark and crime-ridden so you slip out to move your car under a streetlight and when you return you see a large black man dancing naked and when your eyes adjust you see others are naked too and your friend grabs you and says it's time to go the actor who played the older brother on diff'rent strokes is arrested for shooting someone in a drug den in south central los angeles the president or whatever of iran puts a bounty on a writer you've never heard of right around the time you start to think more about the author of the book that the movie you liked was based on and you crank out a handful of short stories some only a few pages long and show them to no one even though you'd like to publish them as a book the last time you wrote something your fifth-grade teacher typed it up for you offering editorial suggestions and even helping you send it off to publishers in new york city most of them not responding but a few sending along form rejections the seriousness of the endeavor left an impression on you writing seemed like something that impressed adults but so did a million things one story you wrote a humorous piece for your high school girlfriend full of puns about having sex with her is found by her mother and you're not allowed to see her for a period of time even though you get an audition with the mother to plead that the story is fiction nothing but which seems to matter not the commercial pepsi paid madonna millions to make debuts during the cosby show but the next day the video madonna made for her song like a prayer debuts and the two side by side are a study in extreme contrasts suddenly christians are supposedly not drinking pepsi you talk the night manager of the fish and chips into cosigning for a car phone for your new ride you wouldn't dare ask your own parents and tread on the freewill parenting plus you know they'd say no the car phone is installed and you pretend to be talk-ing on it whenever you pull in and out of the parking lot of the private school even letting a kid use it at recess the yellow-lit buttons lighting up with a satisfying beep when you turn the key in the igni-tion you're not sure if it's the phone or not but you inch into another group of private-school friends and when you're invited by the kid with the black mercedes to ditch and go see president reagan at arizona state university you agree and zip to tempe with the others in the black mercedes which you note has a car phone too a point you bring up casually you learn the others are all in a young repub-licans club which doesn't interest you until you learn it meets at the house of one of the girls at the neighboring private school and you agree to join them though you forget about it completely when you hatch a plan to join the mormon church in order to enliven the same stale route your relationship with your high school girlfriend is headed down unsure how else to keep the relationship going and also you have the sense that you'll probably get married or at least it'll come up soon because mormon girls start talking about marriage at a very young age and you know you can't marry her unless you're mormon and so the math works out even though math is not your strong suit but you never admit it is a stunt even when your high school girlfriend prompts you to do so when you start attending church regularly on sundays and again when you arrange for meetings with the missionaries in her cousin's house mostly so your parents won't find out you don't tell your friends either and the enormity of the situation doesn't hit until you're wet behind the ears having been dunked into the baptismal waters standing at the pulpit in front of the crowd of mormon friends and their families smiling up at you during the command performance you give the attention welcome and familiar but the words coming out of your mouth invented for the occasion forgotten before they're uttered shortly thereafter a terrible thing happens to a jogger in central park in new york city which is all the news can talk about until it comes out that the actor rob lowe is in a sex tape everyone wants to see but no one has any idea how you hardly have time to practice your new mormonism before you graduate and move into the tiny converted office in the one-bedroom apartment of your old public-school friend who ripped up the carpets without the landlord's consent and spray-painted the concrete floor black the summer filled with parties put on by the foreign exchange club and you heartily attend you feel like a fish out of water too just like the college-aged foreigners far from home but you don't find kinship at these parties mostly because the foreigners close ranks and you don't blame them knowing it's for their own protection a television actress from a show you've never heard of is murdered on her doorstep in los angeles by a crazed fan from tucson and the papers drop the tidbit that the actress became the object of the crazy's obsession when his first obsession the girl from back east who wrote the letter to the russian president died in that small plane crash and it seems weird to share an obsession with a crazy person and you've never considered that the false intimacy celebrity creates could be dangerous two brothers in beverly hills murder their parents with shotguns in the family tv room and try to convince the police that it's a mob hit related to their record producer father's business but the police don't buy it and the brothers are ultimately arrested you put the fish and chips behind you for good when you accept a job as a runner for american continental corporation the parent company of lincoln savings and loan in california run by the already notorious charles keating jr who made national headlines when he tried to buy influence with a cadre of u.s. senators the clip of the question to charlie about whether or not he hoped to be buying influence and charlie's answer that he certainly hoped so a sound bite the press loves also the papers can't get enough of charlie or his lavish lifestyle his beautiful secretaries are referred to as charlie's angels and he lives in a mansion on the same property as his daughter and her husband parents of a kid who attends the same private school you barely graduated from the kid a nationally ranked swimmer and future olympian your job as a runner is to handle the phone calls and open the mail and rotate the company's fleet of mercedeses through the car wash and stock the supply rooms and fetch the catered lunches for the three floors of lawyers all working on the giant bankruptcy case charlie filed to protect himself and his assets from the federal government which has accused him of looting lincoln like it was his personal piggy bank not even the fall of the berlin wall or the fact that the u.s. government has noriega holed up in the vatican or that the mayor of washington dc is arrested for smoking crack or the pictures of the oil-drenched wildlife in alaska

the result of the exxon valdez oil spill can distract the local headlines from charlie and his ongoing battle against the government
old stories about charlie taking on larry flynt the publisher of the
porn magazine hustler back when charlie was an antismut crusad-
ing prosecutor in his native cincinnati as well as newer stories about
his calling former p.o.w. and arizona senator john mccain a wimp
for not standing up to bank regulators on his behalf or the fact that
all of the officers of american continental are related to charlie
either by birth or by marriage a news truck is always parked out on
the sidewalk in front of the american continental offices on camelback road one time they pull into the driveway and you are sent to
ask them politely off the property which they do but not before asking if they can interview you but even after only a month of working for charlie you are in the cult and the idea repels you there's
some pleasure in denying the request charlie is summoned to washington to testify before a committee about lincoln savings and loan
and when he takes the fifth the news goes wild and the phones in
the runners' room light up the mail full of indictments and threats
the one correspondent who faithfully sends a package every week
with epithets and pictures of his father who lost everything when
lincoln failed and took his own life the manila envelope like finding
a rattlesnake in the mailbag every time it appears when you actually
ask what it's all about people shrug and say that maybe elderly
investors in california were persuaded by lincoln employees to move
their savings from safe and guaranteed but low-interest accounts to
high-yield junk bonds so that charlie could then use the money to
build the lavish phoenician hotel at the base of camelback mountain and for other purposes too the dispute seemingly is whether the
investors were greedy or the bank employees were illegally aggres-
sive and misleading no one will ever know the truth about that or
the rumor that the government blocked a sale of lincoln that charlie
had orchestrated which would've kept it from failing and from all

those people losing their money you don't see too much of charlie as his office is up camelback road at the phoenician but one day you arrive at the american continental offices and the parking lot is full of moving vans the caravan idling among the clamor and whispers of charlie's back and you learn that the government has seized the phoenician and evicted charlie your sudden proximity to the boss is invigorating and when you discover a box of yellow buttons that proclaim i like charlie keating you wear them as part of your uniform even on errands like the daily court filings downtown and the airport runs for the cadre of lawyers from beverly hills charlie has hired picking them up on mondays and dropping them off on fridays the one lawyer the lead one telling you how much he regrets not following his first love and becoming a veterinarian which you doubt because of the rolex on the lead lawyer's wrist you wear the button even when you're not working like the party at one of charlie's developer friends' estate where the pips are performing and you notice local celebrities like the center for the phoenix suns and the guy who reviews movies on television people look at you askance but in your heart of hearts you're doing it for the attention you couldn't care less about charlie or his problems but you like the association except when your high school girlfriend's mother bans you from the house because of your employment but by then you're skipping a lot of classes you camped out overnight to sign up for at the registrar's office your first college semester a nonevent and you're seeing even less of your high school girlfriend the ruse of attending church on sundays slipping too the whole enterprise coming apart though you can't see it just yet and when you take stock you apply the corrections suddenly finding your way to class and bombing back and forth between your apartment in tempe and the west side where you find places to meet your high school girlfriend outside of her house adjusting your shift at american continental to accommodate both always in transit and all facets of your life seem to be in a state of equilibrium until you wake up in time to see the metal bumper of the rusted suburban stopped at a red light you've somehow successfully driven off the freeway exit from another crosstown trip but you can't apply the brakes in time and the nose of your sports car the one you still owe many monthly payments on wedges under the metal bumper throwing you against your seat belt as the front of your car disappears the windshield cracking but the radio still blaring as you jump out and wait on the sidewalk to see what comes next that it's saturday night and your roommate can't be reached by the emergency room to come pick you up when you're diagnosed as being fine just a little shaken up and a lot sore is of less importance than the fact that your father warned you to renew your car insurance the previous friday so it didn't expire and it isn't until you're without it that you realize your car was the most important piece of the life you were living and without it everything is in doubt you can't get to work without catching two buses for a two-hour ride each way forget about trips to the west side to visit your high school girlfriend and the punch line is that without insurance you owe the total outstanding amount of your car loan immediately the answer to the vexing problem appears in the classified ads of the campus newspaper an ad about striking it rich working on a fish boat in alaska but the ad is really just to sell you a directory of 800 numbers for ships and canneries and you have to do the legwork but you plunk down the twenty bucks anyway and start making the long-distance calls from the switchboard at american continental after everyone else has left for the day all the jobs are taken have been promised since early in the semester but then one offers to hire you if you can be at sky harbor airport that night a ticket will be waiting for you at the counter and in a desperate few hours you call your high school girlfriend to tell her that you're leaving and have one of your fellow runners drive you to your apartment to pack a bag and then to a barbershop to have your head shaved quitting your job without notice your bewildered family and high school girlfriend meeting you at the airport that night when you say good-bye you have no idea when you'll return the first leg of the flight to salt lake city is like hurtling through a decompression chamber the stress of your recent problems releasing so that you fall into a deep sleep on the second leg from salt lake to anchorage alaska and with some solid sleep you realize that you might've made a huge mistake as you climb aboard the third leg the puddle jumper that will ferry you from anchorage to dutch harbor the village in the aleutian islands where your boat awaits the propellers on the pud- dle jumper are so loud you can't think and the cabin is cold and you try to stay focused on all the money you'll make enough to buy back things as they were the landing strip at the airport in dutch harbor is barely that the terminal not much more than a shack and the two norwegian fishermen sent by the ship to pick you up don't speak english so your panic-induced pantomime about a tragedy back home and how you must return immediately falls untranslated and after you receive the news that your bag hasn't come through you squeeze between the fishermen on the bench of the old ford pickup truck and cruise the harbor of ships gearing up for the sea the ships becoming smaller and smaller as you go until you reach yours the smallest among them and you're awarded a matching blue tracksuit with the words dutch harbor alaska stenciled in yellow down the right leg as clothes until your bag can be found you're instructed to help load the supplies stacked on the dock for the journey men of substance both fictional like jay gatsby and real like charlie keating have about them the myth of the self-made man and you buck in under this pretense the money earned over the summer will be more than you've ever made in your life and you'll use it as seed money to reinvent yourself when you return to phoenix a dream that is quickly deferred when the ship's captain tells you your job is not on the line where cutters who gut the day's catch are entitled to

1 percent of the haul each time the boat docks but in the kitchen as the cook's assistant and at an hourly wage significantly below what charlie keating was paying you the wood-paneled boat quickly becomes a floating tomb and you spend the first two days at sea in the cabin you share with the government inspector whose job it is to ensure that the boat is catching only the type of fish each season allows the windowless cabin enveloped in a fetid stench finally the captain appears in the swaying doorway to tell you that you need to start contributing and you spend all day in the galley working with the cook who plays the appliances tightly strapped to the counter like a maestro though the meals are marginally better than prison food albeit more plentiful you're surprised to learn that you're on trash duty which consists of grabbing up all the bags of trash and heaving them over the side of the boat the captain and crew sit at a wooden table on one side of the kitchen and the rest of you at another under the television wired to an old vhs machine the only two movies are teen wolf too and a mob movie with sean connery and dustin hoffman and matthew broderick and without wondering why and how the movies found their way on board you watch them in a heavy rotation during the downtime between meals when the cook rests in his cabin you run your hand over your shaven scalp to feel your hair growing back incrementally one of the cutters shatters the afternoon routine by appearing with a hook from one of the fishing nets caught in his ear a trickle of blood running into his yellow raincoat he asks you if you can pull the hook out and you tell him you don't think you can and he soldiers on to find someone who can help it quickly becomes apparent that you're to be relegated to the kitchen for the entire summer and when the captain tells you that you are also in charge of cleaning the bathrooms you haul in the power hose used to clean the fish guts off the line and douse the bathroom causing the drain to back up the captain livid a story you try to relay to your high school girlfriend on the

ten-dollar-a-minute ship-to-shore phone calls that will come out of your paycheck along with the tracksuit you've been wearing day and night and when your high school girlfriend says maybe it's better if you stay for the entire summer you jump ship the moment the boat docks after two weeks at sea spending five of your last dollars on a cab ride from the ship to the airport leafing through a discarded people magazine about marlon brando's son murdering his sister's boyfriend while your father tries to get you a ticket on the last plane back to civilization which he does you're back home for a week or so before anyone knows you've returned and in your solitude you hit the books and do extensive research on your thesis that the mormon religion is completely made up by white men and stumble across a documentary called the god makers that proves the salient points of your argument armed with it you show up on your high school girlfriend's doorstep the look of surprise on her face the first clue that you are no longer welcome in her life but she lets you in and you present your case the look of surprise changing to a look of horror the god makers a known enemy propaganda and when you produce it begging her to watch it she asks you to leave and you do hearing through friends that she leaves that summer for an early start on her college career at brigham young university and you're overcome with the idea that you'll never see her again you ask for and get your job with charlie keating back some just assuming you were away on a two-week vacation though you're more weary than when you left the rest of the summer filled with news of the persian gulf war and worry among your friends about what will happen if the draft is reinstated some talk about fleeing to canada but it doesn't come to that the actor who played the older brother on diff'rent strokes is acquitted on manslaughter charges for the shooting in the drug den in south central los angeles you try to focus on your schoolwork as the new semester starts but just as school begins you get interested in writing television scripts and ferret out the advice that you should take a favorite tv show and write an original script on spec to use as a calling card the idea of moving to california to write for television immensely appealing you send away for a sample script for 21 jump street and then work on your own about a white supremacist modeled on a recent local news item involving a high school kid and his plans to kill minorities in churches and at schools which would be a perfect case for an episode of 21 jump street but the idea stalls on the page you take charlie keating to the airport in his custom mercedes so he can fly to los angeles and enter a plea in answer to the charges the state of california have made against him with regard to the failure of lincoln savings and loan with instructions to pick him up later in the day but you never see him again when the judge in california surprises him with a five-million-dollar bail he can't pay the controversial rap group 2 live crew is tried and acquitted on obscenity charges in florida stemming from a concert performance secretly recorded by two undercover police officers a few days before they're acquitted a federal judge declares their best-selling album obscene the government installs a trustee at american continental and a wave of charlie loyalists quit but you sense opportunity and agree to be one of the few runners who stay on the chaos at work is mirrored in the chaos of the atmosphere surrounding the national football league's unprecedented rescinding of the super bowl they previously awarded tempe when arizona voters reject an initiative to create a martin luther king jr holiday the loss of the super bowl means the loss of hundreds of millions of dollars and also black entertainers have called for a boycott of the state which loses more money the shadow of the used-car salesman governor lingering over the gubernatorial election that november which is billed as a fresh start but under the new laws meant to prevent a repeat of the election of the used-car salesman without a majority neither of the two new candidates receives a majority and a runoff election is scheduled for the spring the mayor in washington dc who got caught smoking crack in a hotel room and who has remained mayor all through his trial even running for reelection is sentenced to six months in prison a few days before the election which he loses the musical group milli vanilli are outed as lip-synchers and stripped of their grammy award which causes the kind of outrage found hardly anywhere else the date on the calendar when your ex-girlfriend returns from college for christmas break looms and when she readily agrees to see you you interpret that to mean that she's missed you as much as you have her but when you go into the windup of your apology for everything you've done and say words meant as a means to an end she so easily accepts them that you're taken aback and when she receives a phone call as if the moment is scripted her whispering into the phone it reveals the extent to which she's moved on from you and without explaining the interruption she lets you finish ghosts of your high school romance chase you away as you make a pleasant good-bye knowing you'll never ever see her again there's no one to share your pain with in that your parents and brothers never really knew her and your college friends have long forsaken your collective public school past for new adventures which you attempt to do by moving into the pink stucco apartment complex across the street from campus so notorious for partying everyone watching the war on television it looks like a video game you played as a kid you apply the same nonchalance to the start of the spring semester going stretches without showing up for class but making sure to attend the days of quizzes and tests your new volunteer job at the campus safety escort service keeps you on campus a little more you think it might be a good way to meet women since the girls who turn up at parties at your apartment complex are primarily interested in fraternity guys but you mainly escort married women to their cars after dark sometimes on foot and sometimes in a golf cart you and the other escorts race around campus in during downtime you continue to take two buses each way to your job working for the government trustee installed to wind down american continental and sell its assets for the benefit of its creditors your eyesight goes a little and you need glasses and even though you can't afford them you purchase a pair from the little optique in tempe because the girl behind the counter is cute she seems like she's flirting with you who can tell but on the chance that she might be you ask all the women you work with at american continental to vouch for you by writing the girl a note about you and how she should say yes when you ask her out you collect the notes and have them delivered and then call the girl seems genuinely flattered though she claims she has a boyfriend but agrees to a friend date you borrow your father's pickup for the date which is just dinner at chili's which goes okay you don't seem to have too much in common except your stunt and on the way to drop her back home you drive over a median you don't see because you suddenly realize you probably shouldn't be driving at night which freaks the girl out a little even though you make a small joke about adjusting the glasses you bought from her saying good night is the last time you'll see her you know the video for madonna's new song is banned from mtv and the guy on nightline asks her if she'll make even more money from the song now that it's banned madonna says yeah so what the harvard-educated businessman wins 2 percent above 50 in the run-off election and becomes governor but is immediately embroiled in litigation over his involvement with a different savings and loan from the one charlie owned the girl who played the sister on diff'rent strokes is caught robbing a video store in vegas where she is living and working at a dry cleaner's a girl at one of the parties at your apartment complex mistakenly dives into the shallow end when she's drunk and comes up with a bloody face and no one seems to know what to do everyone too drunk to drive and you would offer but you don't have a car the girl from new jersey who lives upstairs from you and who you think maybe likes you from the road trip you made to mexico with her and her friends offers to drive but the bloodied girl says she's fine and disappears bret easton ellis the author of less than zero the book that the movie you liked as a teenager was based on publishes a new book about a stockbroker who is also a serial killer and his name is all at once everywhere his handsome photo plastered all over the newspaper and in magazines something about his original publisher canceling the book over the violence and another publisher quickly cashing in on the controversy which brings the author a slew of death threats and his fame reignites your long-buried interest in becoming a writer everyone watches the video tape of the rodney king beating on television you are haunted by the image of the famous guitarist's toddler son falling to his death out an open window in new york a high school teacher in new hampshire is found guilty of ordering one of her students who is also her teenage lover to murder her husband warren beatty musing about how madonna doesn't exist if there's no camera the kid from the partridge family who is a radio dj in phoenix is found cowering in his apartment closet when the police come to arrest him for beating up a transvestite prostitute word is gangs from los angeles are infiltrating phoenix and a series of shootings on the freeways seems to confirm the fact two shootings in two weeks and then a third a pregnant woman rumor is gangbangers are driving around at night with their lights off and if you flash them to let them know they come after you so no one flashes anyone after twenty years of marriage your parents decide to divorce both of them young enough for a second act boxer mike tyson is arrested for raping a beauty queen in a hotel room a man running down the street in milwaukee with a handcuff on one arm flags down police and he leads them to the apartment of the man who tried to hold him against his will and the officers find an apartment full of horrors you stop listening at the detail of four decapitated heads you stare at the photo of bennington college the school in a small town in vermont that bret easton ellis attended in the library's copy of peterson's guide to colleges and universities the tuition is outrageous it's one of the most expensive schools in the country and you become obsessed with transferring there the gradeless curriculum the answer to your drowning at a public university and when you ask your latin teacher for a letter of recommendation she reminds you that you're barely passing her class that summer pee-wee herman is arrested for masturbating in an adult theater in florida where he's been visiting his parents and the news explodes across all forms of media pee-wee goes into hiding his career ruined for what some deem hypocritical reasons but the jokes are funny unlike the joke made by the supreme court nominee about his coke can the television endlessly fascinated with the testimony of his former subordinate who claims she was sexually harassed by the nominee some people incredulous that the subordinate followed the nominee from job post to job post even after being harassed but she passes a lie detector and the nominee doesn't want to take one and on and on magic johnson arranges a press conference to announce that he is hiv positive and will retire from basketball immediately and as his team the lakers are perennial tormentors of the hometown phoenix suns some fans are not as compassionate as they could be magic goes on his friend arsenio hall's late-night show to assure everyone he is heterosexual and not gay which gets a standing ovation from the crowd lasting minutes you make the application to bennington college with the same conviction you're always able to muster when you want something to happen and you're momentarily elated when someone from the admissions office calls to request an interview which is the next step but even before you hang up you know you can't afford the flight to and from vermont especially because of the monthly payments for the car you'll never drive again and you reluctantly tell admissions this and they arrange for you to interview with a local alum a woman who is a doctor in downtown phoenix you make an appointment with her and then don't keep it and figure that's that a girl who works with your college friend shows up at a party at your apartment and while she likes your friend he has a girlfriend and so he wants to introduce her to you and you hit it off immediately the fact that she's still in high school no big deal at least to you but maybe a little bit to her parents when you turn up at her house in scottsdale driving the car your parents bought at an auction of old rental cars you start spending all your time with your new high school girlfriend meeting her friends who are also in high school the kick of being the oldest in the group refreshing your outlook more than it should your new high school girlfriend wants to be a writer too and that feels like a real connection one you've never had before but you try not to make too much out of it one of the kennedy relatives goes on trial for raping a woman at the family compound in florida the movie about jfk's assassination fires everyone's imagination especially those who have been living with so many unanswered questions for so long and for you and your friends it becomes the gospel truth about what happened though others are quick to point out that it's simply making an entertainment out of history but it's a compelling and persuasive argument about the events from so long ago but also why would all those famous people in the film agree to portray such historical inaccuracies their celebrity lends a powerful credibility to the whole thing and you check out every book in the phoenix public library about marilyn monroe and her death hoping to unearth some previously ignored kernel of information that solves the mystery surrounding her demise but even though you keep the books long past their due date you don't do more than leaf through them looking at the pictures everyone watching a tv show on mtv called the real world but you don't see much tv and don't have one when you move into the cinder-block studio apartment in the shadow of the pink stucco complex where you wasted time at so many parties none of the faces becoming friends or names you can remember there's a tv in the break room at american continental an old back-projection big screen that you fire up during your lunch and where you learn about an extramarital affair committed by the democratic candidate for president the candidate going on 60 minutes with his wife to do damage control and also the boxer-who-raped-the-beauty-queen's trial and quick conviction the rich texan with the funny name and funny voice who announces his bid for the presidency on a nightly cable talk show even though he doesn't belong to either of the two traditional parties an allegedly new narrative some people get excited about but what little you know about politics doubts the texan is doing more than grandstanding especially when his candidacy is dependent on volunteers getting him on the ballot in every state which is a pretty good gimmick you have to admit the tennis player who contracted aids from a blood transfusion driving home after a late night with your new high school girlfriend it comes across the radio that the comedian sam kinison has been killed driving to las vegas just a few days after his wedding ceremony and it comes out later that a kid swerved across the lane and killed him and there's a rumor that the kid offers up his autograph for anyone who wants it not out of spite but because of his newfound fame charlie keating is sentenced by the state of california to ten years in prison and everyone says it's not a country-club prison but a real prison and he still has the feds to deal with but no one at american continental openly discusses charlie anymore especially the southern lawyer whose apprentice you've become you don't realize until much later how much you counted on becoming charlie keating's apprentice at least in terms of a meteoric rise but also because of the tales of charlie's previous lieutenants all of them making six figures a year to do charlie's bidding but all gone before you were hired the southern lawyer is much more grounded and less egomaniacal than charlie certainly or any of the other lawyers you've encountered he takes an interest in your academic work and rides you about it until you admit that you're not paying it the attention it deserves and you feel some shame about the fact for the first time all of american continental moves from its original compound on camelback road into half a floor of an office building a few blocks away and you agree to become the sole runner and switchboard operator so that the staff can be further downsized you also become a boy friday for the southern lawyer when he buys out of bankruptcy a mansion at the foot of camelback mountain formerly owned by a pair of nursing home administrators errands to home depot and letting contractors in to work you sometimes stay in the guesthouse on the property and you're allowed to use the pool anytime you watch a little of los angeles burning on the tv news borrow the southern lawyer's white mercedes given to him by american continental as one month's pay to take your new high school girlfriend and her friends to the prom staying in a hotel in downtown tempe near the mormon church on the asu campus whose wooden sign you recently destroyed in a drunken rampage when you learned that your mormon ex-girlfriend was getting married that summer a teenage girl on long island shoots but doesn't kill the wife of the guy who works on her car when she brings it in to his auto body shop the friend of the actor who played colonel hogan on one of your favorite shows as a kid hogan's heroes is arrested for colonel hogan's murder at an apartment complex in scottsdale the murder happening sometime in the late seventies long before you even started watching the show and you wonder at the complicit silence among the adults who knew that the actor had had his head bludgeoned in his sleep and possibly as a result of his sex life which included homemade pornographic movies and swinging and who knows what else the friend who is arrested all these years later was always the prime suspect and there's doubt that the evidence will stand up but the news repeats all the salacious details for those not in the know the summer is mostly spent at the southern lawyer's house running various errands and using the pool including some skinny-dipping with your new high school girlfriend and her friends the time you come over and the southern lawyer's current girlfriend is sunbathing nude you sneak back out the way you came but not immediately you continue your work as a boy friday for the southern lawyer to earn some spending money the southern lawyer tells you to bring a copy of your latest work you wonder at the motor home idling on the recently paved circular driveway a large group gathered under the awning filling their plates with food a fleet of rental cars parked two deep rings the motor home a miniature race car is parked where the southern lawyer's mercedes and land cruiser are normally parked and he motions you over and introduces you as the writer to someone who turns out to be the director of the film they're making at the southern lawyer's house the female lead a dark-haired woman in her thirties picks at a fruit salad while the male lead an englishman with a crew cut talks rabidly about the miniature race car he apparently brings with him on every location the director is not that interested in your writing it seems but he gives you his card telling the cast and crew five minutes while the southern lawyer excuses himself to make a phone call you follow the crowd up to the guesthouse which has been transformed into a movie set the sound guy having built a booth just outside the sliding glass doors inside a small camera track circles the queen-size bed the male lead motions for you to take a seat and asks you where you're from he sounds like james bond or at least to you and you tell him you're from montana originally the female lead brushes by in a red satin robe and you turn to the male lead to tell him a funny story about the mulching pit you built behind the guesthouse out of railroad ties but the male lead stands talking about his desire to travel to montana while he slips out of his clothes and it becomes

208

obvious what kind of film they're shooting in the guesthouse though you're surprised by the elaborate production the female lead points at you and says that it's a closed set and so you don't see a thing searching the main house for the southern lawyer but he has for the moment disappeared as does the director's card before you can send him some of your work which oddly you're interested in following through on you promise yourself you're going to spend more time on your classes this go around but your new high school girlfriend means a lot of late nights especially the ones where she sneaks out of her house and so your grades fall off a cliff immediately and are on life support the rest of the way just like your finances so you take a night job manning the desk of the campus law library helping people look up statutes but mostly just reshelving books pulled down by law students too absorbed to reshelve them you lay your hands on madonna's sex book the moment it goes on sale at the local barnes & noble the large-format book with metal covers and spiral binding comparatively tame to what you know about madonna and you give the book to the southern lawyer who wants to give it to a conservative friend as a gag gift you hammer out a couple of short stories including one about a polygamist mormon and his three wives arizona voters approve a statewide holiday for martin luther king jr and are rewarded when the national football league awards the state the right to host the super bowl three years on the actor who played the older brother on diff'rent strokes is arrested when he's pulled over by police who find drugs and a loaded gun the dream of becoming a writer finally trumps all else and you leave the aftermath of the collapse of charlie keating's empire behind and tempe and arizona state university and your old high school girlfriend too and move ninety miles south to the university of arizona to finish your undergraduate degree in their creative writing program taking an apartment just off campus down park avenue which you think is funny you have no furniture no car hardly any money save for what's left over in student loan aid after each semester's tuition but the redbrick campus has a unifying effect and for the first time in your short academic career school becomes the main focus your new high school girlfriend visits a couple of times on the greyhound bus but you both sense that the relationship has run its course no hard feelings charlie keating is convicted again this time by the federal government michael jackson appears on oprah winfrey's talk show and claims to have a skin disease and that he doesn't bleach his skin like some claim a truck bomb explodes at the world trade center doesn't do what it's supposed to knock one building into the other but it does kill a handful of people the actor who played the older brother on diff'rent strokes is arrested for stabbing a guy renting a room from him when he tells the guy to quit yelling at his girlfriend but he's later cleared when the stabbing turns out to be self-defense the little kid from diff'rent strokes everyone loved wins a lawsuit against his parents who squandered all the money he made the actor son of the famous martial artist is killed on a movie set when a blank is fired at him same as it was jon-erik hexum years before you aim to model your writing career primarily on bret easton ellis's since he is a young and famous writer and you want that too so you begin work on your first novel called the vegetable king which loosely resembles a mash-up of fitzgerald's the great gatsby and bret easton ellis's american psycho the television in the student union plays the raid at the waco compound on a loop everyone gathered around as if it's homework a tennis player is stabbed during a tournament and at first people assume it's because of her nationality but really the stabber is just a fan obsessed with the player's rival the campus literary magazine wants to publish your short story about the polygamist leaving a note on your door about it since you don't have a phone tucson empties when summer arrives and you work eight hours a day on your novel sometimes treating yourself to the dollar movie on campus regardless of quality or to an hour in front of the television in the student union where you watch news unfold incrementally prince changes his name to a symbol and nobody knows what to call him the woman in beverly hills who is arrested for running a prostitution ring involving celebrity clients the white house lawyer whose body is found in a park dead from suicide something to do with the real estate scandal involving the president that no one seems to know the specifics of the boy whose father accuses michael jackson of molestation though it might just be a shakedown basketball superstar michael jordan's father going missing his body turning up in a swamp a couple of weeks later the menendez brothers' trial broadcast minute by minute on a cable channel the two dressed in colored sweaters to make them look not like the kind of kids who could level shotguns at their parents you also kill some of the summer at the free wine receptions at the poetry center which is just a little house on cherry street where you hear some great writers including a graduate fiction writer whose first story was published in esquire magazine because the esquire editor happened to be subbing in for the instructor who was his wife and the graduate student's story happened to be up for workshop that day a lucky story that gives you great energy and hope and by the fall you have a finished version of your novel it takes a week to print it out though because you don't have a printer and the monitors in the campus computer labs are tight about how many pages anyone can print at once so you put the different labs on a loop knowing when the monitors change posts so that you can print out a copy of the entire novel which you mail straight off to random house the biggest publisher and the one who publishes your idol every admirer is one part assassin you spend a lot of time wondering what random house thinks of your book while golfing a tennis ball into cups you've set up in your barren living room the golf clubs formerly belonged to your friend who looked like anthony michael hall and you were always meaning to return them and when you finally did after your friend shot himself in the head his mother said he'd want you to keep them even though what she was saying was that she didn't want them in the house you're tapped as the fiction editor for the campus literary magazine and in turn ask a girl in your creative writing class to be the coeditor and she agrees and you set to work on the slush pile trying to make fair judgments on the work submitted a job you come to appreciate as next to impossible though it doesn't assuage your disappointment when a ups deliveryman shows up on your door with a package from random house you momentarily think contains a contract and a check why else would they send it ups but really just contains the copy of your manuscript and a letter saying thanks but no thanks the fibers from your ripping open the ups envelope catching in your carpet and without a vacuum cleaner you have no way to clean them up the actress winona ryder offers a large reward for the little girl from ryder's hometown who is kidnapped from a slumber party your friend from maryland who is as much a fitzgerald fan as you tells you that river phoenix died outside a nightclub in hollywood owned by johnny depp and while there seems to be an insinuation in these facts it's just a terribly sad thing that happened the girl in your apartment complex who tells you the dirty joke you don't understand until much later has a copy of the rob lowe sex tape and shows it to you and after all the years of hearing about it and even the coy allusions to it in that movie rob lowe made as a comeback after the scandal the video of what happened in the hotel room at the democratic national convention in atlanta years previous is tame and a little boring the body of the little girl from winona ryder's hometown who was kidnapped from a slumber party is found your friend the fitzgerald fan goes to the inaugural insomniyakathon with you twenty-four hours of readings at a bar in tucson which you consider a pretty genius gimmick not unlike the entire career of howard stern the dj in new york whose book sells out in a matter of hours with millions more sold thereafter the book signings like carnivals with people in costumes and it seems like stern will say just about anything but you sort of get that he's doing it to do it and it wouldn't be outside the realm of possibility that it's all an act but even more curiously the book seems to be a springboard to movies and television deals stern is on everyone's lips the novelty of so many people who wouldn't normally be reading books suddenly reading one seems only a mockery stern stages a pay-per-view new year's eve special called the miss howard stern new year's eve pageant where women do things like eat maggots and put plastic bags over their heads and while the special grosses a ton of money hollywood executives who have been considering stern for the job of replacing chevy chase as a late-night host change their minds and so too do movie executives interested in bringing some of stern's ideas to the screen an olympic skater is attacked whacked in the knee and it turns out to be a hit ordered by her rival skater your application to be an intern at the university of arizona press is granted and your curiosity about the publishing side of writing brims and maybe they'll even want to publish your novel but after a week it's clear the press doesn't publish books like yours and really doesn't publish much fiction and while the different phases editorial layout cover art publicity are interesting the internship becomes a thing around your neck and you don't get credit for the class when you don't write the final paper about your experience as required radio personality howard stern announces his candidacy for the governor of new york madonna is a guest on david letterman's show and her appearance has to be heavily edited to be shown diane sawyer is sitting in for your favorite news anchor peter jennings and the words coming out of her mouth on the television given to you by your parents cannot possibly be true but it's all over all the other channels too the lead singer of the band nirvana is dead of a suicide in the room over the garage in his house and the facts and rumors and lies about the story consume everyone you know for days and weeks a woman sues the president claiming he sexually harassed her in a hotel room when he was governor of arkansas the issue of the campus literary magazine you helped edit comes out you and your coeditor agreeing to disagree about a post-modern story you want to include just to have one even though it's subpar compared with some other realist fiction stories submitted something about the variety appealing to your nascent editorial sense rumor has it that kojak's son is a student at the university of arizona and that his girlfriend tori spelling has been seen around tucson and that tori spelling's castmate from 90210 jennie garth is from phoenix which matters to devotees of the show you've never seen it though you know all of the characters' names the rumor that you just need to take the university's math placement test in order to have a score of some kind to then be admitted to math x a class for artists and writers that satisfies the university's math require-ment for graduation turns out not to be true a fact you learn only after you've breezed in and out of the test penciling in random answers based on your test score you won't be graduating that december as planned because you need two years of math classes to reach the class you need for credit the test score locking you in also you're so derelict about your studies that while you know you need latin 202 to complete your foreign-language credit you fail to see the obvious that it's only offered in the spring and not between now and when you're supposed to graduate so you make sure you're the first to sign up for the summer class even though the lease on your apartment is up at the end of may you intended to go back to phoe-nix for the fall semester arranging all your classes on tuesdays and thursdays with the idea of attending just on tuesdays to save the money you don't have for an apartment but the more pressing problem is the college algebra class there's really no point in taking the summer latin class if you can't solve the college algebra problem the answer is found the week after oj simpson murders his wife and her friend and then leads the police on a slow freeway chase a mailer for a brand-new community college opening in phoenix arrives in the mail and almost as a dare you call the number on the mailer to ask if you can enroll in college algebra and to your astonishment the voice on the other end takes your credit card information and just like that you're enrolled in the monday/wednesday/friday fall college algebra class at the new community college oj simpson offers a $500,000 reward for information leading to the arrest of the real killer or killers of his wife and her friend radio personality howard stern withdraws from the race for governor of new york rather than publicly reveal his financial statements all of the apartments in tucson are sublet for the summer and after multiple dead ends you scour the dorms on campus for any last-minute cancellations and find luck in that a group of native mexicans enrolled in a summer language immersion class at the university have some missing students and you're given a bunk in a white cinder-block room with a guy who speaks no english but seems good natured enough you never see each other you can't stomach the cramped quarters which remind you too much of your room on the alaskan fish boat and though you don't have any money or a car you find ways to be out of the room either going to dollar movies or walking the halls of the air-conditioned buildings on campus or reading in the library or browsing the new books and magazines in the campus bookstore where you spot the new issue of vanity fair with the article titled who's afraid of bret easton ellis all about what the author has been doing since his controversial book was published a few years earlier and also announcing the publication of his new book a story collection called the informers and even though you can't afford it you buy the magazine so you can read and reread the piece and stare at the caricature drawn of the author you can't afford the new story collection but read it surreptitiously in the campus bookstore you can't make much of it but who are you to judge you write a letter to the editor of vanity fair in support of the author's place in contemporary fiction not sure why but probably mostly because if they print it maybe ellis will see it your last college semester begins and you live ninety miles away so you can concentrate on your monday wednesday friday college algebra class at the new community college on the west side of phoenix you living back home your father dropping you at sky harbor airport on monday nights so you can grab the shuttle to tucson for your other classes on tuesdays you bunk on the couch of your old high-school-aged girlfriend who has just started after a year of community college back in phoenix it's the first time you have any kind of relationship with an ex-girlfriend and there's something dependable about a friendship with someone who knows you so well and you begin to look forward to those nights they break up your otherwise monastic existence the bad reviews for bret easton ellis's book start rolling in and you're not sure why but you write a letter to the editor of entertainment weekly in response to one of the harsher reviews and to your surprise they print it the thrill of your name in the magazine matched only by the message on the answering machine at home that vanity fair is going to print your letter as well the stars aligning when you happen upon a flyer on the fourth floor of the modern languages building on campus where all your creative writing workshops are held for a new low-residency mfa program at bennington college you take in the news stunned a little and then steal the poster so that no one else sees it before you can get your application in you include your latest short story written from the ashes of your failed novel your favorite creative writing professor told you after class that it was probably a publishable story and so you spent an afternoon licking envelopes and stamps to mail it off to all the literary magazines listed in the back of the latest best american short stories collection the book your professor used in class there's a lot of hope and optimism the federal government grinds to a halt and shuts down something you didn't know could even happen though the finger-pointing is less of a surprise former president ronald reagan announces that he has alzheimer's the last the public hears from him one night a few weeks before your december graduation you're out at the pool in your ex-girlfriend's apartment complex and it strikes you that you have no alternative plan should you not get into bennington that you should've applied to a handful of places arrogance isn't to blame you just aren't interested in pursuing the course of study if it isn't at bennington in the shadow of bret easton ellis the coming new year is a blank slate you have no idea where you'll be living what you'll be doing for work nothing the vacuum created by the absence of any kind of schooling too frightening to contemplate vanquished by the phone call from the director of the mfa program who calls during dinner to tell you that you've been accepted and will start in january and then more great good luck the editor of one of the literary magazines in new york city you mailed your story to sends a handwritten note in pencil saying they're considering publishing it so that by the time of your graduation from the university of arizona please stand and turn your tassel along with thousands of others congratulations good-bye your life as a graduate student and possibly a published author has begun you gather your father and two brothers under the same roof in a rented house in a master-planned development in phoenix built around a large man-made lake the first time you've been in the same house in you can't remember how long there's no money to furnish the five-bedroom pink stucco house as it should be but everyone has their living space and you use the extra room as a writing office you're so eager to start your first ten-day residency of the low-residency mfa program at bennington college that you take a red-eye to albany not realizing that you'll have to wait until dawn to hire a driver to take you to the secluded campus in the woods of vermont the slatted sunshine its own miracle as you are expelled from the covered bridge at the foot of campus which is deserted at this time of the morning you survey the landscape you've seen only in pictures the red barn structure that houses the administration the white seventies-style architecture of crossett library the clock-towered commons at the head of the enormous lawn buried under crisp snow that runs out to the end of the world so named because the lawn drops off like a runway your vision taking flight over the green mountains green-and-white clapboard dorms line the lawn and you wonder which one bret easton ellis lived in eager to commune with his ghost you set your bag down on a picnic table and scan the horizon for signs of anyone else bret easton ellis probably sat at this picnic table you think you let yourself into a near dorm all the doors unlocked it seems and think bret easton ellis probably partied in this common room and as your head hits the pillow in an unlocked room the first real sleep since you left phoenix you wonder if he even perhaps lived in the very room you're in it's a possibility until you learn otherwise when you awake dazed to the sound of clanging heaters you get your correct room assignment and scurry off to the welcome reception in the commons disappointed that most of the other writing students have not heard of bret easton ellis or the ones who have just smile talk revolves around the poet robert frost or the writer bernard malamud both dead and lionized and decidedly not very interesting the next day after breakfast served in the commons at communal tables with your fellow students and most of the writing instructors you wander as a lark into the alumni office and tell the girl working the counter that you're a student and want the address of an alum the girl seems skeptical since all the undergraduate students are away in january for winter break and after some discussion with her boss about whether or not mfa students have the same privileges as other students she writes bret easton ellis's address and phone number on a yellow post-it note and hands it across the desk you vamoose before she can recall the information securing the post-it in your wallet after memorizing the address in case the post-it somehow gets lost fresh from victory you head to the library and search the computer for ellis's books and learn that the library has on deposit ellis's student thesis called this year's model which you don't immediately recognize as a song title by elvis costello but you do recognize some of the stories from the thesis as those from ellis's latest collection the informers you also put a request in for the thesis of ellis's classmate donna tartt whose novel the secret history you loved tartt dedicated the book to ellis for helping her and for recommending her to his literary agent which you hope he'll do for you too you fall in love with the other writing students the feel of immediate family permeating the workshops and lectures you volunteer to organize some student readings and choose the laundry room as a suitable venue when no other can be secured the laundry room readings becoming something of a legend severe separation anxiety overcomes you as you board your flight back to phoenix the resumption of your life akin to coming to periscope depth oj simpson's trial for murdering his wife and her friend begins in los angeles you need a job and gravitate toward the camelback corridor where you worked for charlie keating at american continental and randomly put in an application at the family print shop near the old american continental offices remembering how you and the other runners pitched in to buy flowers for the stunning girl who worked the counter the one time someone at american continental wanted some color copies from the print shop the girl had tattoos which you normally didn't care for but she was flirty and it was enough to spring for the bouquet the card signed simply the runners at acc when you get the job at the family print shop running the xerox machines you relay the story to your boss and he remembers it the girl was his girlfriend and the story suddenly doesn't seem so funny though the girlfriend is long gone the print shop is a boon in terms of your being able to photocopy your work for sending off to literary magazines and to the teacher assigned to you by bennington for the semester a writer you've never heard of but whose book you buy with the intention of reading it the literary magazine in new york city that was considering publishing your story writes to say they're accepting it for publication and you pin the acceptance on the wall above your desk next to the yellow post-it note with ellis's address and phone number one of the customers at the print shop runs a mail-order russian bride business and you leaf through the yearbook of women he prints thinking a bunch of different thoughts at once another customer is the daughter of the famed russian ballet dancer vaslav nijinsky whom you've never heard of but you come to learn his life's story as the daughter is working on a book about her father and when she arrives at the print shop you know the next hour or two will be spent helping her copy old news clippings and photos you gather that nijinsky was famous for being the only male ballet dancer who could perform on his tiptoes like you saw michael jackson do on that motown special when you were in grade school everyone wowed by the new dance jackson called the moonwalk you play a practical joke on the good-natured designer who works at the print shop an admitted and avowed marijuana smoker you conspire with your boss who has become one of your closest friends to announce upon the designer's return from his marijuana-fueled honeymoon that the print shop is switching health insurance companies and everyone has to take a drug test you go down to the arizona department of health services claiming to be a college kid doing a research project and in need of a drug test kit the department of health services worker tells you that he can give you the forms and cup but that he has to write the word void across the forms which he does and which is no problem as you and your boss re-create them back at the print shop the designer learns about the test and confides in you that he's going to run out at lunch to buy a masking agent at a smoke shop which he does but back at his desk the masking agent makes him defecate involuntarily and he has to go home for the day the practical joke taking on a life of its own the designer takes the drug test the next day and when your boss tells him he's failed it and his only option is to enroll in drug classes the designer's face gets red and he says no way he's taking classes but that night his wife lets him know that he will in fact have to take the classes so when he comes to work again his face a little hangdog he accepts that he has to take the classes and you and your boss stop the whole thing before it can go any further and the designer is relieved but his wife is angry and calls your boss and gives him an earful oj's houseguest tells about going to mcdonald's with oj the limo driver meant to take oj to the airport rang the doorbell repeatedly before oj appeared looking sweaty the guy tricked into meeting his secret admirer for an episode of the jenny jones show learns the secret admirer is a man and murders the admirer a few days after the show the singer selena is murdered by her assistant who it turns out was stealing money from her the newscaster refers to her as the mexican madonna someone blows up a truck in front of the federal courthouse in oklahoma the galleys for your first short story arrive from the literary magazine in new york city and you stare at them in disbelief your words arranged by an unseen editorial hand three thousand miles away the daughter of actor marlon brando whose brother murdered her husband commits suicide a forensic specialist testifies that the odds against the dna found at the crime scene being anyone else's but oj simpson's are astronomical the actress who played samantha on bewitched dies of cancer the actor who played superman is thrown off his horse and paralyzed from the neck down you spin in circles at an old ice-packing plant in downtown phoenix while former porn star traci lords plays music in her new incarnation as a dj summer in vermont is hotter than you expected but your second residency is made uncomfortable not by the heat but by the secret knowledge you've been carrying that you didn't do the work prescribed by the program between residencies not because you weren't eager but because the writer assigned as your mentor quit responding to your monthly packets and so you quit mailing them all of which is exposed when the writer is fired rumors about a divorce hampering his teaching and it emerges that the other students assigned to the writer had the same experience as you and you're called to account with the administration who threaten not to give you credit for the first semester which is a problem because you're on financial aid and can borrow only so much money surely not for extra future semesters the mercurial irishman who directs the program and whom you once considered an ally seems like the head instigator in your not getting credit the whole thing a cloud over you upsetting because you were so looking forward to seeing everyone again after living your surface life in phoenix but one of the other authors who teach workshops hears of your plight and then something happens that you never really understand and the matter drops with the caveat that you'll have to do two times the work in the upcoming semester and you agree and get on with the residency working late into the nights on the daily fake newsletter some of the students conspire to publish contributing a column under the byline f not fitzgerald late nights at the end of the world under tiki torches you lacquered in bug spray an endless can of beer in your hand sweaty dances in the carriage barn or in the tiny pub on campus flipping through a copy of details magazine in the air-conditioning of crossett library you find a profile of the actor val kilmer by bret easton ellis and feel an electricity of stumbling across ellis's name while being on campus a continuous circle of a kind photos of oj simpson's wife and friend in rivers of blood on the saltillo tile of your youth are all over the news oj tries on the bloody glove a police officer found on oj's property but the glove appears not to fit one of charlie keating's lieutenants is discovered in the early morning in his lexus parked in the parking lot of a toy store a bullet in his brain a few days later another of charlie's lieutenants does the same in his home a handsome actor whose movies you haven't seen is arrested for soliciting a prostitute in los angeles the world agog as the handsome actor's girlfriend is a world-renowned model and actress screen legend lana turner dies a couple of days later but the handsome actor and the prostitute dominate the news oj's doctor says he's too hobbled from football injuries to be able to commit a double homicide but a recent videotape of oj working out while touting an arthritis remedy counters that you read a handful of short stories each week as makeup work and begin writing as many short stories of your own as you can to put yourself back even with the administration at bennington a north carolina judge blocks oj's lawyers' attempt to force a screenwriter who interviewed the police officer who found the incriminating glove for background on a screenplay she was writing to testify to the fact that the police officer is a racist you write a story about a narrator who visits the small town where he was born and finds himself surrounded by racists the north carolina court of appeals grants oj's lawyers the right to hear the tapes of the screenwriter interviewing the police officer you write a twenty-page story that's all dialogue a phone conversation between a man and a woman the news is infatuated with pictures of oj wearing a famous brand of shoes like those that left prints at the crime scene you write a story about a stranger visiting his friend and abusing his friend's girlfriend in some indeterminate way the tapes of the screenwriter interviewing the police officer are played in court but not in front of the jury the officer is heard using the n word constantly contrary to his own previous testimony that he never used it the police officer swiftly invokes his fifth amendment rights there's some debate about whether or not newspapers should publish a rambling antigovernment manifesto by the unabomber a terrorist the government has been after for years the unabomber promises more bombing if the manifesto isn't published in the new york times and the washington post oj simpson applies to trademark his name standing in line at the grocery store getting groceries for you and your father and brothers you pick up details magazine and flip to the last page which features two blond girls posing and giving short answers to a q and a and you can't tell what they do or why they're in the magazine and you come away with the idea that their sole purpose as a quote-unquote group is to become famous and you consider how weird the concept is that someone could be celebrated for just being celebrated and you write an eight-page story called we're so famous around the idea everyone gathered around the small television on top of the xerox machine at the family print shop when they announce the verdict in the matter of the people v oj simpson which you're convinced will be guilty and something akin to shock sets in when it's otherwise and you contemplate for the first time really how much mental energy you expended on the narrative even though you had no stake in the outcome personally a feeling like fatigue settling over you in the following weeks and months as everyone traipses around either in elation or frustration you're all the way back in the good graces of the administration at bennington when the january residency begins you can't believe you're halfway through graduate school when bret easton ellis was your age he'd published two novels and was working on his third the one that would make him famous all over again an unused part of the campus has been rented by a shakespearean theater company so unknown faces known to be aspiring thespians turn up in the dining hall from time to time the one next to you in line complaining about the dining hall running out of strawberries for strawberry short-cake turns out to be the actress raquel welch you make a sympathetic remark about the strawberries before you recognize her but she doesn't seem to hear you madonna reluctantly testifies in court against the man who broke into her hollywood home and threatened to slice her up if she didn't become his wife we've made his fantasies come true madonna admonishes the court which compelled her to testify sitting right in front of him instead of by videotape or some other method one way to meet a celebrity on your terms one of the producers who made all the big movies of the eighties like flashdance beverly hills cop and top gun is found dead in his bathroom from a drug overdose and there are whispers that a botched penile implant is to blame magic johnson comes out of retirement to play for the lakers the hard contacts you've been wearing don't seem to be working and your eye doctor tells you that you have a condition that causes your corneas to elongate weakening at the tip and you'll need a corneal transplant to correct the problem you get on the waiting list for a donated cornea your case different from most in that you need a relatively young cornea and so you're essentially waiting for someone your age or younger to pass away the procedure is outpatient you're awake during it though they put you under to drug up the eye and then bring you back so you can alert them to any problems but it all goes smoothly and your eye doctor tells you seriously not to get into any pillow fights or allow any kind of trauma to your eyes and you wonder how you're going to get through life without violating that mandate howard stern announces that he'll star in the film version of his own book to the delight of his fans the rapper snoop dogg is arrested for allegedly murdering a rival gang member the summer before the arrest taking place after snoop presents an award at the mtv music awards you keep your head down reading and writing in the little office above the garage in the house you're sharing with your father and two brothers enjoying being under the same roof even though you're all living your own lives your youngest brother attending the local high school your other brother and father working everyone home most nights for the dinner you prepare trying to learn how to cook a month or so after your corneal transplant the eye doctor tells you to lean forward and keep your eye open so he can begin removing the tiny stitches your friend from bennington's husband is an actor traveling with a play coming to gammage auditorium in tempe and you offer to put him up he looks like christopher reeve which he gets a lot especially after the accident you see the play with one of your friends who you can tell has an immediate crush on him but he probably gets that a lot too the play goes to los angeles and you and your friend from your charlie keating days drive out to see the actor and his wife your friend from bennington staying with them in the old fifties hotel converted into apartments filled with struggling actors the kidney-shaped pool at the center of the tahitian-themed complex going unused you love the idea of all the little compartments filled with ambitious people trying to realize their dream and feel a sort of kinship even though back in phoenix you continue to keep your head down don't date don't see your old friends who have all scattered here and there no one believes the story the menendez brothers tell about the abuse they suffered at the hands of their father and they're found guilty of murder don't eat meat or you'll catch mad cow disease charlie keating's conviction is overturned and he's released the unabomber is arrested when his brother recognizes the rantings of the manifesto published in the newspapers as those of his crazy brother living in the woods in montana the rapper mc hammer files for bankruptcy and you think man where did all that money go the actress from the superman movies is found hiding in some bushes in a suburb of los angeles with all her hair cut off and ranting she was apparently in the bushes for days you spend what time you do spend socializing with the manager of the family print shop who has unexpectedly become your closest friend the def leppard drummer with one arm is arrested for choking his wife for a small fee you can purchase a vhs tape directly from oj with his side of the story but no one seems to want it the summer residency at bennington is the penultimate residency for you and you feel a mild panic about what will happen to you after you graduate you can't imagine hanging on any longer in phoenix you never felt at home there always a double life and now you have the vocabulary to express it but you also can't imagine leaving your family a vexation you express to one of your mentors on a walk through the woods at bennington and he encourages you to do what you feel is right but you think easy for him to say though you never really know if your family's dependence on you is real or imagined the host of the family feud game show is found hanging in the closet of a hospital where he went for mental observation one of the best customers at the family print shop a psychiatrist with an office in downtown phoenix shoots himself through the heart with a handgun you can't stop thinking about how he must've been alive for a few minutes right after the actor who portrayed one of the leads in the film version of bret easton ellis's first novel less than zero which you saw in a midnight showing is arrested for being under the influence of drugs and then arrested again a couple of weeks later when he's found asleep in a bedroom of the house next door to his assault charges against the old guy who played colonel potter on the television show m*a*s*h are dropped after he completes an anger management course for beating his seventy-year-old wife the year before fans of the rock group van halen are overjoyed when the original front man returns but his second tenure is brief an all-girl band from england records a song that blares from every speaker and the interesting fact is that the band was manufactured as an answer to all the boy bands in pop music different from the usual origin story about a couple of musicians inviting others to join them in starting a band this group was culled from hundreds of applicants who answered a small ad in london a sheep not born but cloned is introduced to the world a jetliner filled with

227

passengers headed to paris and then rome explodes just after take-off from new york and the television is filled with pictures of burning debris floating in the ocean some eyewitnesses allege seeing a missile fired into the jetliner a bomb explodes at the olympics in atlanta and the eyewitness who is at first hailed as a hero is then arrested as the chief suspect and vilified in the press as a lonely wannabe the singer rick james is released from prison after serving time for assault everyone is trying to guess who alanis wrote the song about your high school friend whose sister you briefly dated in high school is murdered in the parking lot of an after-hours club in scottsdale in the police account a kid pulled a gun on your friend and his friends and your friend said you're not going to shoot me but then the kid with the gun did you think back to when you last saw your friend at a grocery store in phoenix buying something for his infant daughter and you feel ashamed that you tried to avoid him but he found you in an aisle anyway and you tried to catch up a little remember the old days you having no plausible explanation for what you were up to only because you were hedging about the fact that you had a foot in two worlds and were conflicted about making the leap everyone doing the macarena at the democratic national convention the rapper tupac shakur is shot in las vegas after attending a boxing match miraculously the letter you wrote to bret easton ellis asking to interview him for your graduate lecture at bennington which is to be a recitation of your literary journey to date is answered your father telling you that someone named bret left a message on the machine and when you return it ellis invites you to come to new york to conduct the interview in person and you immediately agree to the plan tupac holds on for almost a week before dying rumors that he's faked his own death abound the mother in texas who hired a hit man to kill her daughter's cheer-leading rival's mother in an effort to get the rival to drop out of contention is sentenced to prison the mississippi review a small but prestigious literary magazine run by the acclaimed writer frederick barthelme accepts your short story we're so famous for publication the story chosen for the prize issue judged by mary robison another acclaimed writer and the feeling that having published one previous short story was a fluke recedes a little denied a seat at the presidential debates ross perot goes on larry king afterward to rebut the detective who found the bloody glove on oj's property enters a no-contest plea over his lying about not having used the n word in a decade or more in prepping for your interview with bret easton ellis you call the exclusive private school ellis attended to request any info and before you can say ellis's name the woman who answers the phone assumes you're calling about the actor matthew perry you arrive in new york city a day before your scheduled interview with ellis landing at your bennington friend's apartment in queens amazed to find yourself in a place you never thought you'd be the cacophony makes you giddy the landmarks you previously viewed only through the lens of a television screen or imagined from the pages of books big as the sun up close you scope out ellis's apartment in the east village too anxious about the interview but over-prepared too you arrive early the next day with your tape recorder and notebook too early and you're made to wait in the lobby but then you realize you have to pee and the doorman points you in the direction of a bathroom down a hall and you start to worry that ellis will come looking for you and find you in the bathroom meant for the maintenance crew but when you return to the lobby the door-man tells you that you can go up and you didn't consider that ellis wouldn't in fact descend to the lobby to retrieve you the ride to the second floor is quick and when you land the elevator opens on a small hallway ellis's door slightly ajar and before you know it the shy author is shaking your hand and inviting you into his brightly lit but sparsely furnished loft there's no table and so you use a third chair for the tape recorder and the question-and-answer session lasts all afternoon and into the fading light you're astonished at the depth of his answers and your admiration for him grows tenfold he walks out with you when it's over to fetch some corona and limes from the corner deli and when you part he tells you that new york city is a great place to be a writer and it all but seals the matter in your mind bill clinton is the first democratic president since franklin roosevelt to win reelection michael jackson's longtime friend who is also a nurse in jackson's dermatologist's office is pregnant with his child and they quickly marry prince now wants to be called the artist a pint-size beauty queen is found murdered in her home right around christmas and no one seems to know who did it your last residency at bennington begins amidst the january snow with an incident involving a drunken student sexually harassing one of your poet friends so that you have to intervene not knowing the residency will degrade further from there after the student is asked to find accom- modations off campus which he does at his in-laws' house your journey from the midnight showing of less than zero to the alma mater of bret easton ellis culminates with your lecture about said journey you hand out a lengthy xerox of the full q and a of your interview with ellis courtesy of the family print shop back in phoe- nix and deliver your graduating lecture in the subterranean audito- rium known as tishman the doors clattering when you reach the part of your lecture about why and how ellis's notorious novel american psycho was canceled by its publisher when some of the more violent passages are leaked to the media only to be published by a rival publisher you read one of the violent passages as an example your friends alerting you to the fact afterward that some people walked out when you began reading the passage you just shrug thinking whatever but then a chain of letters appears on the bulletin board in the campus mail room decrying your having read the passages out loud and you get a little taste of the kind of contro- versy that surrounds ellis's novel but so what but then someone posts a letter about burning your handout of the q and a and the campus erupts in a first amendment controversy that has you looking over your shoulder and hiding in your dorm room the faculty silent on the matter mostly you think because it involves ellis and not a writer they care about each day more terrible than the next in terms of rumors about what you've done you call ellis and tell him what's happening and he just laughs and says it doesn't surprise him and you adopt his cool attitude while trying to dodge karen finley the artist who was one of a handful who notoriously had their nea artist grants vetoed on the grounds of subject matter she and the other artists sued and won but the end result was the nea folded ending grants to artists someone on the faculty tries to arrange a summit between you and finley but the idea embarrasses you and you avoid her successfully until she sits down at your table at lunch and asks you about your side of what she's been hearing you tell her little and she says maybe you should make a return visit to your birthplace in montana which came up in conversation you go to the movies off campus just to get away from the morass and run into the director of the mfa program heading into a screening of the people vs larry flynt and the first acknowledgment of the brouhaha comes when he says he's preparing some remarks for graduation that'll be the final word on free speech at bennington which he delivers to the confused crowd of parents who have come hundreds and thousands of miles to see their own graduate and know nothing of the controversy the president of the college approaches you after the ceremony to assure you that she's aware of the situation and that bennington will never tolerate censorship of any kind the student who burned your handout is kicked out of the program and you can feel people staring and pointing at you during the graduation dinner and after and the twinning of your narrative with ellis's is the only interesting residual thought you take away as you pass through the gates a graduate on your way to you don't know where oj simpson is forced to take the witness stand in the civil trial brought against him for the wrongful death of the murdered friend of his wife by the murdered friend's father who promises to haunt oj until the end of oj's days and oj brands his ex-wife a liar about all the domestic abuse she claimed to have suffered over the years at his hands his ex-wife unable to defend herself or tell her side of the story because she is dead bill cosby's son is murdered along the freeway in los angeles when he stops to help a stranded motorist the jury finds oj is probably liable for the deaths of his ex-wife and her friend and is ordered to pay tens of millions of dollars to the families of the murdered some employees of michael jackson's neverland ranch sue him for wrongful termination they claim was retribution for cooperating with the grand jury looking into allegations of child molestation by jackson word leaks the reclusive author j d salinger is going to publish a new book or at least a book-length revision of one of his old new yorker short stories a teacher in washington state is arrested for having sex with her twelve-year-old student she's pregnant with his child howard stern stars in the film version of his book private parts and is everywhere heavily promoting his story about growing up a kid listening to the radio to being on the radio and raising his profile via shock-jock antics the rapper biggie smalls is murdered in california after a party at an auto museum just like tupac shakur was killed in las vegas one car pulling up next to another and firing the murders are maybe related tit for tat three dozen or more people commit suicide together in an upscale house in san diego by drinking vodka laced with drugs and tying plastic bags around their heads in an effort to board a ufo they believed was trailing the hale-bopp comet you decide to make the move to new york city which means the end of your family living together in the same house your father and youngest brother taking an apartment and your younger brother moving in with friends your friends warn you that the thousand dollars you've saved for the move is hardly enough but you're impatient to go and the fact that you have a one-way ticket is an echo of the one-way ticket you had to alaska and though you were able to get home from that debacle you need the move to new york to be permanent returning the way you did from alaska will crush your spirits and leave you without options to live your life as you've dreamed the notion of the creative class burnished by your time at bennington you feel the pressure and the same night you land at your friend's apartment in queens you open your laptop and work on the novel you've started you like the symbolic gesture of moving to new york to write a novel based on the short story published by a new york literary magazine during the day you work on the novel but by midday you hop the n train into manhattan and waltz around famous landmarks like the empire state building the new york public library central park the plaza hotel poking your head into the oak bar imagining fitzgerald at the bar a gin in hand imagining the anecdote about him and zelda drunkenly splashing in the fountain out front you spend whole days walking up one side of manhattan and down the other riding the staten island ferry back and forth to see the statue of liberty you follow your friend's actor husband on errands to his agent's office to pick up scripts or to auditions waiting outside the apartment of the actor paul newman and his wife joanne woodward who are casting for a play you look up old friends from bennington who can't believe your talk about moving to new york wasn't just talk you visit one of your favorite faculty members susan cheever whose family you came to know at bennington you tag along with susan when she goes to pick up her son from school or join them on playdates the semblance of family welcome she invites you to her friend's house for coffee and the friend is a photographer who snaps a couple of pictures of you while you're not looking susan also invites you to a panel she's on at freds at barneys the posh restaurant in the base-ment of the famed department store on madison avenue the other panelists are the legendary newsman pete hamill and the actress isabella rossellini who you loved in blue velvet back in high school you can't stop gawking at the actress her skin so white it's translucent a few weeks into your move you realize in horror that your finances have dwindled to a couple hundred dollars well south of what will be required to secure an apartment of your own and a panic sets in about being deported back to arizona reprieve coming in the form of one of your bennington friends who lives in a farmhouse in concord just outside of boston offering up her basement apartment until you can figure out your next move you spend some of your last money on a bus ticket to boston promising yourself that the exile is only temporary the musician jeff buckley jumps into a river in memphis for a swim and his body washes up a week later a judge says mcdonald's needs to stop aiming its advertising at children another judge says the joe camel cigarette ads must be pulled for the same reason new york giants legend frank gifford is caught cheating on his wife with a flight attendant paid by a tabloid to do it the widow of malcolm x is burned by her grandson the person responsible for blowing up the truck in front of the federal building in oklahoma is found guilty and sentenced to death the boxer mike tyson bites off a piece of the ear of his opponent in a highly publicized boxing match and spits it onto the canvas stopping the fight concord is a wealthy hamlet that looks like a movie set the town center built around an ice cream shop a bookstore some restaurants and an old inn with history dating back to the american revolution you settle into the basement apartment and offer babysitting services for your friend's two small children in exchange for a quiet place to write the novel is coming along you think but the days are long and the summer days especially your friend lets you borrow her car to drive into the town center you notice a group of young people drinking at the bar at the colonial inn and fall in with them they're au pairs blowing off steam europeans working for the summer you're drawn to one in particular the belgian au pair and the summer quickly becomes not one of writing your way back to new york but of afternoon barbecues car trips to race point beach on cape cod a jazz festival in montreal you give in to the fact that you haven't had a girlfriend in half a decade and surrender to the welcome notion that someone likes you the way you've been liked before odds are long on you and the belgian au pair having a relationship not just because she's there only for the summer but because she has a boyfriend back home though without any prodding on your part you learn that the boyfriend back home is a long-expired relationship awaiting termination which encourages you but the boyfriend is also coming to america for a planned trip to hike the grand canyon of all places and as the date draws near you're surprised at how jealous you are even though all assurances are given by the belgian au pair robert mitchum dies from smoking and the next day jimmy stewart dies after he refuses to change the battery in his pacemaker the fashion designer gianni versace is murdered on the steps of his mansion in miami after running out for the morning paper the murderer identified as a serial killer on a spree from somewhere in the midwest for a week or so after everyone wonders where the serial killer is and then he's found hiding on a houseboat firing a bullet into his mouth as the police descend hundreds of virgins converge on the white house to celebrate abstinence the former receptionist at a little rock hotel who claims she was escorted by then governor bill clinton's bodyguard to clinton's hotel room and asked for sexual favors gets a trial date for her lawsuit against the president as the date of the belgian au pair's trip to the grand canyon with her boyfriend looms you find yourself in a state of despair then disbelief when your old friend the manager of the family print shop calls with the offer of flying you home to work for a week while he takes a family vacation cheaper and easier than hiring a temporary worker to take his place you agree immediately and the belgian au pair is apprehensive worried that you're engineering something but you swear you aren't though you can't believe your luck the belgian au pair and her boyfriend fly to phoenix ahead of you to take in the city you try not to think about it though you recommend some places worth seeing when you arrive you realize the boyfriend doesn't speak any english you volunteer to drive them to the grand canyon on the two-plus-hour trip north the boyfriend looks up every time you look in the rearview mirror he can't speak a lick of english but he clearly knows what's going on the belgian au pair is in dismay and you learn later that it ruined their trip which you swear to god was not your intention though you underestimated the tells of your body language and feel sorry for the verbal jabs and fights she had to endure while in the grand canyon back at the print shop for a week is old home week you've been gone for only three months and the fear that your attempt to move to new york is a farce drives you to fax your resume with your friend in concord's address and phone number to every literary agency in new york with a fax machine during lunch with your old friend the southern lawyer you lay out your adventures and the southern lawyer loans you three thousand dollars on the spot against whatever you sell your first book for to help get you back on your feet in new york city princess diana is killed when the car she's riding in crashes during a high-speed chase in paris to elude paparazzi as you leave phoenix for concord the governor who barely won election is convicted of extortion and bank fraud and resigns you and millions of others watch princess diana's funeral on television the two little princes walking along behind their mother's coffin it breaks your heart elton john's song about marilyn monroe that your younger brother loves becomes a song about the late princess only one literary agency calls about an interview in answer to your faxing but it's a famous one whose name you recognize you kiss the belgian au pair good-bye at the airport promising that you'll see each other

again the first chance you get making tentative plans to reunite during the holidays on the bus ride back to new york city with the summer behind you and three thousand dollars minus a little in your
bank account you interview at harold ober associates on madison
avenue the clacking of typewriters greets you as you step through
the door stenciled with the name of the firm perhaps as it was back
when it was founded in 1929 your interview is with the president of
the firm and you learn that the previous president a woman who
worked directly for harold ober himself has just passed away you
learn about the agency in full how most of its clients are long-dead
famous writers like f scott fitzgerald sherwood anderson pearl s
buck james m cain agatha christie william faulkner langston hughes
joseph mitchell dylan thomas and of course j d salinger who isn't
dead but just disappeared the interview takes place in the president's office under the low lighting of desk lamps and through a
cloud of cigarette smoke which you guess must not be legal but
everyone seems to be smoking and though you don't you don't
mind you're offered the job but ask if you can start on september 24
not just because it's fitzgerald's birthday but because your old friend
and fitzgerald fan from college who lives in princeton now wants to
go on a pilgrimage to fitzgerald's grave in maryland your new boss
is amused and all is agreed upon you take the train to princeton and
the next morning you and your college friend light out for rockville
maryland where the fitzgeralds are buried one on top of the other
the closing words of the great gatsby etched in stone on a beveled
flat marker where someone has left some cigarettes and an empty
fifth of whiskey what you know about fitzgerald's funeral comes to
you as sad a scene as gatsby's funeral a man who spent his life as an
amusement to friends across two continents buried with few to no
witnesses you can't believe the small catholic cemetery is sur-
rounded by busy streets and commerce in the distance you can
make out the sign for a furniture store and there's something plainly

ignoble about the final resting place the end is the end is the end no matter who or where you wonder if fitzgerald ever daydreamed about his final resting place full of melancholy as he was you know he probably did and you wonder at the gulf between his imagination and reality though it hardly matters you and your friend grab a quick meal for the trip back to princeton eating on the trunk of her car in a shopping center designed by the grandfather of the actor edward norton whose family is from the area or so your friend thinks you take the train from princeton to new york just as fitzgerald did while he was in college so many of fitzgerald's observations about being on the outside looking in resonate and you think about him being from the midwest and you being from the west and now you ride the elevator to the tenth floor of the building on madison avenue just as fitzgerald did when he pushed through the same door you push every morning to start your day toiling in literary matters your job is little more than clerical sorting and distributing the afternoon mail answering the switchboard while the receptionist is at lunch transcribing your boss's daily dictation answering permissions requests to reprint material by ober clients the names and titles of books you love or at least have heard of adding a measure of intangible glamour to the position also a firsthand glimpse of the publishing game wrapping each manuscript as if it were your own anxious to hear back from the editor your boss sends it to disappointed if the manuscript is returned via courier with a declining letter exuberant when a book sells eager to let the author know all of it an inspiration to finish your novel you stay late after eating dinner at your desk so that you can work but also because you're camping out in the west village in the spare bedroom of a friend from bennington the former drummer for an indie rock band everyone loves and his artist wife and you don't want to be intrusive you've been pretending to be a student looking at the apartment postings on the board at the new school and other places but there's nothing you can afford and your friends are nice enough not to mind your residency in the spare room which has already been let to a high school kid who goes to school in vermont and comes to the city only sometimes his parents paying the rent so he'll have a place the kid tells you it's cool with him if you crash in his room and it seems like the perfect temporary housing the apartment is on the first floor above a twenty-four-hour deli on sixth avenue itself a carnival at all hours of the night you have to walk through the deli to the back to reach the stairs to the apartment sportscaster marv albert goes on trial for sodomizing and biting a women he'd known for years the tabloids full of details like a woman grabbing albert's toupee only for it to come off after four days of testimony albert pleads guilty to a lesser charge the promise keepers a christian organization for men founded by a former college football coach march on washington some suspect the group uses the bible to assert men's superiority over women especially in marriage a handful of women allegedly sexually harassed by president clinton are subpoenaed by the lawyers for paula jones after a month of looking you can't find an apartment share you can afford you're only making seven dollars an hour at harold ober but in truth it's a job you'd do for free and plus there's a line of people behind you figuratively who would love to have the job so you accept the invitation of a girl you know from bennington who lives with her husband and infant in a suburb of connecticut it takes two trains from grand central to reach the apartment but you have to agree and you don't mind the train ride though you smirk about being the only one without a briefcase or laptop but the worst part is the last train out of new york leaves at 10 pm so if you miss it you have to sleep at the office and if you miss the connecting train you have to pay for a cab to take you to the apartment the singer john denver is killed when the plane he is flying runs out of gas you go to see the writer denis johnson read from his new book at the new school and wonder if he remembers a time in the not-too-distant past when he visited the university of arizona and you asked him a couple of questions raising your hand when no one else would out of nervousness or whatever a girl you meet who works for george plimpton the legendary writer and founder of the literary magazine the paris review invites you to one of the equally legendary paris review parties at plimpton's house overlooking the east river the room filled with names and at least some faces you recognize from the literary world a famous television personality bumps you off the corner of the pool table doubling as a buffet table to get to the food you muster up the courage to approach plimpton and immediately invoke bret easton ellis's name and plimpton asks how bret is these days and looks at you as if you and only you can provide an update on bret's health and well-being and you shrug and say fine you say some complimentary things about the paris review and then beg off you feel like a fish swimming in the stream even if you're just a little fish the proximity of the big fish is reassuring inspiring you to keep moving on your novel which is almost finished you communicate by fax with the belgian au pair a fax always awaiting you in the morning because of the time difference phone calls are too expensive though the international faxes come out of your paycheck the longing on her end is palpable and you feel the same way and you promise to figure out a way to visit at thanksgiving though you have no idea if you can some friends from arizona visit and you take them to minetta tavern in the west village the dark-wood low-lit bar a block from the apartment of your friend the former drummer–turned–writer who introduced you to the place where you know the bar manager and his brother who is a waiter the bar has a long history the walls covered with drawings of the people who frequented the place all the way back to the 1800s when it was called the black rabbit some recent pictures too of brad pitt and other movie stars who have graced the booths the bar is busy for a sunday but starts to thin you and your friends inebriated thanks to the kind pour all night long the bar manager asks if you and your friends want to go to ac and you exhale loudly and shrug trying to buy time to figure out the code you've learned that half of everything in new york is pretending to be in the know even when you aren't your friends from arizona aren't shackled by the custom and ask what ac is and the bar manager announces that he's leaving in a limo with his brother the waiter for atlantic city and that you're welcome to join them you know you have to work the next day you know it's well after midnight already but your desire for the adventure with old friends overrides all rational thought and you pile into the white limousine when it appears the bar manager grabbing a bottle from behind the counter which you pass around as the limo leaves manhattan having never been to atlantic city you inquire as to how long the trip will take and are dismayed to learn that it's some two hours away your friends doze off and then you do too until you feel the contents of your stomach sloshing working their way back up your esophagus you ask about opening the moonroof for some air which you think might do the trick and you plunge your head through the opening a few minutes later a stream of cartoon vomit spraying from your mouth as the wind whips around you the sign for asbury park is the last thing you see before falling back into the limo and passing out when the limo pulls up under the casino portico the bar manager and his brother tell you to meet in a couple of hours if you want a ride back they're off to the high-stakes rooms you and your friends quickly lose some money on the slots ordering some free drinks that no one seems to want the sun is starting to rise it's after six with no sign of the limo or the bar manager if you leave right now you can still make it back to work you lean your head against the bus window your friends sleeping in seats across the aisle you sprint from the port authority on the west side of manhattan across fifth avenue to your job on madison avenue only to be excused by

your boss who spying the vomit on your shirt asks if you're ill miracle of miracles you finish your novel based on the first short story
you published and bret easton ellis agrees to read it and give you
some feedback and you can't think about him actually reading your
work without getting your hopes up the lead singer of the band inxs
which you saw all those years ago in high school hangs himself in a
hotel room maybe it's an accident maybe it's something else even a
scurrilous rumor about autoerotic sex gone awry your inability to
save any money lends credence to your suspicion that you'll be run
out of new york by the end of the year unless you can sell your book
for some decent money a good word from bret easton ellis would
help but still you buy what you can't afford an airline ticket to belgium to visit the au pair somewhere in all the faxing you've become
boyfriend and girlfriend she talks about selling the house her parents made her buy as an investment when she was young and moving to new york to study poetry which makes you nervous on a
number of levels you portray new york as a hard place to live which
it is though you suspect it's harder for some than others you haven't
spent enough time with the au pair to know which camp she's in
you pass through customs at the airport in brussels flashing the
passport you procured for the trip the transatlantic love affair feels
like the most romantic thing you've ever done though you're not
sure what the immediate future holds but you also try not to think
about it the airport reunion is joyous and you both laugh about how
it's been only twelve weeks since you've seen each other but it feels
like forever the summer in concord a memory the personalities
already ghosts in your memories even though you're exhausted on
the drive to antwerp you're too wired to rest hungry too you stop at
a small outbuilding just outside antwerp and you both point at
rolled meats under fluorescent lights that are quickly dropped into
a deep-fat fryer you both happily munch at the kitchen table of her
one-bedroom house drinking beer which she reminds you has a

higher alcohol content than american beer you're just two lovers playing house making plans for the next couple of days which include meeting her parents for dinner at their house you do a little laundry before the short trip to her parents' but stuff too many clothes into the dryer so that your nice black shirt isn't dry not even close when it's time to leave so you put it on wet hoping no one will notice her father a small but sturdy man looks you in the eye as he grips your hand pumping it casually you've been warned that her father is stern which immediately puts you in mind to win him over her mother smiles nervously as you are introduced her sisters less nervous than curious you take the chair set out for you in the living room and they gather around to ask you questions the au pair translating back and forth though everyone seems to understand english everyone sits down to chinese food and you tell the story about your wet shirt and soon you are offered a warm sweatshirt also offered glass after glass of wine her father leaving the table and returning with another bottle more than once you are twice the size of anyone in the room and are sure you can hold your liquor so when you wake the next morning back at the au pair's house it is a surprise that at some point you slumped over at the table much to her father's amusement you're assured her father likes you and that is really all you were going for why do you sleep on couches she asks disdain in her voice you can't find the words to express how much you love new york how it feels like home to you even though you have no home to call your own it makes no sense to her and you get into a small skirmish when you decline her offer to move in with her you can't imagine what you'd do all day but she offers that you can write which sounds ideal but something instinctively tells you it's not the answer but she feels like you've made a choice between her and something else no one can put a name to when you part at the brussels airport you promise to come back in a few weeks at christmas hoping that you'll receive a christmas bonus large enough to cover the trip the actor chris farley is found dead in his chicago apartment from a drug overdose paula jones's lawyers subpoena a former white house intern in jones's ongoing sexual harassment suit against the president the director woody allen marries the adopted daughter of his former lover the actress mia farrow who played daisy in the film version of the great gatsby when you pack for the trip back to belgium at christmas you let your friend in connecticut know you won't return and you're not sure if that means just to her apartment or if it means something more you're welcomed like a long-lost son-in-law by the au pair's family when you return but outside of a nice christmas dinner at their house you don't see them your old high school friend from phoenix flies to london and you and the au pair meet him there for a planned trip to celebrate hogmanay the new year's celebration in edinburgh you and your high school friend have always talked about attending but first you stop north of london at the house of a girl your friend met in his travels abroad the house is in willoughby waterleys a small village with a pub at the end of the lane the girl's house is a two-story georgian called the old rectory and she's there with her mother and sisters her youngish father having recently and tragically died while working in the garden the house cast in a pall but in english fashion you're received and put up in the part of the house that has heat you're asked to sign the guest book and you notice the actress helena bonham carter has recently signed it too the next day is spent mostly in the pub followed by a lively dinner with the girl and her family conversation ranges from american politics to european art and you have fun playing the cosmopolitan delivering one-liners and laughing at zingers the au pair excuses herself from the table and after she's gone for an uncomfortably long time you offer a meager joke about her having gotten lost and go after her you find her in your room packing her bag what are you doing are you sick you ask i don't know you she says hatefully concentrating on her packing you ask what she means and she says listening to you at the table she had no idea who was talking about all these things you were talking about where do they come from she demands to know you do your best to calm her down you say you have no idea what she means but intuitively you know you've been speaking to her in clipped sentences and simple thoughts which started as a shorthand but has become how you communicate you snatch her passport now you can't leave you say playing for laughter i'm leaving she says emphatically you get her to agree to sit for ten minutes in silence with you and if she still wants to leave you'll help her figure out how and after ten minutes she announces that she's going to bed in the morning you and the au pair and your high school friend light out for the house in crawford-upon-john another village with a pub but this time in scotland where your high school friend has rented a house for hogmanay assuring you that you're welcome to stay too the housemates are of various nationalities german swedish dutch and they greet you and the au pair warmly a trip to glasgow planned for the following day is scuttled by the ferocious winds that rock the house imprisoning everyone trapped everyone resigns themselves to a day of board games and drinking you sniff some commentary from the other dutchman in the house that the part of belgium the au pair comes from is considered backward and uncosmopolitan comparatively you ignore the taunts exuberant after a restless night to finally be on your way to edinburgh desperate to escape the glumness pervading the house the atmosphere in edinburgh is fes- tive and as the day expires the city center swells with eager faces you and the au pair set up camp in the window of a pub on the royal mile and began drinking in earnest your high school friend wants to float down the river of people but the au pair is happy where she is you promise not to be gone long as you're swept up in the momen- tum of the human parade you somehow swim back to the au pair before midnight when auld lang syne issues forth the hogmanay tradition of kissing everyone around you for the duration of the song commences and the au pair is besieged with kisses before you step in for your own private celebration your high school friend kisses his way down the royal mile and has a nasty cold sore in the morning as proof saying good-bye to the au pair at heathrow you truly have no idea when you'll see her again the novelty of the transatlantic romance seems to have worn off for both of you and now real decisions must be made one of robert kennedy's sons dies when he hits a tree while skiing in aspen your friend the former drummer–turned–writer and his wife the artist with the apartment in the west village once again rescue you by letting you stay in their spare bedroom and you promise them it's only temporary that you're going to find some kind of permanent living situation you're surprised when bret easton ellis returns the copy of the manuscript you gave him and it's covered with edits in black ink you can't believe he read the novel so closely and you set about spending all your free time in the conference room at harold ober working on the edits one night one of the agents spies you working and asks what you're working on and she says to let her read it when you're finished sonny from sonny and cher dies when he hits a tree while skiing in nevada the teacher in washington state impregnated by her twelve-year-old student is released from prison early and told to stay away from the student monica lewinsky files an affidavit in the paula jones lawsuit denying she had a sexual relationship with president clinton and a week or so later president clinton gives similar testimony in addition to the helpful line editing on your novel bret easton ellis has suggested some wholesale changes to the structure which you accept without question someone named matt drudge runs an e-mail newsletter about politics and hollywood gossip and he includes an item about a story by a newsweek magazine reporter about some secretly taped conversations that monica lewinsky's colleague at the pentagon recorded where lewinsky admits having sexual relations with the president drudge's story is just about how the newsweek story was suppressed internally but a couple of days later the scandal hits all the press outlets at once it seems bret easton ellis even suggests some lines to add here and there and you add them all a group of texas cattle ranchers sue oprah winfrey over a show she did a couple of years earlier about beef production in the era of mad cow disease the cattle ranchers claim the show cost them tens of millions in lost beef sales you write a letter to charles scribner on ober letterhead asking if you can meet with him to discuss the scribner history as it relates to harold ober you're thinking about compiling a history of harold ober and he agrees the old scribner building is a block away but is also a clothing store now but scribner's current offices are in the neighborhood and you keep the appointment the third-generation charles scribner is affable and lively as he regales you with some clearly well-worn chestnuts about the golden days of publishing but you do learn something you were ignorant of before the fact that fitzgerald dealt directly with scribner on the contracts for his books using harold ober only for the sale of his short stories because there was so much money in short story sales and very little in the sale of books you're incredulous but when you check the ober files for the contract for the great gatsby you see it's true president clinton reiterates his denials about a sexual relationship with his former intern the only question the press wants to ask him your boss helps you arrange a phone conversation with harold ober's son to learn a little more about his father who is described as a blue-blood yankee from harvard and you both chuckle about what he must've thought of fitzgerald that ober was exactly the type of person fitzgerald was envious of his whole life the son encourages your nascent project and asks you to keep him posted which you promise to do the last living ober client who knew fitzgerald personally lives in concord your old stomping grounds and you write a letter asking to interview the writer the letter is answered by his daughter who tells you the writer is ill but is looking forward to talking to you on the train to boston you admit what you've been denying about the au pair that the relationship has probably petered out the international faxes becoming less frequent though she still professes to love you but your concern is that the more time you spend together the more ill-suited you seem and how can anything be known with so many miles between you your bennington friend picks you up from the train station and you realize how nice it is to get out of the concrete city and into the green suburbs if only briefly you call to confirm your arrival the next day for the interview and the writer's daughter tells you the writer passed away the previous weekend and that the writer thought you were supposed to come the previous weekend the unspoken idea being that he'd been holding on long enough to talk to you but when you didn't show that was that the daughter is distracted by her grief and doesn't hear your apologies the teacher in washington state on parole for having sex with her twelve-year-old student is arrested again when the two are found having sex in her car where she becomes pregnant again monica lewinsky postpones the deposition she was to give in the paula jones case now that the whole world is watching you turn in the finished version of your novel to the agent who asked and she reads it over the weekend professing her love for it and the following week she begins submitting it to publishers you can't believe you have a manuscript being read by editors in new york city but you have to keep a brave face when the first editor the agent queries turns the book down there are plenty of other editors you're assured and so the long process of trying to find a match with an editor begins monica lewinsky wants immunity from kenneth starr who is leading the investigation of president clinton and his alleged misdeeds a white male in his thirties is arrested at sky harbor airport in phoenix for verbally abusing an airport employee and it turns out to be axl rose the front man of guns n' roses that no one has seen in years the rumor is he lives in a mansion by the ocean in california and never leaves it just rehearsing and rehearsing music no one will ever hear the au pair surprises you by showing up unannounced in new york for valentine's day since you're just crashing in your friend's extra room you scramble to pay for a hotel with money you can't really afford to waste which sets the tone for her visit you refusing to move to belgium her refusing to believe that you don't want to or at least wouldn't benefit from the stability you can't find the words to explain to her that your life in new york is just beginning or so it seems but also it feels selfish to admit that you're more invested in that narrative than the one that began the summer before and a few days after she returns home you say into the phone that it's best if you both call it off she refuses to agree telling you that you'll have to hang up on her because she's not going to agree and you beg her not to make you but she repeats herself and you replace the phone in its cradle and wipe your slick cheeks before returning to work president clinton argues that paula jones's lawsuit should be thrown out or at least delayed until he's no longer president more editors send polite rejection letters for your novel but you continue to hope for the best knowing it could take a year or more for the agent to work her way through all the publishers big and small a homemade sex tape of the actress pamela anderson and her husband tommy lee the drummer for the heavy-metal band mötley crüe stolen by a disgruntled electrician working on their house becomes available to the public for purchase the actress and the drummer claim the tape has been leaked widely enough that the only recourse is to strike a distribution deal to receive a share of the monies for the video you saw it when it first came out at a brunch thrown by the music video editor for atlantic records you met through your former drummer–turned–writer friend the video lives up to the hype but you can't decide if tommy and pamela are truly that exhibitionist or if they knew in their heart of hearts that others might one day see the video an editor declines to publish your novel saying if he were still working at the previous house where he'd worked he'd publish it in a second which seems like a compliment but doesn't sit like one kenneth starr subpoenas the bookstore where monica lewinsky shops and learns that she recently purchased a copy of vox by nicholson baker a book in the form of a phone sex conversation the agent representing you comes to your desk and says she shouldn't tell you this but she just got off the phone with an editor who is halfway through your book and knows he wants to buy it the publisher is one of the smaller ones so the money wouldn't be spectacular but the publisher is well regarded which could mean some critical success you have a hard time refraining from mentioning this bit of intel to your friends who are curious how it's going the judge throws out paula jones's sexual harassment suit against president clinton one half of the disgraced musical duo milli vanilli the ones who had to give back their grammy when it was revealed they were lip-synchers is found dead in his hotel room from a drug overdose on the eve of the release of milli vanilli's comeback album featuring actual vocals from the duo there's no word from the editor who wants to publish your book but the agent says to give him a little more time a show from britain called teletubbies debuts on pbs and everyone gaggles about how weird the teletubbies are wondering what exactly they're supposed to be and why they have televisions for stomachs the anxiety about the silence from the editor interested in publishing your novel is distracting and your agent finally places a call to see if there's any news and she looks ashen when she reports that the editor left suddenly to go work for aol his office having already been cleaned out you're devastated but relieved that you never mentioned a word of it to anyone and you put all your hopes on the editors who are still considering the book a man follows the pop singer george michael into a bathroom at will rogers park in beverly hills and says show me yours and i'll show you mine and when he does the man who is a cop arrests him for engaging in a lewd act drinks with friends at minetta's for your birthday and you're standing at the crowded bar trying to get the bar manager's attention and when you look in the mirror behind the bar you see the actor who played ferris bueller is standing next to you and it takes everything you have not to turn to him and tell him how much you loved ferris and fancied that you were him when you were in high school and when you wake in the morning with a concussive headache you're proud of yourself for having not said a word president clinton holds his first public press conference since the lewinsky scandal broke and is livid about the inquiry initiated by kenneth starr frank sinatra dies and the empire state building is lit up blue as a tribute you stumble to the subway after a night of drinking and all the bars are blasting sinatra music your colleague at harold ober the other assistant has been asking if you want to hang out he's a lot younger than you are just like all the assistants in publishing and so you put it off but then one night agree and end up shooting pool with him and his friend who is an assistant to one of the editors who read your novel the friend really liked the novel and says so which means more to you than it should the comedian phil hartman is murdered in his sleep by his wife while their two children sleep in their rooms in the same house the wife flees and brings back a friend to try to help her figure out what to do and when the friend isn't looking she locks herself in the house and commits suicide a friend who runs the print shop at memorial sloan kettering cancer center scores two tickets to the yankees game which stops with a rain delay you don't know any-thing about baseball but know the history of yankee stadium how-ever the awe wears off the more it rains and the drunker everyone gets the game finally restarts and the opposing team the hated rival boston red sox score right away and your friend being from boston cheers them on to the dismay of those around you and some guys want to make an issue of it but your friend won't back down and you sit tense wondering what will happen next but then the yankees start winning which is the balm the situation needs you're starting to become a regular at george plimpton's place on east seventy-second street this time for a book party for a novelist who dedicated his book to bret easton ellis which is your only interest in attending save for the free food and drinks you meet the writer jonathan ames who is in awe of plimpton and fitzgerald and seems to emulate both not just fitzgerald's sensitivity but also the tenets of plimpton's participatory journalism plimpton having written about the time he quarterbacked for the detroit lions or pitched to willie mays or took a bullet from john wayne you recall fitzgerald's advice to his daughter when she professed wanting to become a writer you can't do something for the sake of writing about it but george plimpton surely could and did the writer at bennington who helped save you from the debacle of the teacher who disappeared is reading at the national arts club a private club that once boasted mark twain as a member you're concerned about the dress code when you see a sign that gentlemen must wear jackets after 5 pm but the only true hassle is the bartender who refuses to see you your boss at harold ober agrees to let you train to princeton on fridays to root around in the ober archives for your history of harold ober project you stroll the princeton quad passing students roughly your age wondering if they mistake you for one of their own you stand before the house on prospect avenue where fitzgerald lived as a student hunting fitzgerald's ghost in every corner of campus the irony of his being one of princeton's most famous alums even though he never actually graduated you finally settle into a chair in firestone library and summon the first box of the ober archives gingerly flipping through files of yellowed typewritten letters surprising in their lack of detail about ober the man letters devoid of gossip or news of the day your hope of preserving a romantic history fluttering away as you comb through the boxes and you end up canceling the weekly train trips a few weeks into the project one of the spice girls ginger spice announces that she's leaving the all-girl supergroup in order to launch a solo career a respite in the cobbling together of beds and couches comes in the form of a room to rent inside a warehouse in an industrial section of brooklyn called dumbo an unfortunate acronym for down under the manhattan bridge overpass dumbo is little more than artists squatting in their studios there are no services and at night the streets become deadly quiet but the room is cheap and so you move your stuff into a building with a helmet factory on the fifth floor the window in your small room overlooks the power plant next door the east river just beyond and you think about how just up the river is george plimpton's opulent apartment and how that's worlds away from where you'll be resting your head your roommate is an artist friend of the artist going out with the former drummer–turned–writer which is how you heard of the sublet your roommate's art is across many mediums but one of the more recent ones is her painting her body in latex and then performing at local burlesque shows stripping down and then stripping her skin you see one of these performances on a videotape you mistake for a movie one day when you're home sick from work president clinton is subpoenaed in the lewinsky matter a few days later lewinsky meets with kenneth starr and admits to a sexual encounter with the president the very next day lewinsky is granted immunity president clinton agrees to testify voluntarily lewinsky hands over one of her dresses which rumor has it contains some of the president's dna on it the little kid from diff'rent strokes everyone loved is arrested for punching a woman who asks for his autograph while he's shopping for a bulletproof vest for his job as a security guard paula jones's lawyers appeal to have her lawsuit against the president reinstated bret easton ellis invites you to dinner at the bowery bar a chic bar and grill a known haunt of actors and models bret also invites two other writers he knows one of them you know as a writer whose work bret discovered as a zine in tower records bret recommended the writer to someone and the writer got a book deal so you're naturally a little jealous but you honestly think the writer's work isn't very good but maybe that's just jealousy the other writer is someone bret attended bennington with and you're starting to feel like a fish out of water until bret favorably mentions your as-yet-unpublished novel to the others and they pepper you with sincere questions about it and wish you good luck trying to get it published and you admit that you suspect it's not going to happen they suggest starting something new and whether or not you will feels like a test of your confidence in your first novel finding a publisher immunity in hand monica lewinsky testifies before the grand jury you relax on the porch of the davis alumni house at bennington college taking in the summer landscape as you and your friend from boston await the arrival of your fellow benningtonites the former drummer–turned–writer and his artist girlfriend as well as the woman who lent you her basement apartment in concord the five of you chipping in to rent the house to get some work done faced with the reality that your first novel has been seen by every publisher in and out of new york without garnering any interest you know you need to start a new writing project the consistent criticism about your first novel being too dark stung even though books that are dark or called small are considered literary the preferred label of most writers you know your time as a student at bennington impressed upon you that literary distinction is preferable to money or wide readership a theory that your job in publishing has all but erased you wonder if it isn't possible to shoot for both and you have this in mind when you spend your week at the alumni house casting about for ideas for a new book lighting on the notion of using your second published story we're so famous as a springboard for a novel the short story is only eight pages long so there's room to enlarge

the narrative around the theme of celebrity obsession you're thinking about a gentle criticism of society's infatuation with frivolity
and minutiae about celebrities nothing overt or harsh especially
since you're in no way above the fray though part of you feels
manipulated into being interested in things you wouldn't normally
care about you use the first-person voice of the short story and just
start writing and by the end of the week you have close to eighty
pages having taken breaks only for dinner and nightly carousing
with the others you're so excited about the new pages that you show
them to your agent back at ober hoping she'll be excited too but she
frowns and complains that the book makes women look dumb
you're so upset that you put the pages in a drawer and try to forget
them instead researching small foreign publishers who might be
interested in publishing your first novel outside of america which
you're fine with president clinton becomes the first sitting president
to give testimony to a grand jury investigating him he goes on television after giving his testimony and admits that he had an improper
relationship with monica lewinsky but did not have sexual relations
with her there's a rumor in the press that the president has submitted a dna sample to kenneth starr and word about monica lewinsky's unlaundered blue dress leaks out major league baseball players
mark mcgwire and sammy sosa are in a race to break the long-held
single-season home run record and mcgwire finally does in a game
against sosa's team kenneth starr turns in the results of his investigation and calls for the impeachment of president clinton whose
four-hour grand jury testimony is leaked to the networks who air it
in full bret easton ellis calls you at work to tell you that you're mentioned in a new york times article about kgb bar where you and
your former drummer–turned–writer friend will be reading your
short stories published in literary magazines you run across the
street and buy a copy showing everyone in the office the full-page
article staring at your name in print the woman who previously

stalked late-night host david letterman stealing his porsche and sleeping near the tennis courts of his home in connecticut kneels in front of a train in colorado the house of representatives authorizes an impeachment inquiry against president clinton sportscaster marv albert's criminal record is wiped clean after a year of good behavior two teens in wyoming pretend to be gay and lure an openly gay kid to a remote area and beat and rob him and chain him to a fence where he's discovered eighteen hours after he dies less than a week later from his beating president clinton signs legislation meant to prepare the government for the upcoming millennium-bug problem something about banks not being able to recognize the year 2000 because they previously used only two digits instead of four when writing computer software not just banks but lots of problems maybe on the horizon some say it'll be the end of civilization when computers think the year 2000 is really the year 1900 the actor michael j fox who played that kid you loved on that show when you were a kid and all the back to the future movies too announces he has parkinson's disease the new york tabloids are ablaze with headlines about the comedian jerry seinfeld and a woman he met at a health club who was recently married to the son of a prominent theater family the woman ends the marriage after four months and begins dating seinfeld president clinton settles with paula jones over her lawsuit without admitting any wrongdoing among your cherished responsibilities working at harold ober is opening the mail as a kid you would join fan clubs and send away for things just to have a reason to run to the mailbox at ober the mail arrives in two or three mailbags every afternoon and it's your job to sort the query letters manuscripts royalty statements fan mail and the like the most interesting mail is always from j d salinger bearing a typewritten return address somewhere in vermont the envelopes usually stuffed with items salinger considers a nuisance or matters he needs his agent your boss to handle directly the cover letter to his agent your boss is never signed though salinger prints his name anything with his signature is considered valuable and owing to some contracts recently stolen from the agency that handles his foreign rights you spend a couple of days photocopying all of ober's correspondence and contracts involving salinger and shredding the originals under the eye of your boss there is something admirable in the way salinger refuses any of his work to be reprinted or adapted the television show freaks and geeks writes for permission to use a copy of the catcher in the rye as a prop in a scene and ober responds with salinger's long-standing policy against such a thing hoping the producers wouldn't ferret out that when the mel gibson julia roberts movie conspiracy theory asked to use the book as a central prop to the movie and were told no they realized they didn't need permission a start-up called amazon sends over a script for a proposed television commercial featuring delivery of a box to a house in the woods wherein the house's occupant merely slats the blinds as the delivery person walks past a mailbox emblazoned with the name salinger which ober declines even though you all laugh about it around the office but any whiff of infringement is no laughing matter the fbi has been involved in a case going back to the 1970s when someone offered for sale a book of all twenty-two of salinger's short stories selling them all over the country out of the back of a vehicle no one could describe by a bookseller that no one could identify the burgeoning internet provides an avenue for further sales of the bootleg book and when ober notices it for sale on the auction site ebay we write them a letter demanding they remove the item ebay's initial response is the standard fare that outside of body parts and other egregiousness they are not responsible for the content of auctions transacted on their site but a second letter warning them of their complicity in trafficking in copyright infringement brings the desired result and you are assigned a new daily routine perusing ebay for illegal salingeralia the question you field the most from friends is whether or not the catcher in the rye will ever be made into a movie and you say not in the author's lifetime it's his wish for all his work that none of it be adapted for film some story about a disaster the time one of his short stories was filmed with his permission so when an advance article appears in the new york times about an iranian film festival at lincoln center that will feature a film based on salinger's franny and zooey the ober forces mobilize quickly the attorney ober keeps on retainer on salinger's behalf is apprised of the situation and though there's no copyright convention between the united states and iran preventing the making of the film the fact that the film is being shown on united states soil will make it easy to quash on the grounds that it is a violation of salinger's copyright your boss lays this out in a letter to salinger with the note asking for further instructions from him the timing is bad though as your boss is leaving on one of the scarce vacations she takes so in her letter to salinger she tells him just to call and talk to you about what he wants to do your boss tells you that the author is suffering from some deafness and that you'll have to shout into the phone if he calls you don't think he'll really call so you're surprised when you pick up the phone at your desk and the deep gravelly voice on the other end says your name with a question mark at the end in an accusatory way and then says salinger here i think we ought to do something about this thing you tell him you'll give the message to the lawyer and salinger says very good and then good-bye when you hang up you are a little shaken by what has just transpired the same as if you'd seen a ghost the lawyer stops the showing at lincoln center and the whole matter disappears just like that your friend from bennington who lives in brooklyn has been working on a memoir about drinking in bars every night and to celebrate the near end he invites everyone he knows to mcsorley's old ale house where he'll be in residence for twelve straight hours you go for a lot of it happy to celebrate the success of his fieldwork but also the end of another year in new york for you with all its ups and downs bret easton ellis invites you to his annual christmas party one of the more exclusive holiday parties and you make the mistake of attending alone thinking that you aren't allowed to bring anyone but when you arrive you see that bret's loft has been cleared of all furniture save for a stereo system in the corner screeching at levels making conversation intolerable bret shyly hiding in the corner near the stereo console while people approach him you also bring a christmas gift a photocopy of the contract for the great gatsby but no one else has brought anything and you submarine the manila envelope near the catered food and get in line for a drink nodding at bret who maybe does or doesn't see you recognize some faces but not the girl who is standing next to you hanging on the extremely tall guy you recognize as one of the editors behind the new york literary magazine open city but then the girl turns in profile and you see it's the actress parker posey and you just smile and nod rather than make a fuss about how great you think she is the population of the loft doubles and triples it seems and you think there's no way all these people were invited and without finishing your drink you escape grabbing your coat from the coat check bret has set up in the lobby of his building president clinton is impeached by the house of representatives for lying under oath and obstructing justice only the second president in history to be impeached after andrew johnson who was impeached for removing the secretary of war and replacing him with ulysses s grant the new year opens with clinton's senate trial by now the facts and alleged facts of the matter well known basketball player michael jordan retires for the last time and for good you head up to bennington with some friends to hang around the residency see old teachers and participate on a publishing panel extolling what you've gleaned about working in publishing without trying to sound too defeatist you don't let the reality that you're an alum with a novel that failed to sell ruin the homecoming back in new york you see the writer jonathan ames in his one-man show oedipussy and witness firsthand how much ames idolizes george plimpton the show an incredible bridge between ames's work and his persona you think about how having a persona is oftentimes the difference between the mortal and immortal especially when it comes to writers there's always some memorable backstory stories outside the covers of their books that keep authors alive in everyone's imagination none more than fitzgerald but also bret easton ellis whom you have drinks with the following night bret amused by all you tell him about jonathan's show you also let him know that your first novel failed to find a publisher and he encourages you just to move on from it and you remember the pages of the new project you shelved and look them over devising a way to revise the material so that the entire novel isn't told from just one point of view which you suspect is what turned your agent off the televangelist jerry falwell warns parents that one of the teletubbies the one called tinky winky is really gay and bad for children a twenty-two-year-old immigrant from guinea is shot forty-one times on the landing of his apartment in the bronx by four police officers who mistake him for a rape suspect and further mistake his reaching for his wallet as him reaching for a gun you place another short story with a small literary magazine which gives you some much-needed confidence as you dive into the revision of we're so famous the senate votes to acquit president clinton of his impeachment charges the thing over except for everyone's divided opinions about it you pitch the idea of editing an all-interview issue of the mississippi review using your interview with bret easton ellis as a centerpiece and are awarded the commission you tap your closest bennington friends to come on board and interview their favorite writers everyone excited about the project the film critic gene siskel who owns the suit john travolta wore in the movie saturday night fever dies from complications after surgery for brain cancer your friend from college your former literary magazine coeditor blows through new york with her best friend who happens to work for notorious boxing promoter don king and who can get tickets to practically anything and invites you to the broadway show cabaret featuring the actress jennifer jason leigh attending the show you realize there are whole swaths of new york you know nothing about the broadway district one of them that cabaret is based on the writings of christopher isherwood a writer you're vaguely familiar with comes as a surprise you've previously given no thought to the idea of musicals being based on literary works doctor jack kevorkian the euthanasia booster present at a number of suicides over the years is arrested when he actually helps someone commit suicide the magician david blaine is buried in a plastic coffin under a tank of water for a week across the street from trump plaza everyone stopping by to have their picture taken with the entombed magician you move out of the warehouse in dumbo and back into the spare bedroom in the west village apartment of your friend the former drummer–turned–writer and his artist girlfriend the rapper puff daddy is arrested for assaulting the manager of another rapper over a crucifixion scene in a music video you and your friend the former drummer–turned–writer are asked to teach a hemingway story to a class of high school students at the kennedy library in boston for the hemingway centennial the hemingway room at the kennedy library is a memorial to the writer and his life and works you're not much of a hemingway fan having long ago chosen fitzgerald's side of the literary contretemps promoted through legend though you recognize that the idea of having to choose sides is ridiculous same as the east coast/west coast rap thing two seniors dressed in trench coats walk into their colorado high school and open fire killing twelve students and a teacher and injuring almost two dozen other students before committing suicide in the school's library the all-interview issue of the mississippi review comes together easily and you turn everything in eager to

see it in print on the eve of being retried by the government your
old boss charles h keating jr pleads guilty to wire and bankruptcy
fraud and receives a sentence of time already served ending the
legal proceedings against him you sell another short story to a literary magazine a little bit of a roll happening the girl who played the
sister on diff'rent strokes dies of an accidental overdose love letters
between j d salinger and a college girl he famously seduced are sold
by the college girl at auction at sotheby's and purchased by a software magnate who returns them to salinger via harold ober and
you shred them while your boss watches you turn in the final draft
of your new novel we're so famous to your agent but she still doesn't
like it well enough to represent it but you beg her to try a few publishers just to see agreeing to drop the matter if the editors concur
the agent agrees sportscaster marv albert is given back his old job at
nbc bret easton ellis invites you to drinks with jay mcinerney at a
bar called pop around the corner from bret's loft in the east village
and mcinerney makes a crack about bret traveling a long distance
and you watch in amusement as they banter back and forth the
handful of editors your agent sends we're so famous to decline the
manuscript and that's that though you still feel strongly about the
book you send it on your own to your colleague's friend the one you
shot pool with and who said he liked your first book but the manuscript comes back your colleague's friend having left his job the
small plane piloted by john f kennedy jr goes missing on a flight
from new jersey to his family's compound on martha's vineyard
where he was to attend the wedding of a cousin president clinton
orders u.s. navy warships to assist in the search and the wreckage
and bodies of kennedy and his wife and the wife's sister are found
five days later you take the subway down to the loft apartment in
tribeca where jfk jr lived to see the shrine of flowers and photos and
notes no one can figure out for sure if the movie the blair witch
project is real or not you see it even though you don't really like

horror films and you can't tell but think the marketing campaign is to blame for the confusion which is the filmmaker's intention and everyone proclaims the use of the internet in this way as genius the government pays the heirs of abraham zapruder tens of millions of dollars rather than relinquish the footage of kennedy's assassination they confiscated that november day in dallas a couple you don't know personally but who are friends of friends abandon their apartment in queens for a better apartment the rent all paid up on the old place so you buy an inflatable mattress and camping lantern and sleep on the floor of the empty apartment the early-morning light streaming in through the curtainless rooms when the month is over you're able to crash temporarily on the couch in the upper east side apartment of your agent who spends most of her time upstate the literary agent's boyfriend a bartender and the father of the actor dylan mcdermott is your roommate though you hardly see each other the calendar turns to october and you're out of couches and connections to places to sleep so you move your meager possessions into the harold ober offices the hardest part about living at ober is fooling the twenty-four-hour doormen whom you simply befriend rather than insult they look the other way when you sneak a bag of laundry out of the building or when you duck out early in the morning to grab a shower at the health club you join on a trial membership for just that purpose you sleep on your boss's floor because of the padding under her rug which is the most comfortable spot a dancer you meet through your bennington friend writing the bar memoir is called away on tour and you sublet her tiny studio apartment in brooklyn while she's away michael jackson's wife debbie rowe files for divorce a new show on television that claims to be unscripted debuts apparently people are stuck in the wild and have to participate in rounds of challenges to earn points for the right to stay the learjet carrying golfer payne stewart from florida to texas veers off course and the fighters that scrambled to escort it see that everyone inside is dead they follow the jet north and rather than shoot it down they wait for it to run out of fuel which it does and crashes in a field in south dakota you track down your colleague's friend who liked your first novel who is now working at a different publisher and send him we're so famous the mississippi review selects a short story you wrote for inclusion in their prize issue when the dancer returns you're homeless again and your agent lets you stay at her place again as she'll be away for most of november and december for the holidays after some serious deliberations your friend the former drummer–turned–writer and you decide to join the movement of literary magazines being founded in new york by starting your own you use what contacts you have to learn about distribution subscription drives how to keep databases and how to avoid production nightmares you both assemble a staff made up of friends from bennington and from your travels in new york one of the fiction editors suggests calling the magazine post road since half the editors are in new york and half are in boston and all the founding editors are excited for the venture the rapper jay z is arrested for stabbing a record executive your boss throws a christmas party at her apartment and you meet ira levin the longtime harold ober client who wrote rosemary's baby and other famous books you shower him with praise even though you haven't read his work a practice that has now become rote but levin's humility strikes you and you engage him in a conversation about the history of harold ober of which he says he's proud to be a part the beatle george harrison is stabbed in his home by an intruder the rapper puff daddy and his girlfriend the actress jennifer lopez are at a new york city nightclub where a scuffle breaks out shots are fired and the rapper is arrested as the clock counts down to the year 2000 the overzealous wait with bated breath for the end of times but when the calendar turns to january all that really happens is a couple of credit card machines refuse to process sales and a bank of slot machines at a casino in delaware all quit working a friend of a friend knows someone in williamsburg brooklyn where your friend who is writing the bar memoir lives who needs a roommate and you move in your room is fully furnished with the stuff from the previous tenant the best friend of your new roommate but best friend no more as he started sleeping with his friend's girlfriend who was also living in the apartment the friend and the girlfriend having decamped the common bathroom has no lights so you buy some battery-powered lighting for use in the middle of the night you've all but given up on hearing from your colleague's friend and the new year brings the sober reality that you're starting from square one writing-wise but then an e-mail arrives in your inbox from your colleague's friend in his capacity at bloomsbury usa the american publishing arm of the british publisher that has made piles of dough publishing the harry potter books asking if you'd be interested in having your novel published as a paperback original meaning it wouldn't come out as a hardcover and meaning that there wouldn't be a lot of review coverage since paperback originals are hardly reviewed but you hardly care about that and you say yes definitely and your colleague's friend answers that in that case he'd like to acquire the book and publish it your new editor writes back with effusive praise for the novel and says he'll get an official offer to you in a day or two having seen publishing deals at ober fall apart you keep the great news of your impending publication to yourself also genuinely afraid of jinxing the prospect an idea you think ridiculous until your editor seems to disappear two days three days a week goes by with no word you don't want to start your publishing relationship off panicking about the offer so you busy yourself at work glad that you didn't say anything to anyone about the e-mail the colleague you have in common with your new editor has long since left ober and so you have no insight into what's going on you think about whether or not the book deal is real every second of every minute of the day the rapper puff daddy is charged in the incident in the nightclub with jennifer lopez all of the post road editors begin soliciting work for their respective sections fiction poetry nonfiction theater criticism and art the band rage against the machine plays a concert on wall street and the swelling crowds cause the markets to close early for security reasons you look up from your desk to find the film agent and the foreign-rights agent two colleagues that have like everyone at ober come to seem like family the agents smile and hand you the fax from bloomsbury usa with the offer for we're so famous word leaks out quickly and every-one congratulates you your new editor e-mails to say he's faxed the offer apologizing for the delay but he was out for two weeks with the flu offer in hand you tell your friends who all convene at minetta's in the west village to celebrate a reality show called who wants to marry a multi-millionaire airs to enormous ratings the contest pits fifty women one from each state against each other for the chance to marry a millionaire they've never met at the end of the show the bride is chosen and marries the millionaire right then and there walking off the set with a three-carat diamond and tens of thou-sands of dollars in wedding presents because bloomsbury usa is a small office in new york you negotiate your contract with the uk office which means by fax and the old routine you used to employ to communicate with the belgian au pair resumes this time with the woman in the contracts office in london your colleagues at ober help you negotiate a fair contract and the back-and-forth with lon-don is nothing but cordial there's some question as to whether or not the millionaire from the reality show is actually a millionaire and it comes to light that the millionaire is using a fake name and his former girlfriend had to file a restraining order against him when she ended their relationship bloomsbury uk decides to publish a british edition of we're so famous in the summer and you're assigned a british editor as well mostly to work on the cover the bride of the millionaire wants the marriage annulled and tells everyone that the relationship was not consummated on the honeymoon all the police officers who riddled the immigrant reaching for his wallet with forty-one bullets are acquitted the rapper puff daddy pleads not guilty to charges he tried to bribe his driver into saying the gun used at the nightclub shooting was his the video producer for atlantic records that you met through your friend the former drummer–turned–writer has offices in midtown near harold ober and she invites you over for lunch in the atlantic records cafeteria and you can't believe the smorgasbord available for pennies on the dollar to those who can afford otherwise your editor takes you to lunch to celebrate your signing the contract and you meet for hangar steaks at les halles a parisian brasserie on park avenue near your editor's office in the flatiron building proximity is not the only connection the restaurant enjoys its executive chef is anthony bourdain another bloomsbury author bourdain brings your hangar steaks and chats for a bit before disappearing back into the kitchen his ponytail the last you see of him your editor who resembles a young john f kennedy jr reiterates his praise for we're so famous and you touch on what's ahead in terms of copyediting and designing the cover and asking writers for blurbs you say you think you can get a few blurbs easily and he leaves that task to you the marriage between the bride and the millionaire is finally annulled after a late night of drinking with your friend who is writing the bar memoir you're stranded on the subway platform far from brooklyn with a sudden urge to urinate you drift away from your friends and the crowds of people walking into the tunnel a little ways and relieve yourself when you walk back into the light a half a dozen or so off-duty police officers also waiting for the train pull out the badges they're wearing around their necks and you're arrested and released with a ticket on the spot much to the amusement of your friends your editor commissions a photo shoot in a limousine with two girls dressed in '80s clothes for the cover of your book the first part of advance payment from bloomsbury arrives and you write a check to the southern lawyer back in phoenix who loaned you the money he couldn't be more surprised to be repaid so quickly a cuban boy whose mother drowned trying to cross the waters into florida and who has been staying with his relatives in miami is seized and returned to cuba to the boy's father the tug-of-war between the united states and cuba over the boy won by cuba you concoct the idea of an oral biography of bret easton ellis much like george plimpton's book about edie sedgwick you plan to talk to all of bret's friends and contemporaries excited about the idea you bring it to bret who smiles and assents to your exploring it telling you to keep him posted the rapper eminem is arrested twice once for assaulting a man he witnessed kissing his estranged wife outside of a nightclub and another time for waving a gun at rival rappers insane clown posse the copyediting of your book commences you're given a printout of your manuscript with queries from the copyeditor most of which you can answer easily but one about the spelling of one of the singers in bananarama you're not sure about and you hunt through some local record stores for the answer a concorde flight takes off from paris and crashes immediately killing everyone on board an agent in the midst of a divorce rents an empty office at harold ober and you ask him to represent the oral biography of bret easton ellis and he agrees to send it around for you the rapper eminem records a song wherein he describes killing his estranged wife you ask bret for a blurb for we're so famous and he gives you one that nails what you're trying to convey jaime clarke pulls off a sympathetic act of sustained male imagination entering the minds of innocent teenage girls dreaming of fame a glibly surreal world where the only thing wanted is notoriety and all you really desire leads to celebrity and where stardom is the only point of reference what's new about this novel is how unconsciously casual the characters' drives are this lust is as natural to them as being american it's almost a birthright imagine britney spears narrating the day of the locust as a gentle fable and you'll get the idea your editor loves the blurb too and says he'll put it on the cover ditto the british editor and the british edition eminem's estranged wife attends his concert on his promise that he won't perform the song he wrote about her but he does anyway and she leaves distraught getting in a car wreck on the way home once home she tries to commit suicide by slitting her wrists the british cover for we're so famous is a beautiful shot of the hollywood sign traced over in pink the writer and now raconteur jonathan ames also gives you a blurb darkly and pinkly comic this is the story of a trio of teenage american girls and their pursuit of the three big m's of american life music movies and murder this is an impressive debut by a talented young novelist everyone is afraid of contracting the west nile virus which is spread through mosquitoes the bride who had her tv marriage to the millionaire annulled poses for playboy the last blurb for we're so famous comes from bob shacochis a national book award-winning author you know from bennington like a make-up artist jaime clarke is a master illusionist in his deft hands emptiness seems full teenage pathos appears sassy and charming we're so famous is a blithe highly entertaining indictment of the permanent state of adolescence that trademarks our culture a made-for-tv world where innocence is hardly a virtue ambition barely a value system eminem files for divorce from his estranged wife and she sues him for ten million dollars for defaming her in the song he wrote about her all of the pieces that constitute the first issue of post road are gathered by the editors and your friend who runs the print shop at memorial sloan kettering and who is also the theater editor and publisher begins laying out the magazine you head to the print shop every day after your job at harold ober to help with the design and printing all of the editors who can congregate at the print shop after hours and help collate and bind too you come home to your apartment and find all the furniture in your bedroom gone having forgotten that it belongs to your roommate's friend and so you cobble together the couch cushions for the night before arranging for a new mattress to be delivered working the switchboard at harold ober late on a friday afternoon before you're supposed to hop a train to visit your friend who works for the paris review at her parents' house in the hamptons you answer a call for the divorced agent who is soliciting editors with your proposed oral biography of bret easton ellis the divorced agent is gone for the weekend and you say so and the caller reveals himself to be a reporter for new york magazine looking to track you down for a comment about an article they're going to run about bret refusing to cooperate with the oral biography all your nerves are snapping as you pretend not to have any contact information to give and you get off the phone as quickly as possible brooding on the train about what's going on if you've offended bret in some way worried that you've done something terrible the whole episode threatens the nice weekend you've planned with your friend who works for the paris review and when she picks you up at the train station she senses something and you blurt it all out she offers to help says she has a friend from college who is a hacker and who can get into the new york magazine server you say yes please and after an hour or so you're holding a printout of the article new york magazine is going to publish called bret easton ellis evades history which reads bret easton ellis has always had a knack for getting press but young writers looking to hitch their wagons to his publicity mule should look elsewhere the american psycho author tells us he is refusing to cooperate with an oral history of his life and work being written by fellow bennington alum jamie clarke according to inside.com clarke intends to interview such literary folk as tama janowitz jay mcinerney and joan didion so why won't ellis touch the project with a ten-foot pen a friend of his tells us he just isn't in the mood but another tipster says that ellis was put off when he found out that a character in clarke's upcoming debut novel we're so famous is bryan metro a character from ellis's the informers more bad news for clarke who could not be reached for comment comes from an editor at a top publisher who's been pitched the project we saw the proposal and we were like no it does not make any sense to do this says the insider explaining that ellis is too young for his bio to make a good read the literary biographies that work are about the range of a person's life unless you've got a writer in an older stage it's hard to see any evolution well we're sure clarke will dig up something you vow to avoid bret for a while and when you do see him again you ask if he saw the article and he smiles and says he saw it and that's that a pop culture magazine called shout publishes an early excerpt of we're so famous by arrangement with bloomsbury usa and the magazine editor asks if you want to contribute nonfiction and you pitch an article about how the rapper tupac shakur's fans believe he isn't really dead and will rise again on a date in the future you're not much of a rap fan so you consult your youngest brother who is to get the facts straight shout loves the idea and runs the piece the whitewater investigation against president clinton closes without any charges being leveled the first issue of post road comes out and you arrange back-to-back parties in bars in new york city and boston to celebrate both attended by most of the editors and a lot of writers who welcome the magazine into the literary world mister rogers from mister rogers' neighborhood is diagnosed with stomach cancer and announces the end of his show he'll tape a handful of episodes to wind the show down that will air in the coming months your roommates sit around the television giggling about how they voted for ralph nader for president but then disbelief sets in as they watch the election results roll in it all coming down to which candidate vice president al gore or texas governor george w bush wins the state of florida

271

most of the television networks call florida for gore but a couple of hours later they retract and think maybe the votes mostly belong to bush early the next morning gore calls bush to concede but on his way to thank his supporters his aides tell him that florida is too close to call so he doubles back to his campaign headquarters and calls bush to rescind his concession because the margin of victory for bush is so slim the state of florida initiates a recall next day the popular vote totals are released for the election and gore has about 150,000 more votes than bush but neither has enough electoral votes to win gore asks for a hand count in some counties but the results have to be certified within a week and the secretary of state admits they'll be lucky to make the deadline two days later bush wants an injunction to stop the hand recounts next day the hand counting expands to more counties next day a judge rejects bush's injunction to stop the hand recounts one of the larger democratic counties votes against hand recounting next day florida officials vote to delay further recounts until they can clarify if they have the right to undertake the recounts also a judge in palm beach hears a case about poor ballot design which might've led some voters wanting to vote for gore to actually vote for a third-party candidate the secretary of state certifies the election results in bush's favor next day the large democratic county reverses itself and decides to recount the secretary of state files a petition with the florida supreme court to stop recounts bush joins the petition gore threatens to sue for a recount in all counties if bush doesn't accept recounts of the contested counties the florida supreme court denies the request to block recounts the secretary of state says she will not consider returns from counties conducting recounts bush rejects gore's proposal for a statewide recount as well as the suggestion that they meet face-to-face next day bush files an appeal with the federal appeals court in atlanta to stop the recounts in florida gore files a motion in opposition also filing an emergency motion with the state challenging the secretary of state's right to refuse to certify some election results the florida supreme court says the state can go ahead with recounting next day the florida supreme court says the secretary of state may not yet certify results the court of appeals in atlanta denies bush's request to stop the manual recounts next day bush's lead over gore triples when all of the overseas ballots are counted next day another county opts to recount manually next day the florida supreme court hears arguments about whether or not the secretary of state should have to wait for all recounts to certify election results next day the florida supreme court rules in a unanimous decision that recounts may continue and that the totals must be included in the final results all results must be certified in the next five days next day vice presidential candidate dick cheney suffers a mild heart attack and undergoes an operation to place a stent in his narrowing artery bush petitions the u.s. supreme court over the florida surpreme court ruling about counting all ballots a judge in florida says hanging chads cannot be excluded from the recount the county comprising miami votes to halt its manual recount next day gore files papers with the florida supreme court to force the county comprising miami to resume recounting but the court rejects the motion the u.s. supreme court agrees to hear bush's complaints about recounting next day bush drops a lawsuit he filed to force florida to reconsider ballots from overseas military members rejected on technicalities next day the secretary of state denies one county an hour-and-a-half extension of the 5 pm deadline to file totals and thousands of ballots are left uncounted the secretary of state declares bush the winner in florida but there's too much in doubt for it to mean anything five hundred votes separate bush and gore in florida the governor who is george bush's brother certifies the electoral votes next day gore officially contests the election results with the state of florida bush files a motion with the appeals court in atlanta to delay the start of the trial over whether or not florida has the right to recount next day gore asks a county circuit judge to authorize an immediate recount of tens of thousands of disputed ballots the judge wants everything the ballots the voting booths and voting machines brought to his courtroom next day gore and bush file briefs with the united states supreme court over bush's appeal of the florida state supreme court's authorizing selective recounts next day vice presidential candidate dick cheney announces the opening of transition offices funded by private money when the government refuses to release transition funds and office space to bush because of ongoing litigation next day the united states supreme court hears arguments about bush's complaints about the state of florida initiating selective recounts the florida supreme court rejects gore's request to immediately begin hand recounts of tens of thousands of ballots from palm beach and the county comprising miami the court of appeals in atlanta agrees to hear cases brought by private individuals that assert that hand recounts are illegal and unconstitutional the florida circuit judge who had ballots and booths and machines hauled into his courtroom holds a hearing about whether or not the tens of thousands of disputed ballots from palm beach and the county including miami should be recounted by hand two days later the united states supreme court overturns the florida supreme court's decision to restart hand counting and asks for some clarification about the previous deadline for certifying election results the florida circuit judge who had the ballots and booths and machines hauled into his courtroom rules against gore saying recounts aren't necessary in the disputed counties as they're heavily democratic so the totals should stand two days later the appeals court in atlanta denies bush's appeal to throw out manual recounts in some counties next day gore appeals the ruling of the circuit judge who had the ballots and booths and machines hauled into his courtroom to the florida supreme court next day the florida supreme court reverses the circuit judge's ruling and orders statewide manual recounts bush seeks a stay before the recounts can begin and petitions the united states supreme court to intervene next day the florida supreme court refuses bush's stay and begins recounts the appeals court in atlanta also refuses bush's stay but the united states supreme court issues a stay and all manual recounts come to a halt two days later the united states supreme court hears arguments from both bush and gore lawyers on the issue of the recount bush arguing that the recount is a constitutional violation of the equal protection clause because there is no one standard for undertaking said recount and gore argues it's just common sense that the recounting is just to show the will of the people the next day the florida house of representatives approves the twenty-five electors pledged to bush in the afternoon the united states supreme court overturns the florida supreme court's ruling to restart recounting siding with bush that because the recounts are undertaken without a statewide standard for doing so it violates the constitution the next day gore appears on television to concede the election and george w bush becomes president your roommates are beside themselves and get squeamish at various news reports that third-party candidates like the one they voted for likely siphoned off votes for gore the rapper eminem and his wife reconcile the magazine editor at shout who ran your piece on the rapper tupac shakur invites you to a party in chelsea thrown for a new magazine edited by the daughter of the rolling stones guitarist keith richards neither of you knowing in advance that keith richards is going to be at the party the magazine editor says oh my god when he spots the recognizable silhouette of the legendary guitarist you tell him he should go say something to richards and the magazine editor admits the thought makes him so nervous he might vomit you roam a large circle around richards just to check him out and notice the subtle tabs his two bodyguards keep on you and anyone else who approaches richards's immediate area you don't really know anything about the rolling stones and so the glimpse of richards is just a curiosity once an editor you met at bret easton ellis's christmas party said he was casting about for a writer to write a piece about how the rolling stones were the worst band ever and you volunteered for the assignment dropping it when you mentioned the idea to one of your colleagues at harold ober and he looked at you gravely and said you should not write such an article the foreign-rights agent at ober announces that he's leaving publishing and he advocates for you to have his old job which entails securing foreign-rights deals on behalf of ober clients also flying to germany for the annual rights fair the job pays much more than you're making and you covet the idea of being a kind of agent without being a full-fledged literary agent but your boss calls you in to tell you that you're not getting the job and after three years at the agency you're to remain an assistant you're disappointed but don't say so and decide to go part-time to work the other angle writing another novel but you and your roommates are notified that your apartment building is going to be gutted and renovated to accommodate the gentrification of williamsburg and the thought of trying to find yet another apartment coupled with what seems like your fading status at harold ober goads you into throwing in the towel you reluctantly give notice at work and sell what few belongings you have sitting on the bus to the airport you can feel the slow unwinding of your life in new york you know you'll be back to celebrate the publication of we're so famous in the spring but outside of that you wonder if you'll ever see new york again a place that's felt more like home than any other place you've lived but now you're just one of the many people who have come to the city full of ambition only to be bounced back out you move in with your father in his new house back in arizona committed to finishing another novel one that you hope will lead you back to new york you still have a couple of thousand dollars left from your advance for we're so famous and hope that perhaps more money will come in maybe from sales of foreign editions or even film options but for the moment you write eight hours a day on the new book about three characters on a scavenger hunt through bars in new york your editor faxes over the first review of we're so famous by publishers weekly a trade magazine for publishers and booksellers publishers weekly reviews usually setting the pace for how many and what kind of reviews a book will get the publishers weekly review is as harsh as you imagine it can get in its attempt to skewer our obsession with celebrity culture this trifle of a tale about three teenage girls and their quest for fame and fortune only manages to injure itself narrated in three parts the novel follows the exploits of paque stella and daisy talentless teenagers from phoenix ariz with an overwhelming desire for fame obsessed with the british girl group bananarama paque and daisy are avid '80s aficionados the two record an amateur single that gains notoriety when they are linked to a local murder case but this plot line is abandoned and their singing career goes nowhere following a disastrous live performance stella a struggling actress living in hollywood works in a dinner theater reenacting celebrity deaths her obsession with her new boyfriend an actor who can't get beyond failed television pilots paque and daisy join her in hollywood to work on a no-budget movie with a no-name director will paque and daisy hit the big time will stella's stalking of bad-boy rocker bryan metro bear fruit will readers be at all amused by the book's incessant name-dropping pop culture factoids and the postmodern trick of slipping screenplays and faux fan letters into the narrative not likely although those who find nick hornby and bret easton ellis too challenging might be engaged for a moment or two satire needs to be smarter than its subject and unfortunately this fable is neither wicked nor clever enough to wade out from the shallows it purports to spoof a blurb from ellis probably won't do much to boost sales after the first 15 minutes and it's hard to tell who the intended audience is readers under 30 won't be familiar with much of the '80s arcana and those over 30 won't have the patience for the puerile protagonists your editor says to give him a call and you do and he laughs the review off saying it must be an old girlfriend but the nastiness of the review does feel personal and you can't help but wonder if it's someone you know new york city is full of wannabe writers many of them taking jobs as critics and while you don't care about a bad review you can't shake the tone from your head you feel strongly that whoever wrote it should have to sign his or her name to it that publishers weekly shouldn't be publishing anonymous reviews if someone feels strongly about a book one way or the other it shouldn't be done behind a curtain also the review mentions bret easton ellis twice which makes you suspect he's the real target of the reviewer's disdain you immediately recall an episode at harold ober where the editor of the los angeles review of books called the agent of one of ober's authors who publicly hated an author with a new book out the editor wanted to hire the ober author to review the author he hated a setup the ober author rightly declined but the fact that the editor initiated the request spooked you around that time you'd been reading a memoir by the long-dead legendary new york times critic anatole broyard who joyfully confessed that it was the job of the critic to bring writers down a notch which he had done time and again all of it swirling in your head as you brooded about the publishers weekly review for we're so famous the review would likely kill any other reviewers' interest in the book you imagine you are desperate to know the name of the reviewer and wonder how you can find out your friend who worked for the paris review with the hacker friend wouldn't be able to find out because the reviewer's name is likely not filed electronically you hatch a plan a stunt one that at first sounds ludicrous but as you consider it more and more you realize that even if it doesn't reveal the name of the reviewer it will at least raise the profile of your novel and if you know anything it's that a raised profile for whatever reason is better than naught so without telling anyone what you're going to do you send an e-mail to everyone at publishers weekly offering the last thousand dollars of your advance money for the name of the reviewer you also openly cc all the media outlets you can think of and press send before you can talk yourself out of doing it you sleep fitfully that night expecting the time difference in new york to bring replies early in the morning but your barren inbox is a sign either that something is afoot or that no one cares you spend the morning rationalizing what you've done you don't care what people think about you personally all the moving around as a kid erased that from your makeup over the years and you have no agent to disappoint your friends will stick by you you hope your family is family so when your editor calls and asks you what in the world is going on your heart sinks not realizing that publishers weekly would place a call over to bloomsbury usa your editor has been your champion all the way through taking a chance on you and your book and now you've embarrassed him and probably gotten him in trouble with his colleagues something you didn't consider even for a moment mortification sets in and you apologize to him but he's already written you off you can tell and you're in the quagmire of your own making by yourself the publicist at bloomsbury usa calls and asks you not to answer any of the interview requests that are coming in about the bounty and you say you'll do whatever she wants you to forwarding the requests that filter into your inbox straight to her so she can issue a no comment the rapper puff daddy changes his name to p diddy the magazine salon writes a piece about your row with publishers weekly called when authors attack you fly to san diego for a week to meet your friend from new york who is writing the bar memoir who is visiting his friend a hatter who owns a chain of successful hat shops in southern california the music magazine spin publishes a nice short review of we're so famous which you see in a record store in san diego when you return to phoenix the publishers weekly thing seems like a dream until a friend forwards you a piece from time magazine called poor sport disparaging you and what you've done that the journalist is allowed to rail against you without comment from you seems an injustice but you're trying to salvage anything you can of your relationship with your editor and bloomsbury usa a famous hollywood agent becomes your film agent and you know that his interest is a result of the thing with publishers weekly you bounce to new york for a party celebrating the release of the second issue of post road happy to have the distraction you spend a few days seeing friends in new york before taking the bus to boston where there's a second post road party your publicist at bloomsbury usa wants you to speak with a journalist writing a piece about the publishers weekly thing and you agree the journalist starts off by mentioning the blurb for we're so famous from bob shacochis saying that he hates shacochis's work and you wonder what kind of setup you're in for the journalist's piece is called how to make literary journalists nervous and reveals his agenda a more studied approach comes from the novelist kurt andersen on his radio show studio 360 finally you hear someone agree with you that reviews should not be written anonymously a point that's been lost in the maelstrom you give your first public reading from we're so famous at newtonville books outside of boston a bookstore owned by a friend of your friend from bennington and it's a comfort to see so many friendly faces from bennington in the crowd including some of your former teachers the next day the village voice runs a long favorable review of we're so famous which makes your reaction to the publishers weekly review look like an overreaction you travel back to new york as the official publication date nears for a scheduled reading at the astor place barnes & noble the book party will be a few days later and so your entire family flies out arriving at barnes & noble in cabs from the airport just as the reading is about to start you don't see your editor in the crowd and are bummed out that he's probably too mad at you to attend you begin reading to the crowd of friends and some people you don't know and when you look up from the podium during the reading you see the actress molly ringwald cutting through the crowd finding a place in the corner after the reading you're relieved to find your editor in the back of the room though your interaction with him is a bit awkward before you can launch into an apology about the whole thing and explain your side molly ringwald appears and it's clear they are a couple and all else is washed away in pleasantries the editor stops by the book party which you've arranged at a ukrainian social club in the east village with the help of your friend who is writing a bar memoir and who is married to a ukrainian your friend from college the fitzgerald fan drives up and your family is there and you take a moment to appreciate everyone you care about being in the same room at the same moment you bounce back to arizona the next day and drive to tucson for a sparsely attended reading at your alma mater your former teachers attending one of them saying you didn't waste any time which you think is a compliment but who knows you bounce to los angeles driving through the desert with your father staying in a pastel-colored hotel near the borders in westwood where you're scheduled to read when you and your father check in there's a party of some kind in the lobby bar and you see the actor who played crocodile dundee raising a glass at your reading at borders the next day no one shows up save for one former bennington classmate who sits next to your father but as the reading is about to begin the bennington classmate waltzes through the spacious bookstore and gathers up a few souls whom she deposits in the front row you start reading and a half a dozen men in expensive suits file in and stand at the back agents from the office of the hollywood agent handling the film rights for we're so famous you say a quick hello when it's over and they hightail it out as quickly as they

arrived you land back in phoenix the small publicity tour for the
novel done entertainment weekly publishes an unfavorable review
of we're so famous and you smile when you think of the bad reviews
they've written about bret easton ellis's books over the years and
when the unimpressed new york times review appears it hardly
matters though there's vindication in the fact that the times reviewed
the book at all as they tend not to review paperback originals a victory of sorts you take a data entry job at your mother's medical
billing business as the last of your money is gone bloomsbury usa
sends a rejection for your new novel the one about the scavenger
hunt and the tilt-a-whirl finally finally finally comes to a rest an
intern in washington dc goes missing and the congressman from
her district in california is questioned the actor robert blake's wife is
found murdered in the passenger seat of his car he ran back into
the italian restaurant where they'd dined to retrieve his gun which
had fallen out of his jacket to put a coda on the thing with publishers weekly you go on a local radio morning show and announce
that you're donating all the royalties from we're so famous to a local
literacy group it comes out that robert blake's wife would send nude
photos of herself to men as a means of supporting herself she also
ran ads in magazines seeking companionship and then asking men
for money which supported her lifestyle and gave her enough
money to move to los angeles to pursue a film career that didn't pan
out though it allowed her access to celebrities including marlon
brando's son whom she wrote to in prison after he was convicted of
killing his sister's husband after his release she began dating brando's son though she was also dating robert blake and when she
became pregnant she thought the child was brando's son's but a
paternity test revealed it was blake's he married her and moved her
and the child into the guesthouse of his home the local paper the
phoenix new times publishes an in-depth profile about you which
your friends see and you stop to wonder if your old high school

282

girlfriend now married sees it too and all of that feels like a lifetime ago you bounce back to new york city and drive with friends up to bennington for an alumni weekend and feel some love for your novel which though it's recently published feels like another time period you marvel at the fact that it's been only four years since you graduated you spend a couple of days on cape cod with your bennington friend from boston and his family his father the former dean of harvard taking in that your friend and his family have been like a second family to you through the years of bouncing between new york and boston and you feel wistful on the flight back to phoenix bloomsbury publishes the british edition of we're so famous and there are some nice notices you receive an e-mail out of the blue from a record producer in london asking for your address and a few weeks later an envelope arrives with a british copy of your novel signed by bananarama after denying it for months the congressman from the district of the disappeared intern admits that he was having an affair with her but that he knows nothing about what happened to her madonna announces her first tour in over a decade the drowned world tour and you think that about says it all you convince the band fuzzy who appears in we're so famous to go on a tour of colleges with you in the fall and set about using your ample free time looking at maps calculating costs locating cheap hotels the idea that the tour will coincide with the start of the fall semester inspires you to contact some college english departments for help in arranging appearances but because it's summer you don't get a lot of feedback and the idea of touring college campuses fizzles you're chagrined to learn that the film rights to your novel are being shopped selectively when a small producer asks for a copy and your hollywood agent won't send it or even consider the producer the populist in you fires up and with the help of your brothers you create a listing on ebay offering up the film rights to we're so famous to the highest bidder you also fax all the production companies in hollywood and beyond about the auction your hollywood agent calls enraged demanding that you halt what you're up to but you don't listen don't care there's nothing anyone can say at this point that will influence how you behave the singer aaliyah is killed when her private plane is overloaded with people and equipment and drops into the ocean right after takeoff the last episode of mister rogers' neighborhood airs the monday you targeted for the start of your college campus tour passes and you're spent all out of ideas for promoting yourself and your novel and then the unreal becomes real when you wake up the following morning and your father says there's been an aviation accident in new york city and you watch the city you love the only real home you've ever known crumble and burn and people stop thinking about themselves at least for the moment while the man who gave away of all those free gum balls so long ago is put in charge of retaliating against those who ruined that part of new york and a lot of people's lives forever but it doesn't take long for everyone to wonder how long is appropriate before it is okay to resume the intense investigation of the insignificant and welcome the comfort of the trivial back into our lives

Acknowledgments

My thanks to

Josephine Bergin
Charles Bock
Stephanie Duncan
Panio Gianopoulos
Pete Hausler
Michael Rosovsky
Laurel Sills
Erica Stahler

Clarkes, Cottons, Gilkeys, and Kaliens

Mary and Max

A Note on the Author

© John Laprade

Jaime Clarke is a graduate of the University of Arizona and holds an MFA from Bennington College. He is the author of the novels *We're So Famous*, *Vernon Downs*, *World Gone Water*, and *Garden Lakes*; editor of the anthologies *Don't You Forget About Me: Contemporary Writers on the Films of John Hughes*, *Conversations with Jonathan Lethem*, and *Talk Show: On the Couch with Contemporary Writers*; and co-editor of the anthologies *No Near Exit: Writers Select Their Favorite Work from 'Post Road' Magazine* (with Mary Cotton) and *Boston Noir 2: The Classics* (with Dennis Lehane and Mary Cotton). He is a founding editor of the literary magazine *Post Road*, now published at Boston College, and co-owner, with his wife, of Newtonville Books, an independent bookstore in Boston.

www.jaimeclarke.com

www.postroadmag.com

www.baumsbazaar.com

www.newtonvillebooks.com

Vernon Downs
By Jaime Clarke
www.bloomsbury.com/JaimeClarke

'*Vernon Downs* is a gripping, hypnotically written and unnerving look at the dark side of literary adulation. Jaime Clarke's tautly suspenseful novel is a cautionary tale for writers and readers alike–after finishing it, you may start to think that J. D. Salinger had the right idea after all'
Tom Perrotta, author of *Election*, *Little Children*, and *The Leftovers*

'Moving and edgy in just the right way. Love (or lack of) and Family (or lack of) is at the heart of this wonderfully obsessive novel'
Gary Shteyngart, author of *Super Sad True Love Story*

'All strong literature stems from obsession. *Vernon Downs* belongs to a tradition that includes Nicholson Baker's *U and I*, Geoff Dyer's *Out of Sheer Rage*, and—for that matter—*Pale Fire*. What makes Clarke's excellent novel stand out isn't just its rueful intelligence, or its playful semi-veiling of certain notorious literary figures, but its startling sadness. *Vernon Downs* is first rate'
Matthew Specktor, author of *American Dream Machine*

'*Vernon Downs* is a brilliant meditation on obsession, art, and celebrity. Charlie Martens's mounting fixation with the titular Vernon is not only driven by the burn of heartbreak and the lure of fame, but also a lost young man's struggle to locate his place in the world. *Vernon Downs* is an intoxicating novel, and Clarke is a dazzling literary talent'
Laura van den Berg, author of *The Isle of Youth*

'An engrossing novel about longing and impersonation, which is to say, a story about the distance between persons, distances within ourselves. Clarke's prose is infused with music and intelligence and deep feeling'
Charles Yu, author of *Sorry Please Thank You*

'*Vernon Downs* is a fascinating and sly tribute to a certain fascinating and sly writer, but this novel also perfectly captures the lonely distortions of a true obsession'
Dana Spiotta, author of *Stone Arabia*

Selected by *The Millions* as a Most Anticipated Read

'Though *Vernon Downs* appears to be about deception and celebrity, it's really about the alienation out of which these things grow. Clarke shows that obsession is, at root, about yearning: about the things we don't have but desperately want; about our longing to be anyone but ourselves'
The Boston Globe

'A stunning and unsettling foray into a glamorous world of celebrity writers, artistic loneliness, and individual desperation'
The Harvard Crimson

'*Vernon Downs* is a fast-moving and yet, at times, quite sad book about, in the broadest sense, longing'
The Brooklyn Rail

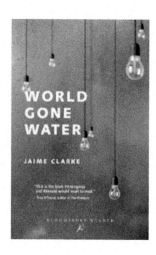

World Gone Water
By Jaime Clarke
www.bloomsbury.com/JaimeClarke

'Jaime Clarke's *World Gone Water* is so fresh and daring, a necessary book, a barbaric yawp that revels in its taboo: the sexual
and emotional desires of today's hetero young man. Clarke is a
sure and sensitive writer, his line are clean and carry us right to
the tender heart of his lovelorn hero, Charlie Martens. This is
the book Hemingway and Kerouac would want to read. It's the
sort of honesty in this climate that many of us aren't brave
enough to write'
Tony D'Souza, author of *The Konkans*

'This unsettling novel ponders human morality and sexuality, and
the murky interplay between the two. Charlie Martens is a
compelling anti-hero with a voice that can turn on a dime, from
shrugging naiveté to chilling frankness. *World Gone Water* is a
candid, often startling portrait of an unconventional life'
J. Robert Lennon, author of *Familiar*

'Funny and surprising, *World Gone Water* is terrific fun to read … and, as a spectacle of bad behavior, pretty terrifying to contemplate'
Adrienne Miller, author of *The Coast of Akron*

'Charlie Martens is my favorite kind of narrator, an obsessive yearner whose commitment to his worldview is so overwhelming that the distance between his words and the reader's usual thinking gets clouded fast. *World Gone Water* will draw you in, make you complicit, and finally leave you both discomfited and thrilled'
Matt Bell, author of *In the House upon the Dirt between the Lake and the Woods*

'Charlie Martens will make you laugh. More, he'll offend and shock you while making you laugh. Even trickier: he'll somehow make you like him, root for him, despite yourself and despite him. This novel travels into the dark heart of male/female relations and yet there is tenderness, humanity, hope. Jaime Clarke rides what is a terribly fine line between hero and antihero. Read and be astounded'
Amy Grace Loyd, author of *The Affairs of Others*

Garden Lakes
By Jaime Clarke
www.bloomsbury.com/JaimeClarke

'An intriguing cross-section of loneliness and power in the
world of boys and men'
Kirkus Reviews

'Astute study in the darker aspects of adolescent psychology'
Booklist

'It takes some nerve to revisit a bulletproof classic, but Jaime Clarke
does so, with elegance and a cool contemporary eye, in this cunningly
crafted homage to Lord of the Flies. He understands all too well the
complex psychology of boyhood, how easily the insecurities and
power plays slide into mayhem when adults look the other way'
Julia Glass, National Book Award-winning author of *Three Junes*

'Jaime Clarke reminds us that if the banality of evil is indeed a
viable truth, its seeds are most likely sewn among adolescent boys'
Brad Watson, author of *Aliens in the Prime of Their Lives*

'In the flawlessly imagined *Garden Lakes*, Jaime Clarke pays homage to *Lord of the Flies* and creates his own vivid, inadvertently isolated community. As summer tightens its grip, and adult authority recedes, his boys gradually reveal themselves to scary and exhilarating effect. In the hands of this master of suspense and psychological detail, the result is a compulsively readable novel'
Margot Livesey, author of *The Flight of Gemma Hardy*

'Smart, seductive, and suggestively sinister, *Garden Lakes* is a disturbingly honest look at how our lies shape our lives and destroy our communities. Read it: Part three in one of the best literary trilogies we have'
Scott Cheshire, author of *High as the Horses' Bridles*

'As tense and tight and pitch-perfect as Clarke's narrative of the harrowing events at Garden Lakes is, and as fine a meditation it is on Golding's novel, what deepens this book to another level of insight and artfulness is the parallel portrait of Charlie Martens as an adult, years after his fateful role that summer, still tyrannized, paralyzed, tangled in lies, wishing for redemption, maybe fated never to get it. Complicated and feral, Garden Lakes is thrilling, literary, and smart as hell'
Paul Harding, Pulitzer Prize-winning author of *Tinkers*

CPSIA information can be obtained at www.ICGtesting.com
Printed in the USA
BVOW06s0337140916

462044BV00004B/7/P